Pr...
laura an...

PARANORMAL SCENE INVESTIGATIONS

Hard Magic
"Readers will love the *Mythbusters*-style fun of smart, sassy people solving mysteries through experimentation, failure, and blowing stuff up."
—*Publishers Weekly,* starred review

Pack of Lies
"Bonnie's intelligence and perceptiveness really make this book go and readers will root for her and the team to solve their investigation."
—*RT Book Reviews,* Top Pick

RETRIEVERS

Staying Dead
"An entertaining, fast-paced thriller."
—*Locus*

Curse the Dark
"Features fast-paced action, wisecracking dialogue, and a pair of strong, appealing heroes."
—*Library Journal*

Bring it On
"Ripping good urban fantasy, fast-paced and filled with an exciting blend of mystery and magic... this is a paranormal romance for those who normally avoid romance, and the entire series is worth checking out."
—*SF Site*

Burning Bridges
"Leaves the reader on the edge of her seat for the next book."
—*RT Book Reviews,* 4 stars

Free Fall
"The best of the Retrievers series to date."
—*Publishers Weekly,* starred review

Blood from Stone
"Extreme fun, nicely balanced with dark stuff... and a scene in a museum that had me whimpering with joy."
—*Green Man Review*

Also available from

laura anne gilman

and LUNA Books:

Retrievers

Staying Dead
Curse the Dark
Bring It On
Burning Bridges
Free Fall
Blood from Stone

Paranormal Scene Investigations

Hard Magic
Pack of Lies

And coming soon:

Damage Control

laura anne gilman

TRICKS OF THE TRADE

LUNA™

LUNA™

TRICKS OF THE TRADE

Recycling programs
for this product may
not exist in your area.

ISBN-13: 978-0-373-80331-6

For Geoff. For taking my hand, and holding on.

prologue

My name is Bonnie Torres, and I'm a student of (in)human nature. More specifically, and according to the business cards we don't actually have yet, I'm a Paranormal Scene Investigator. What that means is that I look at the world a little differently than most, even among my fellow Talent.

I used to be an idealist of sorts. Not that everyone was good— I knew firsthand that we were all filled with conflicting impulses, some positive and some negative, and sometimes the negative ones got out and did damage. I also knew that there were people who didn't feel any guilt about the damage they did. But a year ago, I would have claimed that responsibility was all about your intent; that if you meant well, did your best, and didn't hurt anyone, you could sleep with a clear conscience. Then I was recruited to join PUPI, Ian Stosser's dream of an unbiased, impartial investigative unit designed to ferret out the truth behind crimes of a magical nature or cause.

Ian Stosser had been a certified boy wonder, once upon a time: Golden Boy of the Midwest Council, high-res Talent and general scary-ass smart guy. But something happened in Chicago, something they still don't talk about, and he came to New York with his business partner Benjamin Venec, to hang their shingle here.

Ian said there was a need, that the Cosa Nostradamus needed us, to save it from itself.

The Cosa Nostradamus wasn't all that thrilled to be saved, but Ian had been right—there was a need. After only a few months we—the Private, Unaffiliated Paranormal Investigations team—got our first case, a bad one: a double murder. We solved it, proved what had happened, let the authorities—such as the Cosa has—handle the punishment. And then, once we'd demonstrated we could be trusted to be fair in our investigations, impartial in our discoveries, we were approached to investigate a few more, and they were all bad.

They only call us when it's bad.

Magic isn't an instinct; for most of us it requires forethought to pull current and direct it against someone else. That means Talent mostly don't commit crimes of passion, but ones of forethought and malice. By the time we get called in? The crime's been committed, and all we see is the tarry residue left in the aftermath, the pain and the grief and the greed and the malice and the denial—and, sometimes, the regret and remorse, too late to do any good.

When I took this job, my mentor had warned me: you rarely see anyone's shining better nature in this job. He'd been right.

PUPI did good work, though. We got people answers, closure. We were making sure that there were consequences to actions. From the lonejacks and gypsies on the street to the Council members in their hushed private offices, the word was spreading: we were smart, we were sharp, and we were unaffiliated—something rare in the highly political world of magic. If you came to us with a mystery, we would find the answers, no matter where they led.

We investigated events. We stuck to the facts. But there's no way, I was learning, that you could separate facts and events from the people who drive them. And people? People are complicated. Responsibility is complicated.

Every case we took, from the cold-blooded killer-for-hire to the regret-stricken being who let terrible things happen for love, taught me that some acts cannot be excused, no matter the intent...and that it's possible to sleep soundly, your conscience clear as a cloudless sky, after inflicting terrible harm on someone. People aren't good. They're not bad, either, mostly. They're actions and reactions, pushed this way and that by things we have so little control over.

There is a black and a white, yeah. And a thousand shades of gray, between. Most of us? We think our shade of gray is a hell of a lot lighter than it is. But we each have the choice—maybe not where we stand, but how aware we are of what we do.

Responsibility is complicated. Also, uncomfortable.

Being a pup isn't easy. We look. We observe. We don't turn away.

And if I don't sleep soundly some nights... I have to believe it's worth it, in the end.

one

Every Talent in the city probably felt it when The Roblin arrived, but most of them didn't know what it was, not even after everything was done and dusted. There was maybe a sense of unease, a niggling in the back of their minds, not like they'd forgotten something but that something was happening that they should know about, that was going to affect them.

And then it was gone: fading into the still-chilly predawn air, lost in the quiet bustle of hospital workers changing shifts, police cars idling on street corners, short-order cooks strapping on fresh aprons and firing up grease-skimmed griddles. Those particularly sensitive to bad vibes, Null and Talent alike, shifted restlessly in their sleep, or woke feeling particularly anxious or alert, but there was nothing to tell them why they felt that way, and most of them forgot it after the first cup of coffee, and the first crisis of the day.

But because it was forgotten didn't mean it was gone. The malaise started downtown, and spread, like fingers of a hand stretching out to cover all five boroughs of New York City. Barely touching anything, yet sensing, feeling, absorbing the pulse of the city, finding the weak points, the delicate spots, the danger zones.

And, finding them, narrowing in for the kill.

"All right, people, settle down."

The noise level hadn't been high to begin with, but the restless movements stilled almost immediately. It was Wednesday, and we were all gathered in the main conference room in the PUPI offices, which were on the seventh floor of a nondescript seven-story brick building uptown in Harlem. Outside I could hear the muffled sounds of traffic, trucks and buses and cabbies in their usual dance, sirens cutting in and out like a soprano having diva-fits in a cast of baritones. Seven of us: me, and Sharon, Pietr, Nifty, Nick, and our newest hire, Lou. And Benjamin Venec, our boss.

"After the past few weeks I had planned on spending time working on your defensive work, but—"

"We've got a job? Do I get to—?"

Venec scowled at the interruption. "No."

Nifty was getting itchy. Literally: he'd had a run-in with a molting Istiachi two weeks ago, which was unfortunate, since molting made them both pissy and toxic. He'd ended up with a bad rash—startlingly bright green against his black skin—that he was under strict orders not to scratch. He was also stuck on office duty until it healed, while we'd been out on a case, and that was really making his skin itch.

The first time I'd ever seen Nifty during our group

interview/audition for this job, I'd thought "well-dressed jock" and assumed he was all bulk and no brain. Working with him for the past year had proved that assumption wrong: he was smart and surprisingly sophisticated. But right now, he was more like a petulant ten-year-old than a pro-quality athlete turned paranormal P.I.

"Why can't I..." he started to ask again, his voice not quite whining, but getting awfully close.

"Because you're still contagious," Venec said, not even looking at him. "That's fine here, where we can protect ourselves, but letting you out among Nulls, who'd freak if they started coming over in sparkling green itches? Forget about it, Lawrence."

I hid a smile. Venec would not appreciate knowing how very much more like a parent than a boss he sounded, right then. Benjamin Venec was many, many things: smart, savvy, fierce, an utter bastard when it suited him, and hotter than hell, with dark eyes that I still couldn't identify the color of, because every time I looked into them I got seriously distracted, but he was absolutely not daddy material.

Nifty didn't have the same physical—or emotional—reaction I did to Benjamin Venec, but Venec was the Big Dog, so Nifty subsided, spreading his hands—plate-size, and equally capable of pulling a pigskin out of the air or dragging a suspect to the ground—flat on the conference room table to keep from rubbing at his arms or legs. Since I'd been right behind him when the Istiachi lifted its tail and sprayed, I was sympathetic. That could have been me, if my coworker hadn't massed twice my weight, and protected me from the attack.

It was funny, really. When I'd agreed to work for the mad Talent combination of Ian Stosser and Benjamin Venec, I never thought it would result in me facing down a foot-long land-squid and ducking toxic urine in order to get the skinny on a bank robbery.

J, my mentor, says I need to read more noir mysteries, to expand my expectations about this job. J still isn't really 100% behind my career choice, but he tries to be supportive. I'm not sure Dashiell Hammett wrote about Istiachi, myself. More Lovecraft's style. The land-squid were fatae, technically full and valued members of the *Cosa Nostradamus,* but you didn't invite them to Gathers, and certainly never to lunch.

"Besides," Venec went on. "I need you here to work on those files with Lou."

There was a faint snicker that sounded like it came from down the table, which meant Nick, which wasn't a surprise. Boy still didn't have an inch of self-preservation in him. Nifty glared around the table, and went back to sulking. Lou merely nodded her head, accepting both the assignment and the partnering.

Nick was one of the Original Five. He looked like your basic geek...and okay, he was. But he had skills nobody else could match. Lou was new to our pack—she'd come on board two months ago, when the cases started coming faster and Stosser decided we needed more hands. The oldest of us by a decade, she had actual experience, having worked for a Null P.I.'s office before, but the first time she went out into the field as an active PUPI...

Well. It had been spectacular, and not in a good way. Lou's control was fabulous under training conditions, and not so much in the real world. Now she worked the back office, making sure the research records were in order, the supplies properly kept, and we're never caught without proper background files. At that, she's a whiz. We didn't know how badly we needed an office manager until we had one in place.

Venec waited to see if anyone was going to make any other comments. We weren't. "After the backlog last week—" The Big Dog held up a hand to keep anyone from trying to explain or protest. "Yah, I know. That job was a goddamned disaster, and we were all stressed. But not a single one of you filed paperwork all case, and then every damn one of you dumped it on Lou's desk Thursday afternoon. Tacky, people. She's already gone through her initiation."

"*Así mero!*" Lou muttered, leaning back in her chair, and I tried not to crack a grin. My father might not have taught me much Spanish before handing me over to J, but I'd learned enough over the years to know what she'd said—and even if I hadn't understood the particular slang, her tone made it clear. The rest of my cohorts—middle-class whitebread to the core, even Nifty—were clueless.

"As I was saying, after the backlog of last week, I had wanted you all to do some skill-work—Sharon, you still need to work on your binding spells, and Pietr and Bonnie are due for a refresher course in ducking a tail."

How someone who could disappear as thoroughly as Pietr when he was stressed couldn't manage to shake a tail still amazed me. But it was true: for a ghost-boy, he stuck out like a sore thumb when he was focused on following someone.

My problem, according to Venec, was my hair.

I reached up and touched my short blond curls self-consciously. I'd thought the blue streaks were kicky. Venec had informed me, in no uncertain terms, that they were distracting, and unprofessional. And, apparently, they made me easy to pick out of a crowd.

We weren't supposed to stand out; we were supposed to blend in, the better to find out things people didn't want known. Or, as he put it, "This isn't a peacock show, damn it."

He was right, okay, he was absolutely right. But I'd spent most of my life standing out, gleefully and with encouragement from my mentor, and this...

This drabbing down to dullness was hard.

Even as I let that thought slip, there was a mental touch of something, not quite sympathy—never sympathy—but a rough buck-up sort of pushback, and I sighed. Of course Venec would know I was indulging in self-pity.

There was no such thing as telepathy, beyond the ping—a quick burst of information that was more visual than heard or seen—but about eight months ago we'd discovered that Venec and I could pick up each other's emotions, even thoughts.

Worse and weirder than that: our current kept getting tangled together without our willing it, something that was supposedly impossible. Magic didn't work that way.

The old texts, what Venec had been able to find, called it the Merge. It was rare, annoying, and not something either of us had wanted: We still didn't want it. But, like Nifty's rash, we had to deal with it and not let it interfere with the job.

I, at least, was dealing with it by total denial. So far, so good.

"You had wanted to give us a break?" Sharon asked, her coffee mug—a robin's-egg-blue color that matched her blond perfection, well, perfectly—halfway to her lips. "Implying that you're not going to…or not able to?"

Sharon liked to have things nailed down definite-like, the better to tear them apart. She was probably our best in-field operative. That scalpel-sharp brain, matched to the fact that she looked like a 1940s movie goddess, cool and lush at the same time, made her a killer investigator: people got distracted, and then she zoomed in without mercy, finding exactly what they were trying to hide.

The fact that she had the ability to sense when they were actively lying was just icing on that cake.

"Not able to," Nifty said. As usual, he and Sharon were jockeying for lead dog spot, having to prove they were smarter, sharper, more alpha than the other. Then he ruined the superior attitude by scratching at his arm, making a face like a box turtle's, all scrunched up and sour. We all glared at him, and he stopped, shamefaced.

The rash spread by contact. Venec might be able to treat the infection, but I didn't want to be stuck under house arrest, too, because Nifty couldn't let it heal. If he wasn't careful, we were going to make him stay *home*.

"Not able to," Venec agreed, carefully not seeing Nifty's lapse so he didn't have to yell at him again. "Ian handed over two files this morning."

"Two?" I was surprised, yeah. It wasn't uncommon for us to have two jobs going, these days; the Council overall might still not officially recognize us, but word had gotten out that they'd use us in need, and so the ordinary members of the *Cosa Nostradamus* were calling. But two coming in on the same day? That meant Nifty's desk assignment wasn't make-work; there wasn't time or manpower to do that, even with Lou around.

"And where is Master Stosser, anyway?" Nick looked around like the boss might suddenly pop out of the woodwork—and he might, actually.

Ian Stosser might be the genius behind PUPI, but lately he'd left more and more of the day-to-day stuff to his partner. Since Venec was better at that anyway I hadn't thought much about it. But Nick was right; Ian had been least-in-sight, recently.

"I'll worry about Ian," Venec said, his voice more of a growl than usual, reminding me why we called him Big Dog, other than the obvious PUPI pun. "You focus on what we pay you for. Two jobs. First's a break-in, up in Fieldston. Sharon, you and Nick take that one." He slid a plain brown folder across the table, and Sharon took it.

Ah, paperwork. Magic—current, in the modern parlance—runs in every human, but only a very small percentage of humans can actually manipulate it. They—we—are called Talent, and the ones who can't use it are, rather condescendingly, called Nulls. Magic makes a lot of things easier, yeah. One of the prices we pay for Talent, though, is that we don't interact well with things that run on current's kissing cousin, electricity. You find a Talent who carries a cell phone or a PDA, and doesn't have to replace it every other month, and I'll show you a Talent who can't use current worth a damn.

Okay, unfair. But even those of us who don't use current every day found anything more sophisticated than a debit card got fritzed pretty fast. I hadn't been able to carry an MP3 player since I was fourteen.

I've spent most of my life in openly Talented society, but some days I watch people using netbooks or smartphones, while we have to juggle paper and pen and memory, and I wonder if we really got the better part of the deal, after all.

"Where the hell is Fieldston?" Sharon asked, scanning the paperwork. "I swear, if we have to lug out to Long Island again…"

"End of the 1 line, up in the Bronx," Nifty told her, capping the one-upmanship for the moment.

"Oh. Okay." She wasn't happy about heading all the way out there, but apparently so long as it didn't involve having to leave the city, she could deal with it. Shar was our only born-and-bred New Yorker—I didn't count, having spent most of my teens in Boston—and sometimes that just shone through.

"Client's a Null, he owns a house up there, it got tossed last night and he thinks it was a Retriever. No idea why he thinks that, but if it is…"

I couldn't stop myself from interrupting. "Venec, when was the last time someone actually pinned anything on an active Retriever?"

Retrievers were the cat burglars of the *Cosa Nostradamus,* Talent who naturally went invisible, like Pietr, only they controlled it, used it to get away with everything short of murder. If this guy'd been burgled by a Retriever, odds were that even if we could prove it, nobody would ever get the stuff back.

Those dark, irritated eyes glared at me, but I didn't feel any actual irritation coming off him, just annoyance. "If the client thinks it was a Retriever, then that's his call. You will determine the facts and find out who is responsible. And, if possible, get back the stolen items. Yeah," he said when Sharon would have protested, "I know, you're not the lost-and-found. If this guy did get hit by a Retriever, think about the egoboo, to hit back."

There was that.

"Bonnie, you and Pietr get a floater on the East Side, off 14th."

"Oh, maaaaaaan," Pietr said, in an uncanny imitation of Nick, while I took the file with a grimace. Yeah, Venec was still pissed about the blue hair-dye job.

Lou and Nifty, for a change, looked relieved to be stuck in the office. Nobody wanted a floater. Ever.

Everyone else filtered out, but I stayed in my chair, looking at the folder.

"You guys make it look so easy."

I twisted in my chair and looked at Lou, who had left, and then come back, standing in the doorway. "What?"

"Easy." She made a gesture with one hand at some vague thing in front of her. "I know it's not—god, how I know—but you never seem to hesitate. Stosser gives you an assignment, you absorb it, and head out. You call on your current, and you just assume that the current will do what you want. And it does."

"If you're still worrying about the incident with the piskies, they do that to everyone, first case...." I started to say, but she waved me off. That wasn't it.

I waited. That was the first thing Venec had taught

us: if you wait quietly long enough, people will tell you what you need to know.

"You're what, twenty-four?" She made it sound like a disease.

"Yeah." Twenty-three and a half, actually, but I didn't think correcting her was going to make things better.

Lou stared at the apple in her other hand like she couldn't remember picking it up, then shook her head and looked back at me. She had a serious face to start, and the look in her eyes now, a sort of despairing resignation, just deepened that impression. "I'm a decade older than you. I had solid training, good training. I'm high-res enough to hold my own. And I'm smart enough to understand how everything works, break it down, and make it better."

All of that was true, and she knew it and she knew I knew it, so I just kept my mouth shut and waited for her to get to her point. But she didn't. She just stood there, that apple in her hand, one bite taken out of it like Snow White's last dinner.

I twisted back and stared at the paperwork in front of me, wanting nothing more than to pack up and head out to the floater, get it over with, if Lou wasn't going to say anything more. But she stood there, and the silence drew out and got uncomfortable until the weight of social responsibility as hammered into me by J was like a third person in the room.

"You wouldn't be on the team if you weren't good," I said, hoping that would be enough.

"I know that."

"And you'll learn the control needed to—"

Her snort interrupted me, and I was thankful. I

could lie reasonably well, but I hated doing it. Honestly, though, I had no idea what she wanted me to say, or why she hadn't gone to Sharon, instead. They were closer in age, had more in common... Why me?

"I'm never going to get it. Not out there, during an open case, with all that pressure. It's just...like saying Pietr's suddenly going to stop ghosting."

She was probably right. Pietr hated the fact that he couldn't control the way he faded from sight under stress, even though it was probably going to save his life some day.

"I just... I keep wondering why I can't do it, what's wrong with me...and then I wonder what else is wrong with me, what am I missing, and what happens if we discover that thing during a case? What happens if we screw up because I can't handle something in the field, or one of you gets hurt, or..." She stopped, and took a bite out of the apple, teeth crunching into the flesh with maybe a little too much violence.

I was flailing, trying to figure out what she needed to hear. "That's why we work together. So if one of us misses something, the other's there as backup. We all make mistakes. Venec will be happy to remind you of that fact, if you'd like."

Another snort. "You never doubt yourself, do you, Bonnie? Never once wonder if you're not good enough, worry that you'll do something so wrong there's no re-covering from it?"

"Of course I do. But everything short of death can be recovered from, and death kinda takes the worry out of the situation." I hoped.

"Nice. I don't think I was ever that cocky. Maybe that's the problem."

She didn't mean to be cruel, but the words stung. I had a flash of J, years ago, sitting in his favorite chair in the library. The reading lamp was on, and Rupert, who had just been a brown-and-white mop of a puppy then, was sleeping at his feet. He had been gone for a few days, and I'd been happy to have him home, but he didn't talk much and I'd come in to see what was up, if he maybe wanted dinner, or a drink. And in the light of the lamp, a pale umber glow against his skin, I'd seen the damp track of tears on his cheek.

Whatever he'd been doing, it hadn't gone well.

"J?" I could have closed the door and left; he'd known I was there but he hadn't acknowledged me, and so we could both pretend I hadn't seen anything. But that wasn't how our household worked.

"Not now, Bonnie," my mentor had said, his voice a flat, gentle tone. "Right now I am not able to deal with anything beyond my own inabilities."

I'd been fourteen then, and filled with a sense— nurtured by J—that hard work and skill could get me through anything. The idea that there was something J couldn't do, that he might doubt his own abilities, was as foreign to me as the thought that he might sprout wings and fly.

I was older now, and had seen more of what life could and would throw at you on a daily basis, things that overwhelmed and dispirited as much as they lifted us and showed us joy. But...

"I'm sorry." I was. "I didn't mean to make light of what it is you're saying..."

"But you have no idea what I'm saying, do you?"

I shook my head, then nodded. "No. I mean, I know what you're saying, I just..."

Lou laughed, and it was tired but amused, not mocking. "But you're twenty-four and have never failed at anything, have you?"

I had failed to bring my dad's killer to justice. The bitterness of that still made my throat ache. But I'd dealt with it, accepted the failure as inevitable—and PUPI was my guarantee that never happened again. The failure had not been my inability, but the lack of a mechanism.

So I said the only thing that I knew was true. "We're a stronger team, because you're part of it."

There was silence, and I risked looking back at Lou. She was staring out the window, and the look on her face was one I recognized: deep, fast-moving thoughts under the surface. I saw that look a lot, around here.

"Yeah," she said, finally. "Okay."

She tossed the half-eaten apple into the waste can in the corner, and left. I didn't get the feeling I'd helped her solve anything.

Hopefully, I'd have better luck with the floater.

two

Pietr had been waiting, semipatiently, in the break room. He took one look at my face and bit back whatever he was going to say, just handing me my case and holding the door to the hallway. One of the great things about our office was that we were only a block away from the subway. The downside was that it was the 1 line, which meant leaving the west side required a crosstown bus, or a lot of walking. Fortunately, it wasn't a bad day, weatherwise.

We made it to the subway without speaking to each other, heading downtown toward the floater, and all the related joy therein, our kits—the assorted and alchemical tools of our trade—stashed at our feet, where nobody could walk by and grab them. And with every rattle and spark along the track, I felt more and more guilty about his being sent along with me. Normally, we take the assignments as they come and try not to whine too much. It's not like we ever get handed a bouquet of spring flowers to investigate, after all, and if we did it would be infested by hornets and nose-rot. But I felt like I had to say something to Pietr, anyway.

"Sorry."

Pietr turned his head slightly to look at me, surprised. "Why?"

"Venec's punishing me for the hair disaster, and you're stuck with it by association."

"Oh." His face went all closed and quiet, the way it does when he processes, and I watched him curiously. For all that he liked to cause mischief, Pietr tended to take his time to consider things. He was one of our thinkers—not that he couldn't improvise, and quickly, but not in the instinctive, nearly impulsive way Nick did. Or me for that matter, although I used to pride myself on how well I thought shit through. Not enough, apparently.

Pietr didn't have to think long, though. "You sure it's the hair that's chafing his...mood? Or that you're the real target?"

Ow. I groaned, and looked away. "Don't you start."

The fact that Venec and I had sparks going on— okay, sparks like Macy's fireworks—wasn't something you could hide from a blind fish, much less an office of trained investigators. The guys liked to tease me about that occasionally. Not meaning any harm, just...the usual shit you get, when the job is tense and the laughs few. Pietr, though, had a different take on the situation. He and I were—on a very specifically, intentionally casual basis—sexual partners. So naturally, he figured that was also why he got stuck with the floater—because there was no way an investigator like Benjamin Venec, with more experience than the rest of us slammed together, didn't also know about our off-hours agreement, no matter how much we kept it on the q.t.

He might have been right, in ordinary conditions. But Pietr, and the others, were missing a really important part of the puzzle. The pack knew there were sparks. They also knew I wasn't exactly shy, normally, about going after what or who I wanted. So they had to figure I didn't want to get involved with the boss, or that the boss had shot me down, for work-reasons. Which was all sorta true.

They didn't know about the damned Merge, though. Venec and I both agreed to keep it that way. The fact that our current had somehow recognized each other and decided we'd make pretty babies, or some weird and seriously annoying thing like that, didn't impress me at all, and Venec, well, he really did not like being told what to do by some biomagical force.

All right, it was more complicated than that, and according to Venec's research the Merge is Serious Doings, but I kept control over my sex life my own self, thanks, anyway, Fate, and be damned if I was going to risk not being taken seriously in my career because my current wanted me to make babies.

I have nothing against babies. Eventually. When and if I decided to have them.

But every day we worked together, the pull got stronger. If I let down my mental walls even a little bit, I knew his mood, and if I reached just an inch, I'd get my fingers into his thoughts.

Same for him, with me.

It was making us…cranky. Venec was a fair guy, for all

that he was a bastard, and wouldn't play favorites or punish someone for a screwup once the lesson was learned. My hair color was only an excuse for him to blow off some of that crank into an actual reason. Knowing that rationally didn't make the scolding hurt any less, though.

And Lou thought I never doubted myself? That was almost funny. The Merge had made me doubt my entire personal philosophy, change the way I interacted with people, second-guess every flicker and twinge of my emotions…. I needed to get a handle on myself. A distracted investigator could not do her job, and leaving this job was…not an option.

Pietr touched his hand on mine, lightly. "Bonnie…"

I shook my head, staring at the advertisement across the subway car instead of looking at him, listening to the chunk-chunk-whirr of the car's movement, focusing on the subtle but real hum of current running along the third rail, instead of listening to him. "No. Stop. Work hours."

I wasn't talking about the touch, but what he was going to say. How the two of us blew off steam and gave comfort off-hours was off-hours. Neither of us wanted it to spill into the workday, especially if there was half a chance that it would screw up our professional relationship. Pietr and I worked well together. He backed me up, I pushed him on…we got things done.

That was why Venec had paired him with me, today. Probably. Anything else would be petty, and Benjamin Venec wasn't petty.

Except, of course, when he was.

We rode the rest of the way in a more comfortable,

companionable silence, switching from the train downtown for a crosstown bus that dropped us off at the Manhattan Bridge, and we walked the rest of the way, stopped by the usual tangle of the FDR Drive. Finding a safe place to cross would require some backtracking. Mass transit sucked when you were working a crime scene, but without a siren, cars could be even slower, and Translocation, using current to move someone from point A to point B, was a serious drain on the core of the person doing the sending, with the additional inherent risk of finding a safe place to land. You couldn't actually land "on" someone—magic follows the same rules as physics, mostly, and two objects can't occupy the same space—but you could get knocked over or hit by a moving object or person. As usual with magic, the odds of actually being seen *doing* anything was small. Nulls didn't see what they didn't want to see.

Oh, hell, Talent didn't, either.

We stood there, and watched the traffic moving along the FDR, a steady stream of cars going too fast, and I heard a thoughtful hrmm rise from my companion.

"I don't know about you, but I have absolutely no desire to become a greasy splat on the highway."

The hrmm turned into a heavy exhale that wasn't quite a sigh. "Me, neither."

Especially since there was no guarantee that, in racing across the street, Pietr wouldn't ghost out of sight, and get hit by an otherwise-paying-attention driver. After you worked with him for a while, you started thinking about things like that.

I looked around to make sure nobody was watching

us, and pointed to a spot across the wide highway. He followed my finger with his gaze, and nodded.

Three seconds later, we were both on the other side, intact and unrun-over, the traffic now at our back. The sharp smell of the East River hit my nostrils, overwhelming even the smell of diesel behind us, and for a brief moment I was homesick for Boston, and J's apartment overlooking the bay, where the smell of salt air was a daily greeting.

The moment passed, the weight of the kit in my hand reminding me what we were here for. I checked my core, making sure that it was settled, because the last thing you wanted to do was walk onto a scene with your core-current ruffled. I glanced over at Pietr, who looked to be doing the same.

"Ready?"

"Yeah."

A short walk farther, the smell of the river getting stronger, and we were on a concrete dock that housed a parking lot, a warehouse of undetermined ownership, and, I presumed, a dead body.

We were met on the scene by a cop who looked like she'd rather be anywhere else but there. She was little, by cop standards, with thick black hair cut short, and a tea-stained complexion I'd have killed for. Talent—I thought I recognized her, but wouldn't swear to it. New York's a big city, and Talent don't really clump together outside of Council functions and cocktail parties—or the occasional impromptu gossip session—but only a Talent, a magic-user like us, would have been left to guard this particular body. The NYPD had at least half a clue, even on bad days.

"You the pups?"

As questions went, it was pretty stupid, but there was a protocol that needed to be followed: I didn't know her, and she didn't know us. "Bonita Torres, Pietr Cholis," I said. I waited for her to ask for official identification, but I guess she really didn't care that much. We were here, which meant it wasn't her responsibility anymore.

Pietr bypassed the cop and crouched to look under the orange tarp, and then backed up a step, almost involuntarily.

"What is it?" I asked her.

"You're the investigator," she said, looking bored. "You tell me."

I gave her a sideways stare, and she took it without flinching. Great, now I was trying to tough-out the NYPD? Right.

I thought about pointing out that covering the body was not SOP, and that she might have ruined evidence, then decided that she already knew that and had her reasons.

"Bippis," Pietr said. I was the nominal specialist on fatae politics, but Pietr knew a lot more about the various breeds than I did

"A what?" Distracted, I tried to place the word, and couldn't.

"Bippis. I think that's how it's pronounced, anyway. I recognize the arms."

I went to look at the body under the tarp, and saw what Pietr was talking about. The corpse looked almost human, if you could ignore the dark green skin that glittered like mica, but the arms were twice as thick around as mine, and all muscle, and extended like an orangutan's down to its knees. And the head, which was hairless, and shaped like an anvil, almost. No wonder she'd covered it. Even in NYC, even out here where tourists didn't wander, a corpse like that might draw notice.

"Is the color normal, or did it react to the water?" Weird question, but when it came to the fatae, it paid to ask. Or, actually *we* were paid to ask.

"Damned if I know." He knelt down on the grass and touched the skin before I could remind him that we were supposed to wear gloves. Not because we might interfere with evidence—we collected data a little differently from Null CSIs—but because, well, look at what happened to poor Nifty. Some things bit even without teeth. Or even dead.

"Skin's cool, but dry. I'm thinking the color's natural." He rubbed his fingers together thoughtfully. "No flaking, either."

"You people freak me out." That was our cop, looking a little queasy now, rather than bored.

"Human floaters are better?"

"At least they're human," she said, distaste evident in her voice.

Ah, bigotry, alive and stupid in New York City. She should be glad it wasn't summer, yet. I didn't think this guy would smell too good, a few hours in the heat.

"Somebody tied him up," I said, taking Pietr's lead and ignoring the cop, who returned the favor, wandering off to pointedly look away from whatever we were doing. I crouched beside him and pulled the tarp aside a little more without touching the corpse itself. "Hands and feet—they didn't want him to be able to swim at all."

"Assuming the breed could even swim. He looks solid, all muscle...might have sunk to the bottom, anyway," Pietr said. "Alive or dead when he went in?"

"Oh, sure, give me the crap jobs." I shook out my left hand, and mentally reached in to gather some current, selecting threads from the neat coil of multicolored, static-shivering magic inside my core, and drawing them up my rib cage, along my arm, and down into the fingers I'd just loosened.

Like so many of the cantrips and preset spells we'd been working on in the office the past year, this one hadn't actually been tested in the field yet. It should work, but *should* and *did* weren't always reading from the same page, and we'd had a few go rather spectacularly sour when tried under real-life conditions.

At least nobody was watching, or grading, this time.

I selected a specific thread, a glittery glinting dark blue that was almost purple, and directed it down away from me, into the corpse's chest. The thread slipped through the flesh like a needle, and I could *feel* it tunneling down into the lungs. I don't care who you are or what you did, the sensation of current moving like that at your command *never* got old.

Older spells, and modern traditionalists, used words to direct their current. Venec frowned on that: we weren't here to entertain or impress—or intimidate—but to work. So I kept it simple. "Wet or dry?" I asked down the line of current, imbuing a sense of what I was looking for into the words, and waited. A scant second later, the current sent back its answer.

"Water in the lungs," I said. "Our boy was tossed in still breathing. Cause of death probably drowning, unless there's something funky about the Bippis physiology?"

"Not so far's I know," Pietr said. That meant absolutely nothing; there were more breeds within the *Cosa Nostradamus* than any human could ever encounter, or even read about, and most of 'em had at least a small community living here. New York City: melting pot of the world, and not all the ingredients were human.

"So, it was caught, tied up, and tossed in the water...." Pietr knelt again, opening his kit and taking out a brush and a small vial of something glittering. The brush was just a makeup brush, a very expensive one, and the glittery powder was fine-ground, electrically charged metal shavings. Metal conducted current the same way it did for electricity, allowing us to use the lightest possible touch and lowering the risk that we'd disturb evidence. He added a pinch of shavings to the brush, and swirled it over the top of the bindings, careful this time not to touch anything with his bare hands. His personal current could affect the shavings, even through the latex.

The dust settled, and Pietr cocked his head, studying the results. His current was so light, so subtle, I couldn't even see a hint of it in the air over the bonds. Impressive, as always. I was good at gleaning, my memory capturing details I didn't even notice I'd seen, but when it came to this kind of physical collection, Pietr had me beat.

I waited, shivering a little as the wind off the river reached through my jacket, while Pietr focused on the spell's results. The shavings carried the spell into the dead body's tissue, showing him the muscles that had last been used, and how much energy they had burned. "Yeah, it struggled. Another ten minutes, maybe, and the ropes would have given way." They were thick twine, but definitely frayed, I had noticed that. On a human, they would have been enough to immobilize someone indefinitely. "But that kind of struggling would have used oxygen, and sped up the drowning. Whoever tossed it in knew what they were doing."

I exhaled heavily, feeling the air leave my lungs, thinking about what was being said—and what wasn't. "Which probably means *Cosa,* not just some scared humans looking to clean the world of a freak." We'd been having trouble in the city—actually, we'd been having Troubles: humans—Talent and Null—bashing up against the fatae, and everyone coming out the worse for it. During the ki-rin "he said, she said" disaster, it had looked like the entire city was going to combust, but when we'd been able to prove that both humans and fatae had been involved, the flames died down to coals again.

Died down, but hadn't gone out. I still had nightmares, sometimes, about the sound of the ki-rin's voice when it admitted its guilt…regret and remorse that came too late, after four lives were ruined, one fatally.

I'd always been a sunny-side-up girl, but the world was a very gloomy place, some days.

"Maybe. Probably, yeah."

"Joy." And trying to get answers out of the fatae community was always such a pleasant experience. Even when they were human-friendly, they didn't like to tell us anything. Except when they were telling us things we didn't want to know, or trying to talk us into something to their benefit, of course.

"All in a day's work," Pietr said, putting away the dust and brush, and locking his case again. There were still things to be done, but you didn't leave your kit open, ever.

"You gonna take the body, or not?" the cop asked, coming back from her wander of the perimeter to stand over my shoulder, getting way too close inside my personal space.

"You rush your lab techs this much?" I snapped, annoyed at being interrupted.

The cop showed a wide, toothy, happy-to-annoy-you grin. "Yep."

"Great. Try to rush me again, and I'll hotfoot you in ways that won't wear off for a week." She could try to match me, but we both knew she'd lose. I might not be a natural powerhouse the way some of my pack mates were, but you didn't get to be a pup without picking up some serious skills, and I'd a year's worth of training under my belt now.

She backed off.

I looked over at Pietr, who was still studying the body. "You want to do the gleaning?" It was normally my job, but there didn't seem to be anything particularly difficult, and the Big Dogs like everyone to keep at least their pinkie in with that particular spell.

"Not really. But I will."

Gleaning is our version of videography: we collect all the visual evidence, and replay it, back in the office, into a three-dimensional display. We tried, at first, to glean the emotional record, since current leaves trace, and a strong Talent can usually pick up strong emotions after the fact. Unfortunately, we learned the hard way that when you're talking about the sort of violence we tend to uncover, that's not always the smartest idea. We'd been caught up in it, and our first case had almost been our final one. So Venec laid down the law: physical evidence only.

While Pietr went into fugue-state to glean, I wandered down to the East River, or as close as I could get to it, standing on a man-made concrete pier. It looked like... water. Bluish-gray, little ebbs and currents swirling the surface, underneath... Who the hell knew what was underneath. The rivers, Hudson and East, were a hell of a lot cleaner than they had been once upon a time, but a tidal river could hide anything...at least until it pushed it to shore.

I stared out across the surface, anyway, looking. They'd pulled the body out here—I saw a little yellow flag fluttering in the breeze—but odds were it had gone into the river somewhere uptown and floated down. All the landing site would tell me was what size shoe the finders had worn, and how far they'd dragged him before he'd been wrapped up in official sailcloth and brought up here, in direct contradiction of every rule of Standard Operating Procedure the NYPD was supposed to follow. I looked, anyway. You never knew where or when or how something useful might turn up.

In this instance, though, I didn't even find a candy wrapper that looked suspicious, just a lot of gunky mud

I had to knock off my shoes when I got back up on the pier. I guess I understood why they'd moved the body, but it still pissed me off. I'd bet the NYPD hadn't even bothered to do a basic sweep of the area before calling us in—something this obviously *Cosa* business, their protective filters snapped up and they didn't see anything, didn't know anything, didn't have to write up anything.

I turned back to stare at the water again. I would do a deeper read, but it didn't matter: between the fatae that lived in the local rivers and the ocean waters that fed it, and the power plant upriver, and the general ambient noise of however many thousands of Talent in this area on a daily basis, there was enough magical white noise to cover a multitude of clues, and not even Venec's nose was good enough to sniff anything out of this.

I gave up, and went back to the body.

"I got it," Pietr said, standing up and wincing as his knees cracked loud enough for me to hear.

"You're getting old, old man."

"It's not the years, it's the damned mileage," he said, and he wasn't joking. We were in our twenties, everyone except the Big Dogs and Lou, but some days I woke up feeling like the tail end of a forty-year-old. Current took it out of you. What we were doing, what we were seeing...that took it out of you, too.

I looked at the tarp. Someone had taken it out of our vic, too.

You didn't end up bound-and-drowned by accident. Someone had killed this fatae, for whatever reason. We didn't know who it was, if it left a family, if it had been murdered for cause or on a lark, or if there were other bodies waiting to be found, or if the killing was a one-off or if they would strike again. Hell, we didn't even know the victim's gender, or how to check.

I'd be carrying all those unknowns with me tonight when I tried to get to sleep, and keeping me company in my dreams, and when I woke up again, hoping against hope we'd be able to find even one answer…and knowing we might not.

Sometimes, this job sucked large, pointed rocks.

Pietr pulled the tarp back over the body and nodded to the cop that we were done. They'd cart the body off to the city morgue, to the little cold room in the back that nobody talked about, and stash it there until we figured out who the next of kin were. "You think Shar and Nick are having more fun?"

I glared up at the clear blue sky. "They'd better be."

Sharon's report later was the usual tersely professional recounting, but no, they hadn't been having more fun.

Mass transit didn't reach into their destination, so they had to walk from the bus stop, pausing to check their directions several times.

"Huh. Nice."

Sharon let out a sniff that wasn't entirely disagreement. "Gaudy."

Nick shoved his hands into his jacket pocket and smirked. "I like gaudy. It takes a lot of money to be that tasteless."

The house they were looking at wasn't actually tasteless, although it leaned that way: a gleaming white, pseudo-Federalist structure on a lot not much larger than the house itself. There was enough frontage, barely, to allow for an imposing driveway from the street, and enough shrubbery to suggest privacy without hiding the grandeur of the house from the peasants driving by. Peasants were, clearly, supposed to be aware of their own insignificance in the face of such a house.

Sharon said as much, as they walked up the driveway, each of them carrying their kit in their off-hand, so as not to bump against each other. Nothing in the kits was terribly unstable, but some of their equipment was best neither shaken nor stirred.

"In this neighborhood, any peasants would get knee-capped by the private security force," Nick said, not really joking. They had noted the discreet but blunt signs when they walked down the street: nonresidents were not welcome here, unless invited.

The double doors were white, with lions'-head knockers in brass, and a simple buzzer underneath.

Sharon touched the buzzer, and they waited.

"Yes?"

The woman who opened the door for them wasn't the owner—she was dressed in a neat cream pantsuit that had the feel of a uniform, and had an air to her that was pride but not ownership.

Nick took the lead. Women of a certain age and position, Venec said, would respond more automatically to a man than a younger woman, especially a good-looking man. You used whatever tools you were given. "We're from PUPI. Mr. Wells is expecting us."

"Oh." The woman wasn't flustered, just checking them out, her gaze taking in the details of Sharon's neat, dark blue suit and pumps, and Nick's more casual slacks and loafers. He was wearing a leather jacket, but it was quality enough to pass muster, apparently, because the housekeeper nodded once, and stepped back to let them in.

"Mr. Wells is in the sunroom," she said. "Please follow me."

They both took in the details, not obviously scanning their surroundings. The foyer was larger than either of their apartments, with marble floors and a carpet that was probably worth more than they earned in a year.

"Ouch," Nick said softly, and Sharon's gaze followed his as the housekeeper led them down the wide hallway. The left-hand side of the hallway boasted only closed doors, but to the right there were archways opening to a great room with soaring ceilings and expensive furniture—that had been torn apart. Fabric was shredded, as though huge claws had used it as a scratching post, and cabinet doors were ripped off their hinges, antique-looking carpets shoved in a crumpled pile against the walls.

"I don't think this was a Retriever," Nick said softly.

"No?"

"It just doesn't feel right. Retrievers are pros. They don't leave behind any trace, much less damage."

Sharon nodded. "Although, it could just have been the owner's temper tantrum after being robbed."

"You really think one guy could get that mad?"

Sharon merely looked at Nick, one delicate eyebrow raised. Anger could make even the calmest, most sedate people do things you wouldn't expect; they both knew that. And they had no idea who—or what—their client might be.

"In here, please," the housekeeper said, pushing open an interior door, and ushering them inside.

The sunroom was a surprisingly cozy place after the grandeur of the rest of the house, filled with orchids and small potted trees placed to catch the appropriate light coming in through oversize windows, and a series of comfortable-looking chairs upholstered in dark gray fabric. Each chair had a small table next to it, perfect for a newspaper or drink.

Nothing in this room appeared to have been disturbed, not even a trace of dirt on the parquet floor where a plant might have been knocked over.

The woman stopped the moment they entered the room. "Mr. Wells."

It was less an introduction than an announcement, the way a museum docent might say "The *Mona Lisa*." The client was—to all appearances—an ordinary sixty-something-year-old male. Tall and well built, with skin just naturally dark enough to avoid assumptions of WASPy wealth but not so much that an observer assumed any particular ethnicity. His head was clean-shaven, his face lined and slightly creased around the eyes and mouth. His clothing was rich-man's casual—a pair of expensive twill slacks, and a black pullover sweater that obviously was cashmere, and not a cheap single-ply weave, either.

"These are the—"

"The investigators I hired." His voice was cultured, almost lazy, with an oddly clipped drawl. "Yes. Thank you, Joyce. You may go now. Please remind the staff not to touch anything in the affected rooms."

"Yes, sir."

"Please," the client said, waving to a grouping of cloth-upholstered chairs off to the side of the room. "Be seated."

They sat. The chairs weren't as comfortable as they looked.

"You had a break-in last night." Nick took the lead without checking with Sharon, continuing how they had begun with the housekeeper. It was fifty-fifty how the client would respond, but Sharon's truth-sensing would be a strength here, and it was easier to use it when she could focus her attention entirely on the subject, without worrying about how to phrase the questions. And Nick, while not diplomatic, could do a solid guy-to-guy thing. So Sharon sat and watched, and listened.

"Yes. It happened early this morning, actually. Around 3:00 a.m. We heard the noise."

"We?" They knew already, from the original report, but the more the client talked, the more detail they could pick up, even if the client didn't think it was important.

"My staff—Joyce, my housekeeper, and Clark, my cook. I live alone, otherwise."

"And you did not go down to investigate?"

Wells looked surprised, and a little amused. "I think not. I assumed that the silent alarm had gone off and the police would be arriving soon. Joyce and Clark both know to stay in their rooms in such a case, to ensure that they are not mistaken for the intruder by the police. That would be most unfortunate."

"Indeed. And the police came..."

"They did not. The intruder managed to bypass all the sensors. Neither my security firm nor my local police department knew anything had occurred until I informed them." His voice boded not-well for both security firm and police. "It was then I suspected something out of the usual had occurred."

Magic, he meant, although like most Nulls he resisted actually saying the word.

"When I came down this morning, after the noise had ended, I found..." He sighed, shaking his head. "Wanton destruction."

So it hadn't been a temper tantrum. Or the client was lying. Nick didn't look at Sharon, keeping all of his attention on the client. "What valuables were taken?"

Wells frowned, a slight furrowing of his expression more than any downturn of his lips. "Very little. A few... trinkets, things I've had for a long time, but nothing of particular value beyond the sentimental. The cash in the safe, but none of the papers—securities and whatnot. Most of the truly valuable items are kept in my vault in the bank, of course."

"Of course," Sharon echoed, almost involuntarily. Neither pup believed it for a moment. This was the sort of man who kept everything he really valued close at hand. Sharon would also have said he wasn't a man who had sentimental attachment to anything that wasn't also worth a great deal, financially.

She'd worked for the type before; they made your life miserable, watching over everything you did no matter how good you were because they didn't trust anyone, not really, no matter how many times you'd proved yourself.

It made sense now, that Venec had sent the two of them, and not Bonnie or Nifty. They were good, but Nifty could get his ego tied up in the job, and Bonnie was so honest, someone like this would assume her openness meant she was hiding something. Both those things, with someone like Wells, could cause a problem if he took it the wrong way. Sharon and Nick, on the other hand, looked like exactly what they said they were, and that any sneaky bits they invoked were working for the client, not against him.

Sharon, particularly, excelled in making people believe that she was totally, unquestioningly, on their team. Wells barely gave her a glance now; she had become an appendage, the same as his housekeeper and his gardener.

"I have put together a list of everything I saw that was missing. You will want to examine the site of the intrusion, now?" It was less a question than a gentle order.

"Yes, thank you," Sharon said, standing up when it looked like Nick was going to try and continue the questioning. Her partner, used to following his coworker's cues, shut his mouth and stood up, as well. Rather than call his housekeeper back, Wells escorted them himself.

"The report said that you suspected a Retriever," Sharon said, both because she was curious, and because he would wonder why they hadn't asked, if they didn't. If he had been a member of the *Cosa* it would make sense, but Wells was, unquestionably, Null. "Did you have specific reason to believe…?"

"I have reason to believe that the alarm system I have

set up is suitable to detect any normal means of intrusion," he said. "I also paid a great deal of money to install a spell-detector on the perimeter of my property, to prevent any—" he paused and Sharon and Nick both had the sense that he was about to say "of you people" and changed in the last breath— "unwanted intrusions of a magical sort. Therefore clearly it had to be someone of exceptional skill."

Nick coughed, smothering a laugh. Sharon kept her face poker-still. Their client had been sold a bill of goods—there was no way to detect a spell being cast, short of actually being there when it hit. Venec and Bonnie had been working on it as a side experiment, and the current just wouldn't hold in place long enough to be useful—you could do a short-term thing, maybe a few hours, but after that, it just faded.

The only thing worse than Nulls who were current-blind were Nulls who thought they knew all about current...and didn't have a clue.

Sharon noticed that the client hadn't really answered the question about why he suspected a Retriever specifically, which was interesting. Was that deliberate or was he avoiding giving them some piece of information? She had no chance to follow up on that thought, however. Wells stopped in front of a heavy wooden door, and slid it open. "This is where the worst damage was done."

It was, clearly, his study, and Wells was right, the damage was far worse here than even the room they'd seen before. There was an oversize desk made of some deep red, clearly exotic, wood, that had at one point been placed against the far wall, based on the indentations in the carpet. Now, though, it lay on its side, in the middle of the room. That alone would have taken a lot of muscle power—or a serious push of current. The client was a normal, late-middle-aged human Null. Unless he was hiding a Hulk-like alter ego, he was out from under suspicion in the damage, at least.

The books on the built-in shelves had all been crashed to the floor, and pages lay scattered like feathers after a plucking. A floor lamp lay on its side, the shade shredded much like the upholstery they had seen earlier, and there was the sparkle of glass in the Persian carpet. Out of the corner of her eye, Sharon saw Nick pull a pair of latex gloves out of his pocket, and stretch them on quietly, without fuss.

Not that the gloves mattered in terms of evidence—most of what they collected couldn't be smudged by a physical touch—but protection would keep any of the tiny shards from sticking in his fingers.

"You look over the floor and shelves," Sharon said, with a nod at his gloves. "I'll look over the desk, see if our intruder left any hints behind." If the intruder had used current, there should still be signature left, especially if he was feeling strong emotion when he went on his rampage. So long as she was only testing for it, and not actually trying to collect it, she should be within Venec's safety guidelines.

Neither of them were Bonnie-level in terms of their reading and gleaning abilities, but they could do what was needed.

Sharon set down her own kit, and took out a small object wrapped in a silvery chamois. Unwrapping it revealed a chunk of crystal about the size of her thumb, a hazed pale pink chunk of rose quartz.

It had been a birthday present from Bonnie, a few months ago. Sharon wasn't big on aids, but Bonnie swore that using a focus would help her, and none of them were going to refuse anything without at least testing it. Sharon had planned to do that testing in a more controlled circumstance, but…

The crystal felt warm in her hand, but otherwise it just lay there, more a distraction than not. Bonnie had claimed that it would warm to her, connect her to herself more fully, and deepen her fugue-state without losing touch with the actual world.

Nothing happened. Sharon slipped the stone back into her chamois, and went to work without it

The client stood and watched them for a few minutes, but when they didn't do anything more interesting than run their hands lightly over the furniture, seemingly lost in thought, he gave a quiet snort and left them to it.

That was exactly why Venec had them work low-key, not showy. People who were bored were less likely to hang around and interfere.

After giving the desk a full once-over, Sharon sighed and shook her head, waiting until Nick blinked his way out of his own fugue-state, and looked at her.

"I'm not picking up anything," she said. "You?"

"Annoyance," he said. "But I'm not sure if it's his, or mine. Otherwise, this place is clean as a washed-down whistle."

"Like someone cleaned up after themselves?" The perp, she meant, not the victims.

"Maybe," he said. "Or like they weren't here at all."

Not a Talent, he meant. "Client may not know as much as he thinks he does," Sharon said, "but I'm inclined to agree with his conclusions, whatever I think of his logic. There's no way a Null could have gotten in, and done all this. Not in the time he claimed, without a clear point of entry."

Nick lifted one narrow shoulder in a shrug, a move he had stolen from Pietr. "Fatae? Some of them are pretty good at fast and sneaky, and those slashes might have been claws. That's a guess, though. I'm nowhere good enough to pick up an unknown fatae trace. Hell, I'm not even sure I could pick up a known breed, unless I'd encountered it before. We need to find out more about the client, see if he might have pissed off any of the *Cosa*-cousins."

Sharon considered it, then put the crystal into her suit pocket, and lifted her kit up off the carpet. "If he did, Lou will turn it up, and Venec will let us know. Come on, let's check the other rooms."

They both had the bad feeling they weren't going to find anything useful, but by god, they'd check every inch, first.

three

Not every aspect of PUPI involved investigation. Sometimes, it required suasion and statistics. That particular part of running the company they left to Ian Stosser.

Or, more to the point: that part, he kept for himself.

Ian stood in front of his audience, making eye contact with selected members seemingly at random, and infused his words with the firm and fervent belief he had in his team, his methods, and his results. "In the year we have been accepting clients, our success rate has been a rather significant 87%. Of the remaining 13%, we still managed to bring up enough information to pass along to Null authorities. The fact that my team has not yet been able to close the case you referenced—" organ-leggers, an open ticket that still annoyed Ian "—merely emphasizes the difficult and delicate nature of the work we do. More, that we are the only force that is both willing and capable of taking on cases involving magic."

He did not emphasize the *willing* part, but knew that

his point had been taken, here among those who could do good, and instead chose to hamstring his efforts.

Someone in his audience tapped a gold-plated pen on the table, impatiently. "There are others who work with magic, Stosser. You've been involved with some of them yourself."

"Private investigators, working on a borrowed shoe-string and their own instincts." That was damning the half-fatae detective, who was actually reasonably capable, but Ian Stosser did not let anyone get the upper hand in presentations *he* was making. "My team is trained to use science as well as magic, harnessing their instincts into verifiable and logical routes, using teamwork to pool our respective skills into something greater. Perhaps more importantly, we determine the evidence not by who hires us, but by what the investigation reveals as facts."

The feel of the room remained resistant. The individuals gathered here didn't want to hear, didn't want to know, and most especially didn't want to have to change their minds.

Ian Stosser was too trained, too skilled to sigh, and to turn up his current-driven charisma in a room filled with already-suspicious Talent of comparable skill would be a disaster. Instead, he ratcheted his body language up a notch, using the cast of his shoulders, the cant of his hip, even the way he rested his arm to project a calm, reasoned, pragmatic appeal that would—hopefully, ideally—reassure them without their knowing why they were reassured. That was the trick with the Council: most of them so relied on current, they forgot the basics of human psychology, too.

"What I am asking of you is a rational decision, not an emotional one," he continued. "When a crime has been committed, the offender must be determined, and punished. We are all in agreement about that." A firm, if subtle nod, and he was pleased to see several in his audience nod back, almost automatically. "I am offering you, again, the way to determine, fairly and without prejudice, where the responsibility might rest, in any given situation. That way the proper individuals will be taken to task."

A voice from the far end of the table, previously quiet, spoke up then. "And what happens when you cannot determine, for certain, who that party is? Or, worse, when you accuse the wrong person?"

Once. Once, they had... Ian beat down his irritation.

"We do not claim to be perfect," he said smoothly. "We do claim to be extremely good. And that, sirs, madams, is more than you have right now, with your refusal to accept the results of our investigations into your deliberations."

It was the same song and dance he'd done twice before, for each regional Council, crafting his argument to each specific region's objections, designed to entice each specific Council with what he thought they wanted.

According to *Cosa* history, the Mage Council had been split into regional areas back in the 1800s to keep them from becoming too powerful and overshadowing the lonejacks, or unaffiliateds, in each region. In theory. In practice, it was because the seated Council members didn't trust each other any more than the lonejacks trusted the Councils et al. So far, two Councils had voted to accept his people's testimony to their deliberations. The Eastern Council was not one of those, and their refusal, here in PUPI's base of operations, where they could see the good being done directly, stuck in Ian's craw. He took that personally.

"Already, the Midwest Council has benefited from our work. You know this." The pups had determined the truth of a murder, causing some embarrassment to the Council, true, but saving them considerable danger going forward by revealing the presence of a stone killer for hire, who also happened to be a Talent. "And you, yourself, saw the results of our efforts." He did not go into detail; he didn't have to. The events of the previous spring, where they had exposed a scam that might have set human against fatae, had been covered up for fiscal and political reasons, but they all knew the truth. Had it not been for PUPI, the damage could have been devastating—and bloody.

"You make strong points." Madame Howe, the leader of the Eastern Council, was a delicate woman, but nobody ever made the mistake of thinking her frail or gentle. The Talent who worked for her called her the electric dragon, and it wasn't an affectionate nickname. "And we appreciate your restraint while making this presentation."

She might have been speaking for the entire Council. Or she might have been using the royal "we." Ian merely inclined his head to her, accepting both the reminder that they were his equals, in current-usage, and that his part in this meeting was over.

"I shall leave you to your discussions, then. Madame, Council members."

He left the wood-paneled conference room at exactly the right pace, neither hurried nor lingering, counting off the steps deep in his head. When the door closed behind him, he did not stop or breathe a sigh of either relief or disgust, but kept moving, headed not for the elevator, but the stairs. He needed to *move*.

The hard sound of his shoes in the stairwell gave him something to focus on, and once out on the street, he let his stride lengthen, taking full advantage of the mid-morning lull in street traffic. He pushed all his excess energy, both physical and magical, down through his hips, down his legs, and out into the pavement, a sort of walking meditation and grounding all at once.

Everything was working; it was working exactly the way he had planned. They had enough work coming in that—for the first time since starting this venture—he wasn't paying the bills out of his personal account. If the Council relented, and approved PUPI to their members, they might actually have more work than they could handle. He would need to rearrange the office structure, bring in another investigator, maybe set up a separate lab, so they could work out new spells without worrying about shorting out the entire building....

His mentor would warn him against building a business plan on ifs. Stosser believed that it was almost impossible to fail, betting on the trouble that the combination of magic and human folly could create. Even if this Council refused to approve them, eventually they would gain clients from within these ranks, as well as beyond. Ian Stosser took a long view, always. In the long view, PUPI was needed, and therefore would thrive.

Now that the presentation was over, however, another worry insisted on worming its way into his thoughts.

Benjamin.

Ian frowned, a sudden surge of irritation and worry sparking the air around him, and setting off a car alarm on the street as he passed by. They had been friends since they were teenagers, the kind of friendship you counted on, even if you didn't see each other for years. Ian hadn't hesitated for a moment when thinking of a partner for this venture, hadn't hesitated in dragging the other man away from his life in another city, from whatever else he might have planned, and handing him the team of green Talent to mold into proper investigators.

Ben, as Ian expected, had taken to the new venture perfectly. It had given the other man a focus, a mission, a purpose he had been lacking before, wasted on jobs that were beneath his skills. The fact that the mission served his, Ian's own vision…well, they all benefited.

But the past few months, his partner had been…off his game. Distracted, and even more short-tempered than usual. Ben never took it out on anyone, but Ian, a trained reader of what people didn't want known or seen, saw the pressure building under his friend's skin.

Whatever it was, whatever the cause, it had to be lanced and drained, before it got infected. Ian had his suspicions about what was going on, but he didn't act on suspicions alone.

Stepping off the curb to hail a cab, Ian reached up and undid the clip that had held his flame-red hair in a respectable fashion, letting the strands fall down his back, spreading with current-static against the fabric of his suit.

The tension in his scalp lessened only slightly. When a cab pulled to the curb to deposit its passenger, he strode forward and claimed it ahead of some schlub half a step behind.

"Uptown," he said to the driver, then gave the office address. The car jerked forward into traffic, and he tried to relax against the plastic upholstery. His attempts to figure out what was wrong had, so far, met with "leave it alone, Ian," and then a crankier, more laden "back off, *boss*," when he approached Torres. Ian would be the first to admit that he wasn't any sort of relationship guru, but when even he could see something simmering....

Were it anyone else, once the direct approach was blocked, Ian Stosser would have gone the circuitous route, finding a weak spot in someone else's armor, cajoling and coaxing and out-and-out pulling as needed, wiggling the information he wanted that way. He was a trained politician, a born schmoozer. If he wanted to know something, he could and would discover it.

Except...this was Ben. His best friend. Possibly, if he was going to be blunt, his *only* friend. And for the first time in his life, Ian Stosser didn't feel comfortable about getting what he wanted, not if it meant digging into Ben's personal life after he'd been warned off.

Ben wanted to deal with it, whatever "it" was, himself. And so, Ian was going to have to accept that.

For now.

But that didn't mean he wasn't going to keep an eye on the situation. And, if needed, step in. Ben's life was his own; except where it had an impact on PUPI. Then, he belonged to Ian.

★ ★ ★

"You gonna eat that?"

"Yes." I glared at Pietr, clutching at my pastry defensively. "Paws off."

After we'd come back and filed our report of the scene, complete with a dump of our gleanings, Pietr and I ended up in the front break room with Nifty, pouring pitch-black coffee into ourselves and hoovering up the crumbs from a box of really disgustingly stale doughnuts, trying to figure out what sort of fatae could have taken down our floater.

We'd all agreed that it couldn't have been human, not short of five strong men, anyway. Bippis were not only strong, apparently, they were dense; their bones weighing twice what a human's would. Hard to break, even harder to shove around. Pretty easy to drown, though; Pietr had been right about that. So that meant looking through our roster of the fatae breeds to see if any of them matched the required muscle, and of those, if we knew of any that had a bad relationship with Bippis, or cause to do one harm. Bippis didn't harm each other—it was some kind of built-in safe lock in the breed.

"The problem with looking at possible conflicts," Nifty said now, "is that the odds were this was a totally personal thing, one-on-one rather than breed-specific. So it could be some fatae breed who's coexisted peacefully with everyone for generations, just suddenly having a freak-out. Statistically—"

Pietr groaned. Nifty did love his stats.

"Statistically," Nifty went on, undeterred, "most killings are unplanned, spur-of-the-moment, rage-or-jealousy driven kind of things, and the fact that the vic wasn't human doesn't change any of that."

"They'd tied its hands and legs with rope it couldn't break, and thrown it into the river, still alive. That feels like something more than spur-of-the-moment anger." I looked at the others, and got nods, Nifty's more grudging than Pietr's. "So we start big, determining which breeds could actually manage to do the deed, and then work our way down to the smaller scale of motive."

Somewhere, I was pretty sure, someone had collected data on every single fatae breed ever. It was the kind of thing mages used to do, assigning their students twenty pages a night to copy, or something. Not even Venec's mentor, who was a pretty notable scholar in this age, had access to records like that now, though; they'd probably been lost in one of the Church purges, or during the Burning Time here in America.

What we had was a wooden, four-drawer filing cabinet, *très* old-fashioned, that was starting to fill up with folders on each breed as we encountered it, all the notes and specifics, and whatever photos or drawings we could lay paws on. I was looking through the *D*s, glancing and discarding, when I saw the file for "demon." The label wasn't in my handwriting; it was Venec's. I had the urge to open it, see what he had put in there, and if he'd mentioned the one we'd seen in the diner downtown, last winter. And if he had mentioned it, if he'd mentioned anything about why we were down there.

Stupid. Stupid, and pointless, and the kind of poking around a lovesick twelve-year-old did, damn it. If he did mention being there, the citation would be entirely about seeing the demon, maybe something about the case we were working on then.

He wouldn't have mentioned the fact that I'd tracked him down to a goth club, off-hours, or that we'd ended up in that diner to talk, for the first time, about the damned connection we had that was supposed to make us lifetime soul mates or something.

Neither of us wanted that, particularly, or intended to follow up on it, and sure as hell were not about to put it down anywhere even semiofficial, in writing.

No. He wouldn't have mentioned any of that, no more than I mentioned it to anyone, not even J, my mentor.

My secret. My headache.

Even now, if I let my wall down a little, I could feel Venec's current-presence. I could tell you where he was, more or less, and if I concentrated I could tell you what he was feeling.

And if he let down his walls at the same time, I could tell you what he was thinking. By all research and rules, that was supposed to be impossible. I really wished that were true.

As extra-special treats went, the Merge wasn't. I had no interest in being told by some magical mojo who I was supposed to be knocking boots with, or cuddling up thoughtwise, and I sure as hell didn't want some mystical force determining who I extraspeshul magically bonded with. Oh, hell, no.

Thankfully, Venec had the same opinion of the entire thing. Unlike the downtime thing Pietr and I had going, there was no way to cordon off what was between us, safely; even I, queen of let's-try-anything, knew that. It would change everything, disrupt everything, and neither of us had any desire to screw up the most important thing in our lives—this job—for...

For whatever the Merge actually was. Venec might still be digging at it, trying to find answers, or at least explanations. If he'd found anything, he hadn't told me, and I hadn't asked. For once in my life, I was perfectly content to not know about something.

Yeah, I admitted it. I was afraid that if I started poking at it, explored the possibilities even in my thoughts, it would get stronger just by being exposed to air or something. For once in my life, I wasn't going to take the risk.

I'd just moved my hand away from the demon file and pulled the next one on my list when Sharon came out of the back rooms, Nick half a step behind her. She was as immaculate as ever, Nick was rumpled and scrawny as ever, and yet they shared the exact same look of annoyance. Whatever they'd gotten on their assignment, it wasn't open and shut.

"Bad scene?" I asked, putting the file down.

"Useless scene," Sharon said, dropping herself onto the sofa next to Pietr. "The place was trashed, no sign of entry or exit, no way any of the three people in the house could have done it, even if they had cause, and while the place was wrecked, there were only a handful of things actually taken, according to the owner. He's dead set on it being a Retriever, mainly I think because that makes him feel important, that someone hired a pro. My bet is some Talent with a grudge, and most we'd be able to get them for would be breaking and entering."

"What she's really pissed about," Nicky said, "is that

the client must lie for a living. Even I could tell he was full of shit, but she couldn't pinpoint anything specific to call him on."

"What does he do?" I asked, prepared to hear banker, or lawyer, or CEO of a pharmaceutical company.

"Owns a national rental car franchise," she said. "I wouldn't rent from them even if I knew how to drive."

Huh. "What did Venec say?" I asked. I knew he was lurking in the back office; even with my walls up I could feel him, the way you feel a storm coming, the static in the air almost a solid, living thing. He must have just finished debriefing them.

"He told us that lack of trace was a roadblock not a disaster, the client was probably an ass but he was still the client. And to get the hell out of the office, clear our brains, and let the investigation wait until the morning." Sharon had an odd look on her face, and the more I looked the less it seemed like annoyance, and more like she'd bitten into what she thought was a lemon and gotten a peach, instead. "I don't think he's taking this case seriously."

Nifty pointed out the logic-fail in that. "Venec takes everything seriously."

Sharon rubbed at her face, and nodded. "Yeah, I know. I just… The client's an idiot, the house is trashed but nothing of serious value was taken…. I'm not sure I'm taking it seriously, either."

Sharon, like Venec, took everything seriously. I was starting to wonder about this case. It was almost enough to be thankful for a floater. Almost.

"Screw it."

I looked over at Pietr, who had spoken far louder than his norm. "It's not like we're getting anywhere with this, either." He scowled at our piles of so-far-useless paper-work. "Any trace there might have been was washed by the river. You know it, I know it, even the cop knew it. We could stare at files all night and get nowhere, and it's not like the NYPD will appreciate our exhaustion."

We dealt with the weird shit in an exchange of favors, keeping the unspoken lines of communication open, but nobody ever took formal notice of anything; he was right.

"And it's not like the stiff's in any rush. So I say screw it. We have birthdays to celebrate, anyway."

"We do?" That was news to me; we'd just celebrated Sharon's, and I couldn't think of anyone else....

Pietr closed his own file, and stood up. "Someone, somewhere, is being born. That calls for a drink."

It was tough to argue with that logic. So we didn't.

The after-work crowds at Printer's Devil, down by Port Authority terminal, was the usual mix of depressed-looking newspaper geeks and overly cheerful tourists who'd gotten lost off Times Square. I couldn't remember why we kept coming here, except for the fact that it wasn't convenient to anyone's place, and therefore was neutral ground. Also, they made the best damn spicy empanadas north of Miami.

We'd gotten one of the high narrow tables in the back and crowded around it. With six of us, there was barely enough room for our drinks and elbows, but it beat the hell out of trying to stand in that crowd. Nick, on his second mojito, was waving his arms, retelling a story that we'd all heard three times already. "I swear, I thought the conductor was going to blow something out his ear. And Lou's sitting there, looking at him…"

Lou rolled her eyes, not saying anything. She was still figuring out how to fit in with us, but when you get razzed by Nick you can't really get annoyed, because he takes it so cheerfully when the tables are turned.

But it was maybe time to step in. "Oh, come on, that one wasn't her fault," I said.

"Yeah, but she *thought* it was!"

Nick cracked up as he delivered the line, and even Lou smiled a little. He was right; that had been what made it so funny.

We were all still wound up, but it wasn't quite so bad. Venec and Stosser had meant to make us efficient when they molded the pack, but it had also created a sort of safety zone. We knew the kind of shit we'd seen; we didn't have to talk about it, to explain why we needed distraction.

"Don't turn around, you've got an admirer," Pietr said, leaning across the narrow table to shout in…my ear? Nifty's? I couldn't tell. So, of course, we both looked.

Speaking of distraction. Contrary to some people's wet dream of bisexuality, I didn't drool over everything that breathed. Pietr, yes. Venec, yes, even without the Merge. Sharon had piqued my interest briefly, but Nick, Nifty, and Stosser weren't my type either physically or emotionally. This woman, on the other hand….

She looked right back at me, and smiled, the kind of smile I recognized: Hi, it said. Will you smile back at me?

So I did. She was a redhead, the kind of shaggy strawberry that only comes naturally or with a lot of money, and her eyes were wide-set and light-colored, and she had a body that probably wouldn't raise the pulse of any red-blooded American male, unless he recognized the lean and agile muscles flexing as she walked. Toward me. There was a god, and she was gracious.

"Once again, Bonnie scores, and the rest of us strike out," I heard Nifty mutter, and I spared him a consoling pat on the hand. "You do all right for yourself, guy. But this one seems to be more about the girl parts."

"I'm allll about the girl parts," Nick said in a singsong falsetto, picking up the tail end of our conversation. I wasn't looking at him, but from the solid whap-noise, I was guessing that someone—probably Sharon—had just slapped him upside the head to shut him up before my visitor made it to our table.

"Hi." She had an ordinary but pleasant voice, blandly Northeast, and her smile was even nicer up close.

"Hi. I'm Bonnie." I slid off my chair to move away from my usually-but-not-always-discreet coworkers, and tilted my head to better look at my new friend. She was taller than me, and her eyes were definitely hazel-green and very pretty.

"Joan." She gave me her hand, and it was smooth and soft and strong, and...

I didn't feel anything. Not even the shiver of anticipation that usually came when someone gave me that kind of once-over.

Oh, damn it. Just, damn it.

It wasn't that I was in a guy-phase, either. I'd gotten

hit on last week by a very nice example of my type, slightly scruffy and broad-shouldered, and enough smarts to balance out the bad-boy looks…and I'd smiled and felt nothing other than a passing admiration for the package.

Even my recent off-work time with Pietr had been about release and comfort, not the sort of enjoyable, mutual passion I was used to feeling. I was…not dead inside, but rather unnervingly *calm*. Like a very still lake, when you're used to an ocean.

I'd liked to have blamed it on some kind of off-season flu, or overwork, or maybe some horrible current-disease that was eating my libido but that wasn't it, not exactly. If I let my guard down, or lingered too long, late at night, in my deepest thoughts, my entire body came alive like someone had dunked me in liquid current, every nerve tingling and *wanting*.

Just not for any of these would-be playmates.

The Merge. The stupid, unwanted, unasked for Merge, and Benjamin Venec's own innate, dark-eyed appeal. Damn it, thrice.

I knew it was probably a lost cause, but Joan was cute as hell, and I wasn't ready to give up just yet. Maybe getting to know her over a few drinks….

"You want to join us?" I asked, turning to indicate my for-now demure coworkers. A look of disappointment touched Joan's face: no, she really didn't. She wanted me to go with her, somewhere else, right now.

Some of the shiny rubbed off at that. Even if I'd been at loose ends and hot to trot, a quick hit wasn't my thing. I'm a bit of a hedonist, yeah, but I liked to know the person I was with, more than just a name and a favorite drink. So with a regretful smile, and not really any regrets, I let that fish slip back into the sea and went back to my team.

"You feeling all right, dandelion?" Nick almost, almost managed to sound like he was seriously concerned for my well-being.

"Yeah, I'm fine." I twisted on a grin. "She was...too young for me."

"Young." Nifty sounded like he wanted to challenge me on that—and rightfully so, because she clearly had been well above the age of consent, but he didn't. That, in a way, was worse than if he had ragged on me. It was either pity or worry, neither of which I could deal with right now, even if I had anything to tell them.

If I let them, the team would ply me with drinks and do their best to console me on whatever they thought was wrong, distract me with bad jokes or horrible stories, maybe try to fix me up with someone they knew who would be perfect...and normally I'd let them, accepting their own odd ways of showing they cared. But suddenly, my skin was too raw, my nerves too exposed, and I just needed to be by myself.

"Okay, I'm out," I said, finishing my drink. "This little puppy is going home. Alone. I'll see y'all tomorrow." I grabbed my bag, paid out enough to cover my drinks, and waved goodbye before anyone could get a wiseass crack in about me being the first to leave. Okay, it was unusual but it wasn't totally unheard-of.

Not recently, anyway.

I worked with trained investigators, each and every one of them hired because they were obsessively curious, and incapable of walking away from a puzzle. I would lay odds they were playing paper-rock-scissors even now, to determine who got to ask me what was going on, tomorrow. And once they started digging, they weren't going to let up. Not them.

Great.

I walked out into the night with the beginnings of a killer headache under my scalp, and a roil in my stomach that had nothing to do with the empanadas I'd eaten.

The Merge was starting to interfere, not with my ability to do the job, but my coworkers'. They were going to be focusing on the mystery of me, and maybe not on the work at hand. Of all the problems I thought this might cause, that hadn't been one I'd considered.

"So what now, Bonita?"

The great thing about New York City—you can carry on an entire conversation with yourself, and even without an earpiece nobody gives you a second look. The usual chaos of Port Authority in the evening was weirdly soothing to get caught up in. If you know how to walk with the flow, you can get lost in the swirl of people, like being a single grain in a sandstorm, carried around and dropped off where you needed to be by some weird magic. All you had to do was not consciously think about what you were doing or where you were going, and let the universe carry you there.

I caught the A train uptown. Spring is the best time to ride the subway: everyone's dropped off the heavy coats that overstuffed trains during the winter, and the summer's sweat hasn't begun yet. Considering how full the train was, that was a blessing. Bad enough some hip-hop wannabe teenager tried to hold the door for his pack of slower-moving friends, causing the conductor to bawl something incomprehensible until they were all inside and he let the door go.

On another day I might have been tempted to send a spark from the metal door into his hand, for being a jerk, but my focus was all inward, right then.

Fact one: the thing I'd worried about was here, the Merge was impacting work. That it wasn't happening exactly how I'd feared didn't change the fact. So, one excuse for avoiding it, blown out of the water. Or, at least, taking on water and sinking fast.

Fact two: my coworkers were right; this reluctance to plunge into new adventures with someone attractive and attracted was…very much not like me.

Or, at least, not like me-who-was.

J had always claimed that there would come a day when I'd settle down with, as he resignedly put it, "a nice little household." Even he, who'd known me since I was eight, couldn't imagine me being happy with just one person, either male or female. I had always liked—I still *did* like—variety.

And it wasn't that my sex drive was shut off entirely. Pietr might not set off sparks but it had never been about that; we used each other for mutual comfort and release, full knowledge of what it was, and I…

I…

By the time my train had dumped me out at my stop, and I'd climbed the stairs to street level, the stutter in my brain and the rawness of my nerves had finally resolved itself into fact number three.

I felt guilty.

I felt guilty because I *wasn't* cheating on a guy I *wasn't* in a relationship with, who knew I was having sex with someone else and had agreed with me that he had no right or cause to say anything other than "don't let it get tangled in the job." And we hadn't.

But the stress of it all—and the guilt—was starting to bleed over into my relationship with Pietr, too. The fact that he understood, even if he didn't understand all of it, just made me feel worse. I liked Pietr. A lot. He was easy to be with, he understood me, and didn't ask for anything I couldn't give.

Not even explanations.

"Damn it."

That did get me a look from the woman coming down the stairs, more mild curiosity than anything else. I ducked my head and went back to thinking quietly.

J was right. I was changing. And I resented, not the fact of change—that would be like resenting breathing, or rain: you needed those things for life to go on, and not changing in the face of new experiences and knowledge was just dumb and counterproductive. But I resented the hell out of the fact that this had been shoved on me, without so much as a by-your-leave or instruction booklet, and was demanding change without, as far as I could see, giving a damn thing back in return.

"Gonna have a lot of cold showers until you get this thing licked," I said to myself as I unlocked the front door of my building and dragged myself inside. "And, okay, *licked* may not be the best word to use, in context..."

As always, just being inside my apartment soothed

me. The space itself wasn't much, and the building was drafty, but inside... Someone else might find the vibrant burgundy-and-pale-gold walls too exotic, the mix of antiques and thrift store finds too distracting, but to me, it said "home."

I pulled off my boots and dropped them on the parquet floor, wincing at the sound. It was still early, but my downstairs neighbors were always on my case about every pinprick of noise.

Yeah, the decor was me, but the building...not so much.

I dropped my bag on the nearest sofa, and walked across the open space into the kitchen alcove. It was a decent-size studio, as things went, and got gorgeous sunlight, the few times I was home during daylight hours. The glasswork mosaic that hung on the wall where most people would put a flat-screen TV glittered when I turned on a lamp, a pale reflection of what it did during the day, and I noticed with dismay that a few of the colored glass pieces had somehow slipped from the frame and shattered on the ground.

"Well, damn."

I was way more upset about the broken glass than it deserved, taking my frustrations out on a random bit of bad luck. What was that saying my dad's girlfriend Claire used to trot out, about if it weren't for bad luck she'd have none? I stared at the shards, feeling the cranky surge through me, then let it go. It was just glass, and unlike my personal life it could be fixed easily enough.

I held my hand out, palm down over where most of the shards were, and pulled the faintest trickle of current from my core. Not too much; I didn't want the shreds to come flying up and embed themselves in my palm, just lift off the floor and come together in a glittering little lump, and then follow me back to the trash can, where I released the current-strands, and let the tiny shards fall into the bin.

There were leftovers and some salad in the fridge, but I'd eaten enough at the Devil that I wasn't tempted. Instead, I stripped down to undies, intending to crawl into my bed with a book and read until I fell asleep.

Instead, I found myself climbing the loft ladder with, not a book, but the case file in my hand.

Sketches of drowned corpses and detailed descriptions of said remains were not high up on my bedtime reading. But I wasn't planning on going over the details again. Pietr was right; it was a dead end, pun intended. Without evidence, that area of investigation didn't lead anywhere.

A trained pup, though, had more options than what could be found on the body or around the scene. There was also what was caught in the flow of the universe. More, I could try using the particular skill set that my mentor called the kenning, a foresight that sometimes gave me tiny glimpses of the future, sensing when something was coming down the pike. Sometimes, if I was very focused, I could see the present, too, or at least how it intersected with the future.

Focus, though, required a little help. Mostly a kenning came without being called, without warning, at the absolute worst time possible. That was just how the universe seemed to work. To bring it to heel, I'd have to start with a scrying.

Sitting cross-legged on the mattress, careful not to bump my head on the ceiling, I put the file down on the bedspread in front of me and reached to the little shelf, where I kept my crystals.

Yeah, crystals were ridiculously old-fashioned and quaint according to most modern Talent, including J and half my coworkers. They could go jump; crystals helped me scry, and anything that helped was worth keeping.

Venec had broken my favorite shard, back when I tried to scry who was calling me in for the interview. He called it cheating, then. I suspected now he'd call it a "useful tool," so long as I used it for work, and not to see what he was up to. I didn't plan on asking his permission, or for his approval.

Something stirred on the fringes of my awareness and I quashed it. I did not need, nor want, the Merge anywhere near me, right then.

For once, it took the hint, and subsided.

I reached for the plain wooden box, flipping open the lid. It was about the size of a shoe box, and lined in thick, nubby, cream-colored cloth. Inside rested my two remaining pieces: a rose quartz ball about the size of my palm, and my traditional, kerchief-and-skirts style scrying globe of clear quartz, with a jagged imperfection, like a cloudy lightning bolt, through the center.

I really needed to replace the clear shard, someday. I'd gotten good workings with it then; who knew what I could do now that I had hard-core training?

Distracted by the thought, my hand reached for the rose quartz as though by instinct, but I stopped just before my palm touched it.

Rose quartz was really useful for me; I resonated to it, found details I didn't always with another color, or clear. But it worked on a more emotional level, instinctive and visceral. I had the gut feeling—pun intended—that if I picked that one up, all the walls in the world weren't going to protect me from knowing Venec a bit more than I wanted to.

I didn't want to know what he was up to, not that way.

And I *really* didn't want him to know that I was checking what he was up to, or think that I cared enough to look.

It wasn't logical, I knew it wasn't logical, and that was probably why I hated what the Merge did to me so much. I was completely in touch with my hedonistic, sensual side, sure, but, I still thought rather than emoted, considered rather than reacted. It was how I was built, to bulldog through everything in as practical a manner as possible, and this…this threatened to overwhelm all that.

No, better to stick with the clear crystal, until I had a better balance going.

Coward, a little voice whispered in my ear, a rusking, rattling voice like dry leaves and empty husks, and then was gone. I acknowledged the charge, and ignored it, along with everything else I was ignoring.

Current required control, and being in control. Especially if you were going to open yourself up to scry.

The clear globe was heavier than I remembered, filling both my hands and forcing them down to the bed with its weight. I let my arms lower, relaxing my shoulders, letting the breath ease out of me on a slow exhale. The moment the back of my hand touched the files spread out in front of me, I felt the downward-upward spiral of current that meant something was stirring, and I had to scramble, mentally, to get into proper fugue-state before it hit me.

"Ten...nine...eight..."

Too much, too fast, before I hit seven I was in it, caught up in a net of current-threads, sparkling deep green and blue around me. I pulled a breath in before I got dizzy, but it wasn't enough. Sparks flickered like lightning strikes against the inside of my eyelids, leaving a shimmer of sparkles behind that made me want to throw up, the way you do when vertigo hits. It was almost a struggle to stay grounded, something I would die rather than admit to anyone. And then I found my ground like a click and a snap and I could soothe the current swirling in and around my core, taming it back into something useful, something controlled.

I opened my eyes, mage-sense firmly in place, and looked down at the globe.

Sparks were already flicking inside the stone, mimicking what I had seen with my eyes closed, running from my fingertips down to the imperfection in the crystal, where they fractured and bounced back to the surface. More blues and greens, but darker, emitting a faint but clear warning of danger.

Current *was* dangerous, and it could give off a definite sense of menace, if the signature was malign enough, but my own current? That made no sense.

"Ground and center," I whispered. "Control what you see."

There wasn't any control at all in the actual scrying. That was one of the reasons why it wasn't popular anymore: you opened yourself up and waited for something to show up. Like deer hunting, J said, although the thought of my oh-so-patrician mentor actually sitting in a blind, freezing his ass off...

Actually, he probably had done it, at least once. There was a wicked-looking crossbow hanging in his library that I'd always assumed was a gift from someone, but he'd be able to pull it, no problem. When he was younger, anyway.

Useless thought, Bonnie. Distractions. Clear the mind. Ground the core. Open your awareness, Bonnie, and see what waits.

Scrying requires trust as well as Talent, because that lack of control cuts both ways. You don't ask for specifics, just open and wait, and brace yourself for what might or might not come.

There was no way I could brace myself for the scrying that hit.

I was wide open when the kenning came hard on its heels, the two of them twining into a braided rope that nearly knocked me off my magical ass. My vision—my entire awareness, was filled with a night-blue sky filled with electrical fire, tilting on dragons' wings and shattered spires. Hissing, out-of-control cables: lashing and spitting like a serpent's tongue. I tried to focus, to draw the vision in more closely, and was dropped into a long nauseating swoop down, like a bungee cord from hell, and then stark white filled that awareness, splattered and stained with the red that's only and ever the color of spilled blood. The cord brought me back up again with a spine-breaking snap, flinging me up into the sense of a great beast moving even farther overhead, blotting out everything, even the fire, its spread wings wheeling overhead.

Dragon, my mind told me.

I knew a Great Worm. She was an ancient, elegant lady, who would never project such anger, such fury....

The head turned and stared at me, and in its great, glimmering eye I saw nothing but madness and hunger. And deep inside, the shock of recognition, awareness. It knew me. It knew me, and it did not like me.

The feeling of hard, sharp claws pressing against my skin, pulling me down into the gaze, was purely magical, not physical, but that made it more dangerous, not less, as open as I was just then. The dizziness came back, along with the need to throw up.

Bonnie!

Not a ping, the brief current-carried shorthand we used among friends. This was deeper, like the hit of an axe into a hundred-year-old tree, and the shock of it shook me free of those devouring eyes, knocked me out of the clawed grip.

My physical body jerked backward, my hand releasing the crystal, my head hitting the ceiling with a reassuringly painful thunk.

"Ow."

I blinked against the sting of tears and stared at the crystal, trying to recapture what I had seen, but it was already starting to dissipate. Visions faded like that, unreal and therefore impossible to hold. Even so, I had the oddest feeling that I'd kenned something like it before, not recently but within the past year or so. Not the visuals, nothing at all like those visuals, but the sense of something angry, something wild circling, hunting...coming closer.

If I'd felt it before, odds were it had nothing to do with the case at hand. But the increase in intensity, the addition of visuals, meant it was coming closer on the timeline, whatever it was. I reached for my notebook and a pen. My hand was shaking, but I got the details down, best I could, before they were gone entirely.

You never ignored a kenning, especially not one that came that strongly, that tied to a scrying.

As I was writing, trying to force the ink to flow steadily, there was another push at me, somewhere between core and gut, except it wasn't physical at all. No words this time, just a sense of concern, and a willingness to pull back, if shoved.

I knew who it was. There was only one person it could be, with that kind of a connection. He was worried, and he was annoyed, but the feelings were distinct from each other. He wasn't annoyed at *me*.

As much as the Merge irritated me, it pissed Venec off even more. I got the feeling that he was constantly riding the need to check up on all of us, anyway, and not knowing where the line between boss/trainer/Big Dog ended and the Merge began meant he'd been constantly second-guessing himself. For a guy like Venec, who was totally used to being the one calling the shots and making the decisions? Oh, yeah, having something external trying to shove him anywhere would not be appreciated. Unlike me, though, he couldn't ignore it. Hence the annoyance. And if he'd felt even a little of what I did, with that eye glaring at me...no wonder he'd reacted. Normally I'd tell him to MYOB. This was work-stuff, though, even though he didn't know it, so I reached out with just a hint of current to ping back, keeping it brief and impersonal. *scrying. report tomorrow*

His acknowledgment was equally curt, but when I put the crystals and files away and crawled under the spread to sleep, I could feel the flavor of him lingering, like candied ginger on my tongue. Even when we tried to shut the Merge off entirely, it was creeping in.

Yeah. Time to do something about that. Eventually.

My last coherent thought was that I should probably stop by and pay Madame a courtesy visit. If there were any others dragons in town, she would know.

four

Thursday morning I woke up with a head filled with unsettling dreams and an intense desire to kick some investigative ass, since it seemed like that was the only part of my life that held any upside, right now. I bopped into the shower, scrubbed myself down, and practically threw myself into my work-clothes. The solid sound of my boots on the sidewalk was like a drumbeat moving me forward, and even a delay on the subway and a busker trying to play an out-of-tune ukulele couldn't ruin my mood.

The boyos who used to always linger on the stoop between the subway and the office, catcalling in a friendly way, weren't there, and I realized suddenly that I hadn't seen them in weeks. And I hadn't even noticed until now, getting to the office so early, and leaving at odd hours. Had they all gotten jobs, or gone back to school? I didn't know—and had no easy way to find out. I didn't even know their real names.

I decided that yes, they had gotten their asses back into

class, or were gainfully employed. Anything else was... not acceptable, today.

"Hi, honey, I'm home!" I chucked my coat into the closet, and checked the sign-out board in the front room. Lou had put it up when she decided she was tired of trying to remember who had gone where. Everyone's name was listed, even Stosser's, and there were columns for "in," "lunch," "out," and a wider space for details of where we were and what we were doing there. Half the time we even remembered to use it.

Nick, the board informed me, had been sent out to do follow-up interviews on the break-in. Everyone else was in. I checked myself as "in," grabbed a cup of coffee and went in search of the rest of the team.

I found Sharon, Pietr, and Venec in the main conference room, where Sharon was glowering at my report from yesterday like I'd done something to personally offend her.

"What?" I asked, trying to curb my instinctive defensive reaction.

She didn't even bother to look up. "You didn't test the body."

"Test it for what?" My hackles rose, slightly. "There wasn't any current on it, the bastard had drowned to death from the water in its lungs, which I did test, yes, to verify, and the rope burns were pretty clear indicators of why it didn't swim to shore. Unless you have some hidden store of knowledge about the breed you'd like to share with the class?"

"What kind of water was it?"

I stopped, mid-rant, and stared at her. "Son of a *bitch*."

I'd checked that there was water in the corpse's lungs. I hadn't checked to see if it was salt or fresh. The East and Hudson rivers were both tidal—they were salty. If it had been freshwater…

Freshwater would mean that our Bippis had been killed somewhere else, in another body of water, and tossed into the river after the fact.

When I screw up, I own it. Nodding an apology to Sharon, I turned to Venec, who was in his usual hold-up-the-wall pose, his eyes closed and his face not showing much of anything at all, a stone-cold poker player. I couldn't get even a tremor of sensation out of him: both our walls were up, and holding. "I fucked up. Boss, you want I should—"

"Send Pietr." He opened his eyes to look at me, and I tasted that hot candied ginger again, even though neither wall budged. "I want to hear about that scrying you did last night."

Pietr, who had already hauled himself out of the chair and was heading for the door, checked himself, barely, before moving on. He didn't have even a hint of foresee in him—most Talent didn't—and was fascinated by it. While I'd read his tarot cards once or twice as a lark, I'd refused to scry for him. I don't scry for people as a rule, least of all friends. I didn't always get something, but when I did it was always accurate, probably due to the additional whammy of the kenning. Nobody needs to know their personal fate, and I didn't need to be the one to give it to them.

I stopped, struck by that thought. Was that why I was so pissed about this stupid Merge? Not because it was trying to make me do something, but because I thought it was trying to tell me what my capital-*F* Fate would be? If so, that was pretty stupid. No matter how strong this Merge thing ended up being, or how it would change my life if I let it, that wasn't fate, or destiny.

I could feel a crease etch between my eyebrows. Was it?

I really wanted to follow that thought, the analytic cast of my mind and my Need to Know warring with the fact that I was on office-time, and Venec was standing there, waiting for my report.

"Now?" I asked, stalling. We weren't exactly a formal organization, but usually reports were written—or presented in front of the entire team—for brainstorming. Nifty and Nick and Stosser were conspicuous by their absence, even though the board said they were in the office. Ian could be anywhere, from his back office to Timbuktu. He ignored the board unless someone else checked him in or out.

Venec frowned at me, all Big Dog. "Now."

Verbal report, then, not written. "It was mostly visual. Fire-current-fire and real fire. Metal spires, shattered, but I think they were representational, not real." It was tough to tell how, exactly, but real things felt different somehow. A lot had been written up about scrying, but as usual with current, it seemed to work slightly different with each person. That was part of what made our job... interesting.

"A dragon, turning overhead." That had felt real. Physical. There was something else, something I wasn't remembering....

"A dragon?" Sharon had been trying not to listen in, but that caught her attention. I kept my gaze on Venec, the way his eyes drooped a little at the corners, and his nose really didn't fit the rest of his face, and the tiny imperfection in his lip, that made it seem almost crooked. It should have been distracting, but somehow his features focused my memory into its usual razor-sharp perfection. "It could have been a projection of emotions, anger, or power. Maybe." My tone would have told a deaf person I didn't believe that. "I was being shoved from viewpoint to viewpoint—" that had been the bungee cord "—so a lot of people are going to be involved, somehow. I don't think it's associated with this job," I said. I looked at Sharon as though waiting for some connection to kick in—or not—and then considered the residue of the scrying. "Either job. It feels…"

"Another scrying of danger." He stared at me. "Still in the future?"

Right. That was why it all seemed familiar. I'd had a shimmer of something months ago, during the ki-rin job. That was what I'd told Stosser and Venec, then; that there was a distant sense of danger, of something off-kilter, but I couldn't identify the source.

"Yes. Closer now. But not immediate."

I hoped. If I was wrong, and that beast was circling overhead even now, even if it was, please god, only metaphorical…

Venec picked up on what I wasn't saying, although that was probably just his own instincts working again. "Bad?"

His words triggered details I didn't remember seeing

the first time; I saw the splatter of blood against the snow, smelled the stink of something burning, the feel of those claws on my skin, and nodded slowly. "It will be, yeah." I hadn't known that for certain before, hadn't even known until he asked. But I knew, now. That's how the kenning worked. You don't always know what you know, and sometimes you don't know what it was until someone else tells you. Combine it with a strong scrying, and I was never, ever wrong. Even when I wished I were. "In winter, I think." There had been snow, ice. "Not now."

"All right." He seemed satisfied, for the moment. I didn't trust it. "You wrote it down?"

I swallowed, tasting the stink of that burning and the blood in the back of my throat, as though I'd breathed it in, deep. "Most of it, yeah. In my notebook." I'd had to, dumping it out before I could fall asleep.

"Get me a copy." He switched gears. "I'm switching you up on the cases—Sharon has your notes, you take hers. See if there's anything that bites you on the nose."

That was the PUPI philosophy—nobody got ownership of a case; we all worked everything. It hadn't been a problem when we started out, and had one job every couple of months; everyone was chomping to get their teeth into something and who was working what didn't matter so much. Now, with different cases at cross-times, things might get a little complicated, even confusing. Venec wasn't going to let that slow him down, though, and we'd damned well better keep up. Like the in/out board, we needed to track things. Lou, bless her, was working on a system for that, too.

I hadn't lied when I'd told her we were a stronger team for her being part of it.

With Venec's gaze still on me, I sat at the table across from Sharon, creating a tiny spot of current on the table to act as a combination coaster and coffee-warmer. It was a crappy waste of current, but I hated the taste of even lukewarm coffee. Sharon shoved a folder of notes across the table at me, and raised one of those elegant eyebrows at my current-coaster, but didn't say anything. We were still not forgiven for the pizza-grease stains faintly outlined in the middle of the table.

I opened the file. Sharon's notes were neatly handwritten, readable as a printed page. Nick's...not so much. And it wasn't a guy-thing, because the others all managed to make their notes legible, and Nifty's handwriting was better than mine, for all that his hand dwarfed most pens.

"Someday, one of us is going to have to put some effort into a current-run printer," I said, trying to puzzle out a word in Nick's initial overview. The bastard had run over into the margins, and not rewritten his notes for the file when he got back to the office. I was so going to kill him. "A dictation machine or something."

"Nice retirement plan. You go for it."

Sharon wasn't being sarcastic—I was one of the better improvisers in the office, and something like that, if I could make it work, could be worth a small but nice bundle in the community. Something to think about later. Much, much later.

I gave up on Nick's notes, and moved over to Sharon's, figuring that I could use his to add color commentary, later. I'd just gotten into a nice comfortable groove, making checkmarks where something caught my eye, when a roar tore through the office.

"Goddamn it!"

Once I'd gotten my heart back into my chest enough to determine that (a) the bellow belonged to Nifty, and (b) he sounded more pissed off than angry or scared, I drew the current that had automatically sparked on my skin in defensive mode back down into my core, and spent a minute getting my control—and my heartbeat—back to normal levels.

Sharon recovered faster than I did, and was on her feet and poking her nose out into the hallway. I noted in passing that the previously closed door now looked like it had been pulled off its hinges, hanging sideways like a post-Mardi Gras reveler, and that Venec was nowhere to be seen. The two facts were not unrelated. Big Dog had scary-fast reflexes.

Sharon followed her nose out into the hallway, and I followed her. The hallway was empty, but the door into the second conference room was open, if still attached to both hinges. Looking in, we encountered Venec, his back to us, a rather sheepish-looking Nifty, who was covered in a soft gray soot, and Lou, who looked...

Smug. Really, quietly smug.

I laughed, reading the scene quickly, with the ease of familiarity. Nifty had done something stupid, and Lou felt she was finally out from under the mockathon. If he'd blown anything up, she was right.

"Anybody dead?" I asked. Venec turned his back on the tableau, and glared at me.

Oh, boy. His hair looked like he'd just run his hands

through it in exasperation, his eyes were dark like whoa, and if you really looked at his body language you'd think he was about to start swearing, but his wall was down just enough that I got hit with a full-body blast of tight-wound hysterics just waiting for privacy to explode.

Whatever had happened, Venec thought it was funnier'n hell, and I was the only one who knew. Laughing, though? Not a good idea right now. Especially if Venec had to read Nifty the riot act over something he'd done wrong. I turned away, looking out the sole window in the room to give myself time to recover, and blinked.

A pigeon had just flown past the window...backward. Oooookay. Maybe J was right when he said I needed some downtime, maybe a vacation in the tropics somewhere....

I was still staring out the window trying to decide if I'd really seen that or just hallucinated it, most of my awareness still on the scene behind me, when the sound of the office's front door slamming open bought me back to the scene in the room.

"Lawrence, go get cleaned up. Make sure you get all of that off your skin, or it will just make the itching worse." Venec's voice was the usual low rumble, not even a hint of amusement in it. "Lou, can you re-create the steps prior to Mr. Lawrence's mishap?"

Uh-oh. I didn't quite hold my breath, but I bet Sharon did. Looking over my shoulder, I saw that Lou's smirk had turned to uncertainty. Damn it, I thought, but kept it within my own walls, don't push her like that!

Lou was just as skilled as the rest of us in theory—she wouldn't have been hired, otherwise—but her control of anything external was crap, making her use of active forensic magic...iffy. So far the calm of the office kept her steady, but this would be the first real under pressure test since her rather public screwup with the garbage truck.

Although blowing it up like that *had* exposed the body hidden inside that we hadn't known about. So in the end, it had actually been a plus.

Lou didn't see it that way, though, and neither had Venec.

At the moment, she looked exactly like she had the moment the spell went bad, wide-eyed and panicked. "Ah..."

I would swear under oath that Sharon started edging out of the conference room without seeming to move at all. She'd clearly been taking lessons from Pietr, who was almost Retriever-like in his ability to disappear when stressed. I was torn between wanting to beat Shar out the door, and being fascinated by what Lou might do.

"Yes or no?"

Lou, stung by the cold tone, met his question with a flat stare I admired, knowing firsthand how knee-quaking his glare could be. "Yes." If she had any doubts whatsoever, you couldn't tell from her voice, or her body language.

"Good. Do so. Sharon, stop that. You're Lou's second. Make sure she doesn't go splat, too. Bonnie, go fetch Nick and get back to work. When Nifty finishes cleaning up, update him on the break-in. I want to see dioramas of both scenes when I get back."

We didn't exactly snap off salutes, but nobody argued.

And nobody asked Venec where he was going, when he headed past Nick, and down the hallway toward the elevator.

Ben didn't let himself relax until he was in the elevator, and the doors had shut securely in front of him. Then there was a brief pause, and his shoulders began to shake and his eyes teared, as the laughter he'd been holding back finally escaped.

It really wasn't funny. The scene that had met him when he burst in: Lawrence flat on his back and covered in spell-soot, Lou crawling out from under the table like a morning-after reveler, had damn near stopped his heart. Now that everyone was safe and accounted for, he let the laughter come, knowing that it was as much stress-release as amusement.

Nifty could have been hurt—Lou could have been seriously hurt, if the explosion had caught her off guard. But it hadn't. His newest pup might not be able to control her current well enough to be a field operative, but there was nothing wrong with her brains or her reflexes, and she'd gone under the table fast enough to avoid being hit with the spell's debris. He hadn't chosen poorly when he hired her. That was a relief.

Alone in the elevator, laughter dying down, Ben allowed his muscles to relax, the exhaustion he'd been repressing finally surfacing for a moment, and he found himself considering the ramifications of the event. Some days it seemed as though the simplest of spells—simple in theory, anyway—caused the biggest boom when they went wrong, and went wrong more often than the com-

plicated ones. And those booms were happening more
and more often, in the past few weeks. It wasn't because
his pups were being careless: he'd beaten that out of them
the first month they were on the job. No, there had to
be something more to it.

Bad luck? Ben didn't believe in it. A hex? Those he did
believe in, having seen them placed—and dismissed—
more than once. There was an old-style conjure woman
back in Texas who could hex up a mess of trouble, if
you gave her reason. Just because they hadn't heard of
anyone like that in town didn't mean they weren't here.
And there were people who'd have cause to hex the pups,
either in payment for what they'd done, or to keep them
from doing something in the future.

He wished to hell he'd been able to talk Ian out of accepting both jobs, giving the pups the chance to not only
hone their skills but stand down for a bit, but his partner
wanted—*needed*—to prove something. That meant never
backing down from a challenge. Understanding the goal
that drove the other man didn't make it any easier to deal
with the inevitable cock-ups that would happen because
of it. All he could do was try to limit the damage done if
someone dropped the ball due to exhaustion or inexperi-
ence.

But, god, he was so tired. Between the job, and keeping Ian focused, and trying to find out what was going
on with this Merge, without letting it get its hooks into
him...

Giving in to a rare self-indulgent impulse, Ben let his
mental wall down a bit, and reached out deliberately with
a thin tendril of current, like the streamer of a pea plant

unfolding. Bonnie was distracted, her thoughts tangled, but her core hummed like a well-tuned car, focused on her task, and the sound of it soothed him. If there was anything bothering her, he couldn't tell, not without going deeper.

He pulled the tendril back and rebuilt the wall, ignoring the hum within him that protested the loss of contact. Bonnie might fling her emotions and affections around, but that wasn't his thing. He needed privacy, distance. The urge to know where she was, what she was doing or feeling: that was the Merge pushing him, not his own needs.

The elevator doors opened, and he strode out into the lobby, nodding politely at the older woman waiting to enter.

"Have a nice day," the woman called after him, as the doors closed. There were a dozen offices in the building, and he wondered, sometimes, what the other tenants thought of them, the odd assortment of twenty-somethings, their eccentric leader, and the dour man riding herd on them all hours of the day.

He was halfway down the block, wishing that he'd brought his leather jacket with him against the cooler-than-expected breeze, before his brain finally started to sort out why his body had taken him outside. He could have escaped to Ian's little back office if he just needed to laugh without being seen or heard, so clearly he needed to walk something out, away from the confines and demands of the office.

The thought occurred to him that, outside the warded office, he was vulnerable, but he dismissed it as occupational paranoia. Nobody was gunning for him; not right now, anyway.

He lengthened his stride, moving quickly to keep warm, and let his body go on autopilot, allowing his brain to do what it did best: process and place.

Ian was the brilliant Idea Guy, the Concept Man, and the consensus-wooer. He, Ben, was along to kick those ideas and concepts—and employees—into productive, working shape. "You're my gut instincts," Ian said, when his old friend had first called him with the idea for an investigative team that would keep the *Cosa* in line. "I can see what they're doing, even when they don't want me to, but you know what they're up to."

Ben was starting to think that his partner had over-estimated his abilities. Because right now his brain kept returning not to the cases on hand, or even the mental or magical state of his pup-pack, but a greater—and harder to track—uncertainty. His gut instincts were telling him that the human/fatae trouble they'd seen earlier in the year during the ki-rin job, was still there, simmering... waiting for a single spark to blow up under their feet. There hadn't been any proof—the flyers advertising the so-called "exterminators" had disappeared, and the whispers of violence had died back down to their normal level—but his gut wouldn't shut up, wouldn't let him sleep without worry. Bonnie's new kenning added fuel to that, so much that he couldn't focus on the jobs at hand.

Bonnie... He was tired enough that the thought of her was like a mild gut-punch of a different sort, taking him unaware even when he knew that it was coming. He let it roll over him, still walking. Bright eyes and a ready smile, her expression almost fey, with her short curls and pointed chin, a mind that was tough and sharp and moved almost as fast as his own. And her body... She was slender, and slightly built, and under the long-sleeved Ts and pants or long skirts she wore most of the time her muscles were warm and firm. He remembered that from the few times he'd touched her, before the Merge made that too complicated to even consider.

He wanted her, physically. Not a big deal. He'd wanted women who were off-limits before. Knowing how to look and not touch was part of surviving adolescence. It was more than that. He wanted to listen to her talk, to dig into her mind and see what was there, how she thought and why she reacted. He wanted to— Not own her, it wasn't that kind of crazy, but a level of possession that made him feel deeply uncomfortable, like someone else was poking at him, trying to dig into his secrets.

"Enough," he muttered. "You've already got it covered, sorted, and spliced. Worry about the stuff you don't know about. Like where the hell Ian is, and what he's up to."

Even as he was talking to himself, Ben felt the tingling awareness that someone was watching him. Not the same tingling, poking sensation he'd just shaken off, something external, and less magical than physical. He'd followed enough people to know when someone was watching him—and when that watching went from casual interest to a focused hunt.

"All right, then," he said, his lips barely moving out of habit, in case someone was watching him. "Shall we play a game?"

He picked up the pace a little, not fast enough to lose anyone but moving past the other pedestrians with the air of a man late for something. He went the length of the block, and then stopped, bending down as though to tie the lace of his shoe.

The sense of someone watching stayed close, but no closer than it had been before. A maintained distance.

That meant his stalker was human, not fatae. The fatae tended to let him know they were there, to try to make him uneasy with their regard. Only humans hid. Ben felt his mouth draw into an unamused smile. He could test the air, see if his tail was Talent or not, but that risked letting the other know he or she had been spotted, and spoiling the game. There were other ways to tell, though.

Slowing his steps to a more casual pace, he circled around the block, and headed for the nearest cogeneration building.

The miniature power generators that had become popular recently didn't have the same catnip appeal of the big'un power plant, but a cogen attracted the attention of every Talent who walked by the same way a pretty girl caught the eye. If his tail was Talent, he would know the moment they crossed the street; they wouldn't be able to help themselves.

I spent the rest of the day looking over Sharon's notes, not so much looking for something as looking for what wasn't there, a missing element or fact that would open up a new level of questions. All I got was a slight case of eyestrain: Sharon might not have my perfect memory, or Nick's ability to make intuitive leaps, but she was exactly as methodical as you'd expect for someone originally trained as a paralegal.

"You checked the rest of the house?"

"Yes." Nothing in Nick's tone let me know what an insulting question that had been, which I appreciated. "The kitchen was spotless, and surprisingly Spartan. I guess he doesn't entertain much, or have any interest in food.

"Upstairs was nicer, but still pretty plain," he went on, tapping a finger on the table as though the beat would jog his memory. Hell, maybe it did. "I mean, nice but not lush, the way you'd think somebody that rich would do it."

My mentor had that kind of money, or maybe even more. His apartment in Boston was… I thought about the casual way he slouched in a nineteenth-century armchair, and how Rupert was allowed to sleep on a hand-knotted Persian rug, and allowed as how maybe my idea of *lush* was kind of skewed.

"Cheap-looking, or…?" If he was skimping on the private rooms, that might mean a lack of ready cash, or some other cause for trouble.

"No. I mean, not that I'm any judge of it, but no I don't think so. I've seen enough of your stuff to know quality, and this was all good. Just not…" He was struggling to put what he'd seen into words. I waited.

"Sparse. Like he only cared about the rooms where he spent time, where people saw him. Everything else had the minimum for living but…" And I could practically smell Nicky making another one of his leaps, sussing out people in a way I could only wonder at. "He doesn't care about other people. Not about making them comfortable, or seeing to their needs. It's all about him."

"A narcissist?"

"No. That's all about perception and self-interest, right? This is more…he isn't aware that anyone might have needs or wants, beyond where they connect to him, or that they even exist, when he can't see them? Like a sociopath."

Oh. Oh, that was not what I wanted to hear. At all.

"So…what does that add to the case?"

Nick shrugged, which drove me crazy. I hated shrugs; they were so utterly useless as communication because they could mean too many things. Lazy, my mentor used to say, and he was right. "Nothing, really. Not yet, anyway."

"Right." Because why should even simple cases be easy? I went back to my notes, and let Nick do the same with mine.

And if there was a part of me that was *listening* for the touch of Venec's core against mine, I wasn't going to admit to anything.

It said a lot about how trained we'd gotten in the past year that when Venec didn't come back that afternoon and Stosser never made an appearance all day, we still remembered Venec's Law: Nobody Pulls an All-Nighter without Big Dog Approval. At least, I think we all did— when I left at six, Sharon was still going over her notes, looking at the diorama she and Nick had started putting together. But of all of us, she was the least likely to lose track of time—or to use that as an excuse to disobey standing orders.

Lou, who had managed not to blow herself up during the spell trials, was putting on her coat when I headed out, and we walked out together, after I made sure the coffeemaker had been turned off for the night.

I'd headed for the stairs at the end of the hallway when Lou stopped me with a puzzled question. "Why don't any of you use the elevator?"

It was a good question. Easy to answer, except for the fact that none of us were willing, or able, to talk about it, even now. Also, if I made Lou paranoid, too, Venec would kick my ass. So I didn't tell her about the teenage boy who had been killed during an attack on us when we first opened shop, when power shorted out and the elevator plummeted into the basement. I just shrugged, and pushed open the door, giving her a lesser truth. "It keeps us in shape."

Truth, but not the entire truth, and it came out as natural as honey. As a painfully self-aware teenager, I used to insist on the whole truth and nothing but the truth, because anything else was a lie. I'd thought black was black, and white, white, and the right answers were obvious to anyone, if you only thought about it.

I had been an arrogant twit back then, and it's a wonder J didn't lock me in a closet until I was thirty.

With everything else going on, between the two new cases and the underlying worry about where Venec had disappeared to, that thought about lying should have come and gone. Instead it nagged at me. Lou and I went our separate ways on the sidewalk and I—on a whim—decided to walk home rather than taking the subway. It was only a couple of miles, and I felt the need for fresh air, rather than being packed into rush-hour mass transit. I stopped in the local bodega for a bottle of water and a halvah bar to have for dessert, and started walking.

We had been funded not to hand out judgment but to establish the facts—the where and the who—of a crime, which would lead us to the why and the how. But facts didn't exist in a vacuum, neatly cut and packaged. We had to shake them out of the messier tangle of human emotions and motivations.

Black and white. Truth and lies. The ki-rin hadn't been able to lie, but it had deceived. Aden Stosser, our boss's sister, lied about us and what we did, and thought that it was the truth. Sharon suspected that our newest client was lying about the break-in but he was so good at it, she couldn't tell. Sociopath. Maybe.

Oh, what a tangled web we weave, when first we practice to deceive. Sir Walter Scott, not Shakespeare. Deception and truth and half truths. It was the reason we did this job; so that nobody could hide behind magic and deny their actions or deeds. And if sometimes we allowed those actions to be buried again, for the greater good...

"It's not our job."

I swear, I thought I'd said it out loud until I realized that Venec was walking alongside me.

"Motherofgod." It came out in a hot breath, and I shuddered at how easily he'd managed to come up next to me, without my even noticing. "Also, goddamn it. I thought you said this thing would make us more aware of each other, not less?"

The one time we'd talked about it. God knows what

he'd have discovered by now. I swear, every time I adjusted to this shit, the universe smirked at me.

"I found you," Venec pointed out, sounding like he was talking about a particularly boring weather report.

Yeah. He had. How? I touched my wall, and was surprised at how thick it was. He found me through that? Hell. I thinned it a little, and the heat of his presence came through, like standing next to a sunlamp. We walked the rest of the block in silence, as I tried to adjust it so that I could tell where he was, but not feel like he was quite so damn close.

Except he was. His arm kept touching the sleeve of my leather jacket, and I would almost swear he was walking close enough that the fabric of my black skirt brushed his thigh more than once, but when I looked down, there was a professional foot-plus between us.

I thought about asking him where the hell he'd disappeared to, this afternoon, but didn't.

"It's not our job," he said again, finally. "To save the world. It's not even our job to tell the world that they're in danger."

I had no idea what the hell he was talking about now. But he wasn't really talking to me; I knew that even without the Merge. He was working something out in that twisty, very smart brain of his, and I was just the audience. So I just walked, and waited.

"I was followed this afternoon," he said finally, not so much getting to the point as putting it aside. "Human, but not Talent. He, I'm pretty sure it was a he, or a very butch woman, followed me for almost an hour, always keeping half a block behind. Didn't do anything, just watched."

I thought about that for a few steps. "You think it was the Bitch, sending someone?"

I didn't really think that naming Aden Stosser would summon her...exactly. But I wasn't going to take the chance. Big Dog's sister hated us, for reasons only she and Ian and maybe Venec understood, and had tried to shut us down before, first through intimidation and then direct attack.

Ben sighed at my use of the extremely unaffectionate nickname, but he didn't bother scolding us any longer. She had earned it. "Maybe. Ian swears the Council is watching her too closely, after the last dustup. Won't stop her—nothing short of a nuclear blast stops her—but he expects she'll go through the Council now, try to worm her way into influencing votes, keeping us from being recognized, maybe block anyone from aiding us. And that sort of manipulation is Ian's territory, not ours. Thank god." He shook his head, and I felt the overwhelming need to run my hand through those messy curls, push the dark hair away from his face so that I could see him better.

My fingers stayed locked by my side.

We were two blocks from my apartment, and I was starting to wonder where this was going. If he asked to come in...what was I going to say?

The old Bonnie wouldn't have blinked: a hot guy with good manners, smart and built, and definitely interested? Duh! Only I'd already determined that I wasn't the old Bonnie.

And I couldn't afford to take a tumble with Benjamin Venec. Not because I thought he'd fire me if things went bad. I knew better, now. That wasn't his style. I wasn't even worried that it would make working together uncomfortable, at least, not between the two of us. I knew me, and I knew him. It was the rest of the team. For all that they joked, I had a feeling that they would freak if they knew what was really going on, and Stosser...

Did Ian know? Had Ben told him? My brain couldn't even go there. Anyway, I wasn't going to and he wasn't going to and that had been decided already. And even if they handled it fine, I chose my partners, damn it. I didn't need some mystical matchmaker shoving me.

I could hear J sigh, all the way from Boston.

We walked another block, but he didn't say anything more.

"We need to fine-tune the organ-check spell," I said, moving the conversation back firmly onto work ground, where we both knew what the hell was going on. "I knew that there was water in the lungs, so our DB definitely drowned, but the body's already been released, which means no way to check what kind of water." There was an organization that claimed fatae bodies when they ended up in the morgue, and disposed of them either through the breed representative, or on their own. Bad luck for us; this once they weren't backed up. "Anyway, even if I'd thought of it...salt water from fresh? I'm not sure we can do that, the way the cantrip is structured right now."

You had to be very specific when you were working with forensic magic; we'd learned that the hard way.

Ask a vague question, and you got run over with too much information. Too much information was worse than none, because you couldn't figure out what was important. But finding the right balance meant that it was harder to create a one-spell-fits-all cantrip; everything had to be more specialized than we'd thought.

That was where I excelled; fine-turning the details. But we couldn't spare me from the field, not with two open jobs.

Venec nodded, accepting my assessment. "Do you want to work on it, or should I put it in the fishbowl?"

The fishbowl was exactly that—a glass bowl on a table in the smaller conference room, the windowless one that was best shielded for current-use. If you had an idea, or a problem, you wrote it down and tossed it into the bowl, and whenever someone had spare time and energy, they'd go fishing for a problem to solve.

"Fishbowl, for now, although I'll keep poking at it. The body's already been disposed of, so no way to go back and check." I'd never asked what the fatae normally did with their dead; I suspected asking would be rude, and I wasn't sure I wanted to know, anyway. J always said that sex and burial traditions were where most cultural misunderstandings happened.

We turned a corner, our steps almost perfectly matching. I wondered if he was aware of that.

"What's your working theory?" he asked.

"On the drowning? It was either a personal grudge—" the most likely explanation when dealing with the fatae, who tended to have short fuses and long memories "—or money." If it wasn't some personal insult, it was money. The fatae just didn't get het up about sex the way some humans did—at least far's I'd ever heard. Money, though, they were just as wound up as any spending species. "Why else do you get dumped in the East River?"

"Drugs? There was a nice little trade in heroin a while back, nasty pure stuff that would kill a human in one dose." Venec went thoughtful again. "The craze seems to have faded, but there could be a new joyjuice on the market. You might want to ask Danny."

Danny Hendrickson, former NYPD, current P.I., and one of the few human/fatae crossbreeds I knew about. Danny was a good guy, and had helped us out before, so long as it didn't interfere with his own cases. He was also fun to go drinking with, not that we'd had time to do that, much. I nodded. "I'll call him when I get home. He keeps weird hours, I might be able to reach him, or leave a message."

The fatae, being *of* magic but not *using* magic, could enjoy the benefits of modern technology like laptop computers, cell phones, and answering machines. I tried not to be too jealous.

"Do you think we might have a drug war among the fatae? Christ." The idea kind of creeped me out. Fatae were scary enough on their own; they didn't need drugs, especially drugs that led to violence, added to the mix.

Venec went from peer voice to Big Dog voice without blinking. "Don't rule anything out until we know it's not a viable theory."

I winced. Okay, I deserved that. "Right. Drugs, or drug-trafficking. Danny. I'm on it."

And then we were at the stoop of my building, and

I paused, my hand reaching out for the railing. The air around us was the dusky thickness that made it almost impossible to read someone's expression, even if they were right next to you. I could have let down the walls a little more to feel what was going on...but I didn't.

There was a hesitation in the air, like the entire damn city was waiting to see what we'd do.

I wanted him. Every damn cell of my body wanted him, and even knowing that it was one of my worst ideas didn't dull the ache.

"I'll see you tomorrow, then," he said. "Sleep well."

And then he was gone, walking down the street like the UPS guy who'd knocked-and-dropped, and was on to his next delivery.

A wave of hurt swept through me, so unexpected that I almost called after him to demand an explanation, an apology.

Instead, I pulled my key from my shoulder bag, and let myself inside.

The shiver of unease that passed over the city days before had settled, for the moment, at the edge of Central Park. The usual steady noise of evening traffic on the avenue had been overlaid with a snarling mess of human voices and barking dogs. Two of the ubiquitous food carts that lurked along the perimeter had somehow slammed into each other, causing their contents—roasted nuts, for one, and hot pretzels and soda for the other—to spill all over the walkway, and the two owners to stand over the disaster, screaming at each other in two different languages, neither English, clearly insulting each other's patrimony, while the two cops called to the scene tried to get someone to tell them, in English, what had happened.

Another vendor, off to the side and out of the direct line of sight, served up sodas to people who were drawn in to see what the fuss was about. The atmosphere had become less bucolic and more like an arena, spectators gathering to watch the blood spill.

"What happened?" one of them, a tall blonde with a small blond dog at the other end of a bright green leash, asked. The dog looked mournfully up at his mistress, who seemed oblivious, so the vendor slipped it half a hot dog that had fallen on the ground earlier.

"Damnedest thing. One minute they were doing bang-up business, you should pardon the expression," the vendor said, deftly fitting the woman's hot dog onto a bun and handing it to her, "and the next thing there's a crash like you wouldn't believe, and they're going at each other like gangbusters. If the cops hadn't shown up, I bet there would have been blood."

"You didn't see it?"

"Lady, I got a rule. I don't see nothing if it don't involve me. One guy hits another, somebody steals some lady's purse, your dog snitches one of my hot dogs..."

The blonde looked down just in time to see the last of the purloined sausage disappear into the dog's mouth, and let out a horrified cry. "Damn it, Snooks, you're going to throw it all up tonight, aren't you? Damn it."

The vendor grinned, as though pleased at the distress in the woman's voice, but when she looked up again, his leathery face was solemn, and his gaze was more on the still-arguing combatants than his customers. The cops had managed to calm them both down, hauling them to separate corners to get their reports, and, show over, the bystanders had started to move on. "Huh." The vendor sounded disappointed. "I really thought they'd have done more than yell at each other."

"It's a good thing the cops were nearby," another man said, coming to the front of the line. "Pepsi, please."

"Did you hear about the fight that broke out on the 72 crosstown last month?" his companion asked. "Speaking of cursing. The driver had to pull over and haul them off each other. Man, never ever piss off the little old ladies. They're fierce."

They accepted their sodas and walked on, leaving the square that, fun over, was rapidly emptying of people. The hot dog vendor cocked his head and pursed his rubbery lips thoughtfully, his nostrils flaring as though scenting something pleasant. "Buses. I hadn't thought of buses. And subways!" The eyes that had seemed sunken and tired before now sparkled with a literal light, a muted dark gold. "Everyone trapped, tired, and anxious... Oh, that will be fun!"

His hand—oddly gnarled and twisted in the wrong direction, if you looked at it carefully—made a flat pass over the top of his cart, and the metal construct—hot dogs, sodas and all—disappeared.

A second later, so did the vendor.

five

Much to my surprise, I'd managed a hard seven hours of dead-to-the-world sleep, got up in time to not rush through my shower, and still made it to the office by 8:00 a.m, even stopping on the corner to grab a bagel with a-schmear from the coffee cart guy.

The teenagers were missing from the stoop again.

I forced myself to take the elevator, shivering slightly as I did so. But the doors opened safely on the seventh floor, and that felt like victory. Someone had just gone into one of the two offices across the hall—the photographer's—closing the door softly behind them, but other than that the hallway was empty.

I unlocked our door, shucked my jacket, and hung it in the closet. Only one coat there—Pietr's—but the weather was nice enough that that didn't mean anything. There was the low murmur of conversation from the small workroom, and a light showing under the door, down the hallway in Stosser's office. Since we'd long ago tossed the idea of nine to five out the window, I wasn't surprised not to be the first one in, despite being early.

I went back to the break room and grabbed my mug—Sharon's gift, with a brightly feathered, very dead parrot painted on the side—out of the cabinet, filling it with coffee and doctoring it to a proper consistency, and took a long hit, feeling my brain start to kick in for real. There were, as I saw it, two options. I could hang around and see what was happening, or I could get to work.

I got to work.

"Steady…"

It took real willpower not to growl at the helpful—and unwanted—voice in my ear. "I do know how to do this."

The voice backed off—a little, and the sense of current up against my back, supporting me, faded. "Right. I'll go fetch you some coffee then, shall I? Decaf?"

I waited until Pietr left the room—double-checking to make sure he actually *had* left the room, and not just disappeared—before letting out a heavy sigh and lowering my shaking hands to the table. I shouldn't have snapped. He was right; I wasn't at top form. There were too many other things crowded into my head—Venec, mainly, and the damned Merge. But I was still better at reconstruction than he was, so his advice really wasn't all that damn useful, and he knew it.

I looked down at our work, trying to see it with an impartial eye.

The diorama Venec had asked for was an outgrowth of the re-creation spell we used to glean and then display crime scenes, when we needed an overview rather than an eyewitness view. The thing was, the diorama was made entirely of current, built out of the observer's original memory made three-dimensional. That meant the caster had to maintain control at all times, or it would snap back and burn you. Not fun. The spell Lou and Nifty had been working on when he got ashed, apparently, was a variant that would make a stable diorama, allowing the creator to anchor the current used to create the display into the diorama itself, so that it would self-maintain. So far, no matter what they tried, it still snapped back the moment they took control off. That had been what caught Nifty.

Lou had been able to avoid getting powdered with current, but even with their newest modifications, the spell still required the caster to be aware of it constantly.

In terms of pure current-use, a gleaning display was easier for me to set up and maintain, but it left the remains tucked into your head like pond scum, which was both unpleasant, and allowed for shifting memories or external influences to blur details. The diorama-spell scraped everything out and put it into real, if miniature, form, leaving your own memory free to fade normally. I preferred the risk for that return, me. Some things you didn't want to remember in that much detail.

The real added benefit to the diorama, though, is that it wasn't a gleaning-display but a true re-creation. A gleaning showed you exactly what was there, forever static. A diorama, you could play with, run scenarios... play hunches and see how they worked out.

I moved the concrete-block building back a little more, trying to gauge exactly how far it had been from where the body was, and added a few more cars to the parking lot, rearranging the scene to my satisfaction, and then stood up, looking at it from all sides. The current was solid; to anyone looking with plain sight, it appeared like a solid model of the dump scene. Or, more accurately, the discovery scene, where the NYPD Harbor Patrol had spotted the body, and laid it out for display. Where the actual dump occurred was what I wanted—needed—to find out.

All I had to do was set things in motion.

Since the diorama was constructed from my own current, I didn't have to draw down anything more to trigger it. With my hand palm down a few inches over the surface of the water running under the concrete pier, I commanded it: "Water, flow naturally. Bring the body back to me."

The uneven surface of the East River stirred and began to move. A tiny lump—the corpse—disappeared from under the tiny orange tarp as the magic cycled back through its movements in time. Sympathetic magic, with a twist. The body should appear from upstream, caught in the currents, and hit the underground net where the cops found it.

Instead, it appeared across the river, barely a few feet upstream from the net, and splashed into the river without a sound. I sucked my cheeks in and leaned back from the table in surprise.

"Huh." Either the spell wasn't working—entirely possible—or our theories had just been thrown for a very interesting loop.

c'mere

Nick's ping was like a horsefly: unwanted, irritating, and impossible to ignore. *busy* I sent back, a flick of irritation and a sense of actually being, yes, busy.

now That came from Venec, not Nick, and carried the flavor of an order. Venec knew what I was working on, so if he wanted me to leave it…something was Up.

"Damn it." I glared at the diorama. Shutting it down was difficult enough, but letting go wasn't an option. I had no idea if I'd be able to re-create it so well a second time, and the fact that the body had been dumped so close meant it had also been dumped much later than we thought—once it hit the net and the sensors went off, it couldn't have been more than an hour or so before someone was sent to investigate. That was the point of the city-installed nets, after all.

Could I freeze it successfully, without snap back? If I could, yay. If not…ow. And the ow could hit whenever the snap happened.

I decided to risk it.

Sliding back into a faint fugue-state, I looked at the current with mage-sight, noting the weave and warp of the threads. Seen this way, it was a chaotic and yet ordered mass. I wondered if that's what atoms looked like to Null scientists, when they broke us all down to our basic parts. J might know, or he'd know who to ask.

"Freeze and hold," I told the combined threads, my voice scarcely above a whisper. It wasn't volume but control that made it work. "Hold and wait."

The threads shimmied, like they were trying to break free, but the motion of the water halted, and a stillness fell over the diorama, like a cold winter morning seemed to make the world quieter.

I swallowed hard, and moved my hand away from the display.

It held.

I stepped backward, one careful shuffle.

It held.

I turned my back on it, slowly, and felt a quiver from the current-shape. I stopped, and it stilled, just like J's sheepdog, Rupert, when he'd been a puppy learning his commands.

"Hold," I told it again, my voice as even and composed as I could make it, willing myself not to brace against any anticipated snap back. "Hold."

It held.

When I followed the voices toward the break room at the front of the office, I could feel the diorama still waiting. It took everything I had not to flinch, not to anticipate it breaking control and recoiling back into my core...until I walked through the open doorway and saw why Venec thought it worth dragging me away.

A klassvaak. Not on the same level of a Great Worm, thank god, but it was like being visited by the Pope, if you were Catholic—you knew damn well you weren't worthy, and the place was a mess, and why the HELL was he in your living room?

"This is Bonita Torres," Venec said, indicating my late arrival. I guessed that the others had already been introduced. Pietr was forgiven for not coming back with the coffee.

The fatae made a sort of half bow, its elongated head

dipping toward its chin. I had no idea how to respond, so just returned the gesture, dipping my head slightly lower than it had, and hoped that was right. Of the entire team, I probably had the most formal training in dealing with dignitaries, because of J's once-and-future status within the Eastern Council, but my mentor had never covered this particular circumstance.

"This is our entire team," Venec said, glossing over the fact that Stosser wasn't present. Where was the boss, anyway? "Will you now share with us what you came here for?"

The klassvaak turned back toward him, seemingly with relief. I had no way of reading the fatae's body language, but I thought it was uncomfortable as hell, with everyone looking at it. That made sense, I guess. It wasn't exactly an exhibitionist.

I ran over what little I knew of this particular breed, which wasn't much. Not because I hadn't been paying attention to J's lectures, but because there wasn't much to know. The klassvaak had come over with the first Dutch settlers. It was, as far as anyone knew, the only one of its kind, although opinions were mixed whether that had always been the case—making it closer to an Old One than I was comfortable with—or if the others had died out or otherwise drifted out of the mortal world. The klassvaak was a night-dweller, its moon-pale skin a little too reminiscent of a corpse's tinge for human comfort, its eyes round, lashless, and deep blue over a tiny little nose and thin mouth.

I wondered, suddenly, if the klassvaak had been the inspiration for Nosferatu.

"No pleasure in being here, me," the klassvaak said. Its speech was thick, as though it didn't use English—or any human language for that matter—very often. I wasn't even sure how its needle-thin lips could form the words, honestly. "But warning you deserve. The Roblin's come to town."

"The Roblin?" Sharon asked, leaning forward, and then realized her mistake when Venec glared at her. The klassvaak didn't even seem to notice or hear, still looking at a spot somewhere to the left of Venec's head. That was high-end manners, among the fatae—a direct stare was a challenge. Like cats, they preferred to look indirectly, even when in the middle of a conversation.

Most Westerners, human ones, anyway, found it distressing or rude, historically labeling it an indication of sly deceit. Venec didn't seem bothered by it at all.

"The Roblin's come to town," it repeated, as though speaking to a slow but not disliked child. "Mischief calls it, and mischief it will do."

I looked at Venec, trying to gauge if he knew what the hell the klassvaak was talking about. His face, and his core, were still, not giving anything away. Nobody else had a clue: I could tell that from the way they were watching Venec, waiting for a cue, the same as me. There was—not tension, exactly, but a sense of frustrated impatience building.

"Mischief toward whom?" Venec asked, and his voice was that low, not-quite-cajoling tone he used when we were working our way through a problem, the one that said "you can say anything to me, no matter how crazy, I'll back your play."

"Mischief it does," the klassvaak repeated. Its gaze shifted from the side of Venec's face; just for a second, but I caught it. Exasperation? No, annoyance. And a desire to be gone, clear as if it had shouted. The fatae was not used to interacting with those who spoke, only those who dreamed. It was uncomfortable here, being confronted and questioned.

"Elder Cousin," I said, in passable-but-not-fluent German, playing a hunch. "We do not know this name, The Roblin. Inform us?"

I hoped to hell that's what I had said, anyway, and that I used the proper formal verbs. My language classes were years ago and I hadn't had time to travel and polish them since well before graduation.

The klassvaak switched to German with what seemed like relief. "The Roblin is."

Well. That was helpful.

The klassvaak shifted its too-pale body again; whatever had driven it here, out of its comfort zone, to talk to us, clearly done and dealt with. It wanted to go now.

"Thank you," Venec said, standing and bowing like a Japanese diplomat. Our unexpected visitor didn't even bother to acknowledge it, but was zippity gone. I didn't know anything that old could move that fast. At least, not without wings.

I rubbed at my eyes, feeling a headache building.

"What the hell was that, and what the hell is a Roblin?" Nick was the first one to speak after the door closed, of course. From being fanboyishly intrigued with fatae when he first started, through to a deep distrust of them, Nicky now usually projected a very New Yorker attitude of "yeah, yeah, whatever." But this had been bizarre even by our standards.

"I have no idea." Venec turned the straight-backed chair he'd been sitting in around, and sat back down on it, straddling it like a cowboy. I forced my brain not to go where my body wanted. "Lou, go through every source you can find, look for any reference at all for this 'Roblin,' any spelling variants you can think of. Don't limit yourself to the *Cosa*—if it's as old as our guest, you're more likely to find it in the fairy tales."

Lou nodded, and whipped out her notepad, taking notes, I presumed of any variant spellings she could come up with. Nifty leaned over her shoulder, idly scratching at his arm, to make suggestions.

"Can we trust it? I mean, it's fatae, and..." Nick saw the look I gave him, and stared back, refusing to be cowed. "Give me a break, Bonnie. I'm not being a bigot—you know what I mean. Fatae—especially the older breeds, the ones that don't much like humans— they're tricksy. History proves that, over and over. What if our visitor *is* this Roblin, or whatever, messing with us, trying to get us chasing after something, distracting us from, hell, I don't know, something going on, or something it wants to do?"

I blinked, and leaned back against the door frame. Okay, that was tricksy, worthy of a fatae. I was impressed, and admitted I'd never have thought of it. My thought process was too linear, in a lot of ways, but Nick more than made up for it, the way he could swerve and dodge.

"No." Venec was positive of that. "Unless this Roblin's a shape changer, that's not it."

There were seven known, verified shape changers among the fatae breeds, and each of them moved from one specific form to another, not whatever caught its fancy. Of course, if there was a breed that could do that, how would we ever know?

That thought gave me the very unpleasant woogies.

"All right, everyone back to work," Venec said, breaking the shocky, contemplative mood. "We can't do fuckall right now, until we get more information, and meanwhile there are paying clients waiting on us. Bonnie, why were you so het over leaving the diorama, before this?"

I had completely, utterly forgotten about the diorama. With an unpleasant jolt, I reached back to check the status of the current-hold…and found nothing

"Damn it." I smacked the flat of my hand against the door frame, taking a weird comfort in the sting against my flesh. "I lost the diorama, and I had something useful there, too." Or I thought it was useful, anyway. And I hadn't had time to really study it, worse luck, so my near-perfect memory was utterly useless.

"Did it burn you?" Venec was in my face all of a sudden, taking both my hands in his and turning them over like he was expecting to see current-burns scarring my skin.

"No." And that was weird. No, that was really weird. Not only should I have felt it, I should have gotten at least a current-zing, like a first-degree burn, when the control snapped, even distracted by our visitor.

I stared at my hands, like the answer would ooze from the lines on my palms. "It was like it melted, instead of breaking. I didn't even notice it, and I should have…"

"Um. That might be my fault."

Sharon stood next to us, although I noted, vaguely, that she was keeping a little more distance than was normal when we were in the office, like she was afraid to intrude on a private conversation. Pietr was hovering on the edges, the others hanging even farther back.

"How?" Venec asked, not letting go of my hands. I didn't mind, exactly, but it made it kind of difficult to focus on what Sharon was saying.

"Last night, I was building my own diorama, and I was worried, being alone—I didn't stay late," she added quickly, "but I was the last one out and I was worried if there was a problem, if my concentration broke like Bonnie's did, I wouldn't be able to get help."

Which was exactly why Venec didn't let us work late, when the Big Dogs weren't around. There wasn't anyone else in the building we could call on, and by the time someone heard and Translocated, it could be too late.

"So I...sort of upped the wardings. A little."

I wondered if Venec was aware that his thumb had started stroking the inside of my palm, in slow, thoughtful strokes; it was less seductive than reassuring, but the action still sent a shiver right up my spine.

"Enough to dampen the shock of a break in control?" Now that she had his full attention, the thumb motion paused while he looked at her. He didn't let go of my hands, though.

"I don't know. I guess so? I thought I'd taken them down, after, but it might have lingered in the wardings we already had established?" Sharon sounded uncertain, which was unusual for her.

Wardings were old-school, something Venec had taught us when we started. Unlike the Old Times, most modern Talent work on the go, so you don't have specific places set up for rituals or anything like that, which was all very nineteenth century. It made sense that Sharon hadn't really thought about what layering in protections on established protections, building up over time, might do.

"Thank you," I said, breaking into what I could tell was some heavy-duty self-questioning going on in her brain. I meant it. Sharon might not have left it there on purpose, but I would have been in a lot of pain—and felt really stupid in front of our visitor—if I'd gotten burned while it was speaking.

"No problem. And speaking of that stuff, um, you, um, think you guys could stop that, now?"

I blinked, surprised at her blunt reference, and looked down at my hands, and then blinked again as I saw what she was referring to: lazy sparks of deep purple current arcing from my hands to his, or maybe the other way around.

For all my awareness of Ben's touching me, I hadn't even noticed. From the way Venec reacted, neither had he. He dropped my hands so fast I almost felt them go into free fall, and my nerve endings protested even as I was taking a step back, out the door.

As I fled down the hallway, I heard someone—Nick—snicker, and Pietr offer to up the bet-holdings.

I didn't want to know what, specifically, they were betting on, or what the under/over was. I retreated into the workroom and closed and warded the entrance behind me, then leaned against the door like I'd just outrun a giant purple Talent-eater.

"That," I said to the empty room, "was Not Good."

And then, because I was a professional, damn it, I went to work trying to reconstruct the diorama, one memory-detail at a time.

Ben waited for a moment, giving his remaining pups a glare that dared them, just dared them to make a single comment, and then made as dignified a retreat as he could. The moment his back was turned, he heard them upping bets about when he and Torres would admit that something was up, and sighed. Not that he would have wanted them to be cowed by him, exactly, but it would be nice if they had a little bit of fear to go with the respect.

Bonnie was back in the workroom; he could feel the hum of her current as she, he presumed, tried to reconstruct the busted diorama. He was curious as to what she'd found, but there was no point in pushing; when she was ready, she would be ready. Jumping to present evidence was as bad as waiting too long and letting it grow stale.

He had barely gotten back to the small office at the far end of the hallway that Ian had claimed for his own private retreat, and thrown himself into his usual chair in the corner, when there was a whisper of incoming current and Ian himself Translocated in from god knew where.

It took their fearless leader a second to recover from the shift in location, and notice that he had company.

"You look particularly pissed. Which of the children are misbehaving?"

Ben was in no mood to play. "Where the hell have you been?"

Ian gave a slight shrug, shaking out the nonexistent wrinkles in his dress shirt. "I had things to deal with. You were handling everything here perfectly well without me. Was I wrong?"

Ben stared at his partner. Beyond the unusually flippant speech, Ian's normally narrow face was even more drawn, and his hair had a dull sheen to it, making it seem more orange than red. He was dressed in an expensive-looking suit, with his hair tied back, and looked not only tired, but dispirited. That was not only unusual, but alarming.

"If I asked you for details, would you give them?"

Translation: is it your idiot sister Aden causing trouble again? Do I get to dump her in the river, this time?

"It's nothing that involves the team," Ian said, taking a seat behind his desk and leaning back to stare at the ceiling, and Ben knew that was all he was going to get. But at least it wasn't his partner's crazy-ass sibling making more mischief; Ian would have dodged that question differently.

Without looking away from the acoustic tile overhead, Ian deflected the question back at him. "What's been going on here, to make you look so off-color? Is there a problem with one of the cases?"

Benjamin Venec could do an end run around a question just as well as his partner. Ian was his best friend as well as his partner, but there was no way in hell he was

going to tell the other man anything about the unexpected current-surge he'd shown—in front of the entire
damn pack—with Torres. That loss of control was something he was going to deal with himself.

Fortunately, there was enough to tell Ian, without going anywhere near that.

"We had a visitor. A klassvaak."

Just that one word, and Ian abandoned all fascination
with the ceiling, leaning forward across the desk, and
listening intently.

Normally, focusing on a problem isn't a problem for
me: Nick may call me "Dandelion" but I'm not at all
scattered—what I might lack in relative current-power, I
made up for in control and concentration. And yet, after
an hour or so of trying to manipulate my memory of the
scene back into diorama-shape, I gave up. It wasn't going
to happen; my brain was too busy buzzing around all this
new information to really focus.

I shut everything off, took down the wards, and
checked out at the board, leaving a Post-it to say that I
was following up on a long shot lead.

And then I went to see Madame.

The difference when you traveled from our not-quite-
the-Barrio to Madame's neighborhood was significant.
No teenagers hung out on the stoop, here, only rows of
uniformed doormen, and livery cars cruising the street.
The same little maid as from my previous visit met me
at the door of the penthouse suite and took my coat with
a welcoming smile. Unlike last time, though, because it

was after 5:00 p.m., there was a small cut-crystal glass of sherry waiting on the sideboard.

"Madame is in a good mood," Li told me, her wide eyes sparkling with delight. "A someone sent her roses."

I took the glass of sherry and sipped at it. I wasn't a huge fan of the stuff, but it was only good manners to accept the house's hospitality. "Roses, hmm?" I had an instant's image of Madame holding a bouquet up to her snout, sniffing delicately.

But no, when I entered the solarium where she held court, it was to find the Great Worm not sniffing roses, but eating them.

"Thorns and all, Madame?"

"Bonnnnita." She delicately spat a peach petal out of her mouth, and I watched as it lazily floated its way down to the parquet floor. "If you would like, take sssssome home with you. They are a treat, but my digestion is nnnnnot what it once wassss."

"Thank you, Madame. Will your admirer mind?"

"If he doesssss, he will nnnnnot dare ssssssay anything," she said, a delicate whiff of rose-scented air accompanying her words. "He wishessssss a favor of me? Let him earn it through kinnndnessss to my friennnds."

Being named the friend to a Great Worm is...it takes your breath away. Never mind that I claimed her acquaintance solely because J had once done a rather diplomatic favor for her back when he was my age, and she now found me amusing; I treasured the moment.

I knelt to pick up the petal, and placed it in the pocket of my skirt, thankful I'd thought to dress nicely this morning. Madame might not note the difference between cargo pants and a skirt on humans, but I did. Respect was earned, but it was also demanded in certain situations, and I would have felt awkward coming here in my grubbies. As it was, I hid my stompy boots under the hem of the skirt, and was glad I'd at least buffed them to a gloss over the weekend past.

"But you did not come to discusssss horticulture with me." Madame's great head came closer as her neck arched down, her body adjusting so that she could meet me, more or less, eye to eye. "Yesssss? Thissss isss a work call, little Bonnnnita?"

"I am afraid that it is, Madame." I met her gaze, struck again by the jeweled tones of her eyes. Her much lesser cousin, the cave dragon, had eyes the color of fired clay bricks, his entire body barely twice the length of her neck. His voice had been like hers, though: smooth and cultured, like rose water and honey. The old legends of serpents with smooth tongues? They'd been speaking, literally, of dragons.

"So." Madame settled herself comfortably, a great-aunt indulging a favorite niece. "What isss it you wissssh to know?"

What did I want to know? That was the question, wasn't it? What didn't I want to know? Madame was an Ancient, older and wiser even than today's visitor. Anything I asked her, she would either know, or know someone—or something—who knew.

But even before I'd gone to study with J, my dad had me reading fairy tales. And one of the first rules ever when dealing with dragons, no matter how polite, is don't waste your questions on things you can find out for yourself—or things you really *don't* want to know.

"Madame, you know I have the kenning?" It wasn't the sort of thing that you brought up in polite conversation, but the skill set was unusual enough that odds were J had told her, sometime over the years I'd been his student.

She tilted her head slightly, waiting. Yes, she knew. My pulse raced slightly, my heart pounding a little harder. I wasn't frightened of Madame...exactly. No more than I should be, at least. But I didn't know if I was violating a protocol here, pushing a boundary I couldn't see, and that unnerved me more than I'd realized.

"Last evening, I scryed a dragon, Madame." She knew me, she knew J, she knew I didn't scry lightly, or speak often of what I saw. "My vision showed it flying overhead. Filled with rage and fire...attacking the humans below."

Her head pulled back, sharply, and the half-dozen bouquets of peach-petaled roses crashed to the ground, the vases spilling water over the parquet floor.

"You sssssaw thisssss?"

"Madame. I did." I was so very damn impressed that my voice didn't shake or stutter, and that my body hadn't flinched at her outburst. "But I do not know what it means. Have any Ancients bearing ill will toward humans come to ask your leave to enter this island?"

Because this was Madame's territory, from South Ferry to Inwood, Hudson to East River, and no one would dare intrude without her permission...unless they meant to take it from her.

"None. None would dare. This island is mine."

I'd misjudged her. Madame didn't lose her cool. Her voice didn't thunder, and she did not hiss fire. In fact, her voice got damned near frosty, with none of the usual near-lazy sibilants and slurred *n*'s I'd thought were indelible speech patterns.

I stood my ground, but clasped my hands respectfully and bowed over them, my gaze hard on the sparkling scales of her left shoulder. "My kennings are often of things yet to come, Madame. But they are always true. Be watchful."

Her eyes went half-lidded and her delicate chin-whiskers twitched as she considered my words.

If Madame thought I'd come to warn her, so much the better. I had what I'd come here hoping for: the knowledge that there were no other dragons nearby, and none with ill will toward humans. Even if they'd been in another borough—and I suspected, based on things I'd heard, that there was at least one in Queens, albeit not of Madame's status—they were not likely the one I had seen. That meant we had a little time yet, at least.

"Madame?" So long as I was here, and she thought I'd done her a favor... "Have you heard of a fatae called The Roblin?"

That got her attention, in a way I hadn't expected. Her eyelids rose again, and a faint puff of burnt-rose smoke rose from her nostrils. "The Roblin? Here?"

"Yes." My mouth had gone dry, but I got the words out. "A fatae, the klassvaak, came to the office, to warn us...said it came to do mischief."

It was difficult to tell with dragons, but I thought, rather nervously, that Madame looked worried.

"Missschief he isssss, missschief he doesss," she said. The same thing the fatae had said, earlier that day.

"Madame?" I was hoping for something a little more specific—or useful—than that.

"Sssstay far from The Roblin, Bonnnnita," she said, drawing back and curling her body into a pose I recognized as dismissal. "Sssstay far from it, and hope it ssstays far from you."

And that was all she would say. I took a single bouquet of the peach roses, the scent of their bruised petals filling my nostrils, and went home.

"Attn pssngrs. The gee trn will be making all stops to sebthmurph and then going express. Pls take the mumble train to...splutterstatic.... There will be no service on the...splatterstatic.... Shuttle buses will be available."

It was a normal enough occurrence in a city the size of New York, with a mass transit system as old and vast as the Electric Apple, even without the added complexity of Talent occasionally shorting things out. Except, when the passengers piled out of the station and looked, there were no buses waiting; the drivers had received orders to assemble two stations down the line. A series of grumbles, groans, and exasperated sighs met this turn of events, which also would have been a normal enough occurrence, except that across Queens, similar areas of confusion broke out as trains were diverted for no reason, buses didn't arrive, and transit workers and passengers alike began to lose their cool, trying to get home.

With digital communication carrying the news across the city via mobile phones and laptops, the mood soured, feeding the feelings of persecution and annoyance until it felt as though a chain of riots would break out, with everyone blaming the transit authority, and the transit workers not knowing what was going on, either.

"Folks, just wait for the bus—"

"There is no bus!"

The cop was outnumbered, and out of energy. "There will be, ma'am, if you'll just wait..."

"Don't you tell me that! I've been waiting for half an hour already. There is no bus!"

A mutter of agreement greeted that, with more than one person checking their cell phone or watch again to prove how long they'd been there.

The cop glared at the commuters, almost daring them to do something. His eyes were odd in the evening light, the blue turning almost to gold, and several of the passengers shuffled away, suddenly awkward or nervous despite their anger.

A black sedan slid along the curb, with two others coming down the crowded street behind, like sharks drawn to a blood-spill. The window of the first car rolled down and the driver, a middle-aged man in a suit, asked "Anyone need car service?"

Two minutes later, he was full up, pocketing cash, and the next livery car was taking his place even as he pulled away. The cop watched, frowning, as the crowd faded, either waiting for more cars, or setting off on foot, their anger pushed aside under the grim determination to not waste any more time, but get home.

Too quickly, what had seemed like surefire chaos became an empty street corner, not even the usual pedestrians normally visible this time of evening left to stir up.

"That wasn't as much fun as I thought," the cop said, rubbing his chin with one oddly gnarled hand. "What is it with this city, anyway?" He took off his cap and scrubbed at his white hair, then slammed the cap back on as inspiration hit. "More challenge, that's what's needed. These people are all too simple—simple wants, simply fixed. I need something—no, some*one* more complicated." It cocked its head as though listening to something, its leathery nostrils twitched, scenting something, and then a disturbing grin spread across its face, showing more, and more jagged teeth than a human would have.

"Yes, yes. I remember you. I caught scent of you when I came in…. Not larger, but trickier. Sometimes a small trick is the best. Let's do that then, yes," it said in satisfaction. "But first, to find out where your prickly, pokey, pullable spots are…." It grabbed at the air in front of it, like opening a cupboard door, and was pulled through a hole that didn't exist, and out of sight.

Left behind, the broken loudspeaker continued to squawk instructions and directions nobody could understand, befuddling the passengers of the next train that pulled in and out of the station exactly on schedule, as though nothing had ever been wrong.

six

As per the Big Dogs' rules, we were supposed to take off at least one day every six, and if it wasn't a matter of life or death, two days in a row were preferred. It's not a suggestion, either: they know that we're all a little... compulsive, mainly because they trained us to be that way. So when Friday night rolled around, we were kicked out of the office and told not to show our faces again until Monday morning.

Or, as Stosser put it "go pretend to have a life."

Obediently, I spent the weekend doing things that had nothing to do with the job. Or tried to, anyway. There were just too many questions about too many things unanswered for me to really relax. But I stayed away from the office, didn't pick up my crystals, and if I did some quiet digging into the name "Roblin" and spent most of my Sunday night dinner with my mentor asking him about potential inter-fatae politics involving Bippis, well...what did the Big Dogs expect, really?

"I'm sorry, Bonita," J said. He had made veal piccata,

deceptively simple and mouthwateringly delicious. "What little I know matches what you have already discovered. I could ask around, see if my contacts know anything, but…"

But his network was at a considerably higher pay grade than the vic's, so they weren't going to be much help with the specifics. Now, if we had some kind of high-end political collision going on….

I made a quick "avert" sign with my fingers, discreetly hidden by a linen napkin. J frowned on my more old-world superstitions, although he'd just sigh and look away, if he caught me doing it.

"I wish I could be of more help. I worry about you— which you know."

He did. But he also had stood by our agreement, never to poke his nose in unless specifically requested. For a moment—not even a moment—I was tempted to tell him about The Roblin, to see if he could elaborate on Madame's comments. But odds were he wouldn't be able to add anything, and then he would *really* worry.

My mentor wasn't a young man anymore. I couldn't stop doing my job, but I didn't need to tell him every whisper of trouble that floated in.

So I went home—J giving me a Translocation-lift from Boston back to New York—without any useful answers, and first thing Monday morning showed up in the office, filled with well-fed energy, ready for something to break wide open.

Unfortunately, nothing did. In fact, Monday was filled with nothing but a lot of frustration, despite working until nearly ten in the evening trying to tear everything known apart, and put it back together usefully. Nearly a week after the cases landed on our desk, there wasn't a single peep on the street about who might have ransacked our client's house, or why, and I had utterly failed to reconstruct my diorama, even with Pietr's help. And we were no closer to knowing what The Roblin was or why we were involved. Morale, in a word, sucked.

We gave up on the diorama for the moment, since frustration did not lead to fine-tuned current, and instead spent most of Tuesday morning loading the whiteboard with every detail we had been able to dredge up on the floater, going through the last-time-seen and the river tides to put together a timeline, and not coming up with any plausible leads. The break-in investigation didn't seem to be going anywhere—the client was stalling us on a list of things that were taken, for some reason having to do with his insurance company—and none of the fatae wanted to talk about the dead Bippis, not one bit. Since the only thing the fatae as a rule liked more than themselves was gossip about other beings, we weren't sure if they were scared of something, or nobody had an honest, or dishonest, clue. I'd even tapped Bobo, the Mesheadam my mentor had hired as an off-again on-again bodyguard for me, more for J's peace of mind than my actual safety. Bobo was always willing to help, but he hadn't come up with anything yet, either.

Around noon my stomach rumbled, so I left Pietr staring at the board like it was the Rosetta stone, and booked out to grab some fresh air, and lunch.

Heading down the street, mindfully breathing in the air and letting it clear both my lungs and my brain, I spotted one of "my" missing boys sitting on the stoop. Weirdly, that made me feel better. I ended up in a little corner deli down the street from the office, getting an extra-loaded ham-and-Swiss grinder to go and contemplating adding a couple of cookies to that, when Nifty walked in, clearly in the same "feed me or die" mood. Chasing leads and current-use both burned calories at an impressive rate, and it wasn't like he was any kind of a delicate flower.

In fact, Nifty's dark-skinned bulk seemed to almost spark in the air as he walked, his core getting past him in ways that would have made any mentor worth their salt send him back to schooling. I didn't say anything. An entire office filled with frustrated Talent? It's a wonder things weren't sparking and failing throughout the entire building: I guess the money the guys had put in for shielding and grounding was paying off. And knowing that The Roblin was out there somewhere was making the fact that nothing had actually hit us even worse: we all knew that the quiet was not going to last. Venec had told us he would look for signs of unrest elsewhere, and we were supposed to focus on the cases, but...well, that was a lot easier to say than do.

My coworker leaned over the counter and gave his order. "Two tuna subs and a large Coke."

Nifty was a big guy, I was surprised he hadn't just gone down another block and gotten a whole pizza.

"How's the rash?" I asked him, when I saw he had noticed me.

"Rashy." He watched as I pushed money across the counter, and pocketed my change while the guy behind the counter wrapped up my order. "I'm more itchy to get the hell out in the field again, cause I can't still be contagious after this long. Hell, I'll wear full-length opera gloves, set a new fashion. You think you can put in a good word with Venec for me?"

I thought about playing dumb, decided it wasn't worth it. Even as my irritation boiled over, everything I'd been worrying about, everything I'd been repressing, escaped in a single unguarded, overtired moment.

"I'm not sleeping with him, and even if I were, what makes you think he'd listen to a damn thing I said if he thought otherwise?" I didn't wait for Nifty to answer, but took my lunch and stalked out of the deli.

I knew it. I *knew* it. Never mind that Nifty hadn't actually implied that he disapproved of whatever he thought was going on, or given me real grief, it changed the dynamic. The fact that they suspected something was going on inevitably made me less one of the pack and more... what? Venec's chew-toy, someone he kept around merely for his own amusement?

No. I took a deep breath, and let it out slowly. I was pissed, but not so pissed off I lost track of reality. Nobody who'd ever met Venec would think he took chew-toys. Me, yeah, maybe. But not Venec.

Did they think that Venec was *my* chew-toy? The thought was so delightfully absurd I actually stopped dead on the sidewalk, and then had to apologize when a very irritated older woman nearly bumped into me. She glared at me from under perfectly dyed purple bangs, and moved on past.

Huh.

I grinned, my unusual spurt of temper fading, and decided that I would *not* mention that chew-toy thought to Venec. Not that the topic would ever come up, but if it did I suspected he wouldn't find it as amusing as I did.

For the first time in weeks, I was able to think about the Merge with something other than annoyance. Yeah, okay. Maybe, as long as I was rolling with it, I'd see if I couldn't get myself cut into the betting action in the office, after all.

"You work for Stosser."

I stopped, a chill hitting my veins. The growling voice came from behind me, slightly to the right, which meant the speaker was on the curb or in the street, and lower down than my shoulder, which meant that they weren't human-adult height. And the question wasn't asked like they were looking for someone to hire.

"I do," I said. No point in denying it. I reached into my core with a mental hand and gathered a pool of current, letting it slow around imaginary fingers, passive, but ready.

"Tell him to lay off. Nobody wants his nose in this."

This? This what? The break-in? The dead body? Something else Stosser was looking at without bothering to tell any of us? Some case we hadn't even taken on yet? I hated imprecise threats.

"If you want me to carry a message," I said, proud of how calm my voice sounded, "you're going to have to give me more detail than that. Stosser puts his pointy nose into a lot of things."

The voice didn't think that was funny. It growled, and then something hard and sharp hit me just behind the knees, and I went down onto the pavement, hands flat to keep me from going nose-to-gravel, exactly the way we weren't supposed to fall.

"Humans have no place in fatae business," it said. "Keep to your own kind."

I lay there as the sound of heavy footsteps—bare skin, flat feet, I noted mentally—stopped, and the sound of a car door being slammed and a car taking off replaced it.

The floater, then, most likely. All righty.

I waved off the offer of help from a passerby who had carefully not seen anything odd happening, and got back to my feet, checking to make sure my sandwich was un-mushed. It was. I wish I could say the same for my pants; there was a tear in the left knee that not even a skilled tailor was going to fix. Damn it, I'd liked these pants, too. They were a dark gray wool that moved like silk, and had cost me a small fortune.

The front door to our office building had been magicked way back when by Venec to recognize our signatures, so I didn't have to worry about trying to get my keys out of my jacket pocket, but merely pushed the handle with my elbow, and slipped inside. Someone came up behind me, and I held the door open with my foot, just out of common courtesy, without looking. If it was my fatae unfriend come back for another round, it was welcome to come up to the office and make its case to Stosser directly.

"That's particularly stupid," a gravelly male-human-voice said. "What if I'd been a mugger or rapist?"

"Then I'd kick you in the balls and fry your nerve endings with current," I said, letting Danny move past me.

The P.I. was looking his usual hot self in jeans, leather jacket over a button-down, and scuffed-up cowboy boots, an NYPD cap jammed over his brown curls. The cap was less for weather protection than it was to hide the small nubby horns that peeked out through those curls. Danny was half fatae, half human, and all guy. He'd be a fabulous chew-toy if it weren't for the fact that I'd sussed right away that he was waiting, if unconsciously, for True Love. Poor bastard.

"You're out and about early," I said. Fauns weren't night owls as a rule, but Danny had told me once that he got most of his real work done between four in the afternoon and four in the morning. It was barely 1:00 p.m., which meant that for him to get here, dressed and awake, he had to have gotten up at least an hour ago.

"I had a morning meeting with a client," he said. "Figured as long as I was in your neighborhood, I'd stop by and steal some coffee."

"Bullshit. You have something. What do you have?" I started for the stairs, expecting Danny to follow, rather than wait for the elevator. The clomp of his boots on the metal stairs told me he had. Normally, a cutie on my tail like that, I'd put an extra wiggle in my backside just for the heck of it, but this was a business visit. And, anyway, I wasn't feeling it, today.

Danny, being Danny, was checking out my ass, anyway. I don't think he could help it. Genetics are a bitch, especially faunish ones.

"Is it about a pending case, or a future one?" I asked on the second landing, when he didn't respond to my earlier question. He usually didn't hold back, not with me, but this might be more than gossip.

"In the office," he said when we hit the third landing, his voice not at all winded. I'd expect no less from him, either the discretion or the physical conditioning. When it came to business, Danny was 100% human.

There was someone coming out of the office across the hallway from our door, which surprised the hell out of me—twice in one week, seeing those doors open, was unusual. We'd taken over two of the office suites on the east side of the building; the other two on the west side housed a tiny literary agency and a one-person photography office, both of which got a lot of mail delivered, but very little actual foot traffic. I let the woman—a pretty blonde, but too hard-edged to be my type—pass, and then ushered Danny into our office.

He went straight for the coffee machine, not even bothering to take off his coat or say hello to Nick, who was sitting on the sofa weaving current between his fingers. Some people doodled when they thought; he played with current.

"I don't know how you people do it, but your coffee's the best in the city."

"Because it's free?" I suggested.

"Well, there's that. Also, the surroundings are pretty."

Danny and I flirted like other people took in oxygen, but neither of us were really in the mood today. I knew what my reasons were...what was up with him? He lounged against the kitchenette counter and looked at Nick, his gaze flickering back and forth between fingers, watching the threads of blue and green and orange and red weave in and out like some kind of electric cat's cradle.

Actually, I realized, that's exactly what it was.

"Anyone else here?" Danny asked, while I shucked my coat and put it in the closet, then sat down on the sofa—a careful distance away from Nick and his thought-process—to eat my lunch before I collapsed from hunger. The vague warning-and-shove from my mysterious fatae could wait until after I ate. It wasn't as though Stosser was going to listen to it, anyway. The first rule of the office, even before "don't work at night alone" was "don't let yourself forget to eat." Most Talent didn't have to worry about being called on for a sudden burst of current, without warning. We weren't most Talent. Also, I had a bad tendency, still, not to top off my core on a regular basis—holdover from being raised, as J said, like a civilian. Being hungry just made the problem worse.

"Sharon's in the workroom," Nick said. "I don't know where Nifty and Pietr disappeared to."

"Nift was getting lunch right behind me," I said around a mouthful of grinder. "He should be back soon, if he doesn't eat there." Mostly we came back to the office, but I could understand him needing a little away-time. I wouldn't snitch him out to Venec. "Pietr was down the hall half an hour ago—hell, he could be anywhere."

As though on cue, we all peered around the room, trying not to look obvious. But no Pietr materialized out of invisibility. He must have gone somewhere else for food.

"How about your fearless leaders?"

"They've been in the back office powwowing all

morning," Nick said, finally getting tired of his cat's cradle and letting the current-threads slide back under his skin. "You want we should call them out, or you want to go back in?"

If Danny went private with what he knew, expecting the Big Dogs to dole out what we needed to know, I'd kill him. He knew it, too.

"Call 'em," he said. "Politely—it's interesting but not urgent."

I let Nick do the honors. I might be getting the hang of dealing with the Merge pushing at me all the time, but ever since Venec walked me to my door last week, and that little spark-show in the office, we'd been keeping a very careful distance from each other; walls up, if not so thick we couldn't sense each other at all. And now, with Nifty's comment still warm in my ear…yeah. Let Nick ping him.

Thinking about that, I decided to hold off telling Stosser about the warning a little longer, until Venec wasn't around. It had been a message for Stosser, anyway, right? No need to stress Venec about it.

The sigh I heard in the back of my head was definitely a memory-remnant from my mentor, disappointed in my decision-making, or my avoidance skills. Or both. I ignored it.

"We're supposed to go back to the main room," Nick said.

While the three available pups filed in, joining Sharon, who was already there, Benjamin Venec took the seat at the table farthest away from the P.I., and leaned back, trying to give every appearance of casualness while studying the other man intently. It wasn't that he didn't like Hendrickson; the guy was smart, and professional, and had only been helpful, not to mention carefully polite. In any other setting they'd probably be friends, if not drinking buddies.

The only complaint he could bring against the guy was that he was a terminal flirt—and that Bonnie responded. Considering their respective personalities and inclinations, the flirting was hardly surprising. Ben swallowed the annoyance. He didn't have any right to complain—hell, he didn't have the right to say anything if they were all over each other outside the office. Same way he had no right to frown over the fact that Bonnie and Pietr occasionally warmed sheets together. So long as it didn't have any impact on their work—and it hadn't.

The Merge didn't see it that way at all. It wanted him to drop-kick the faun out of the office, and Pietr likewise. Ben squelched the urgency the same way he would hunger pains, or the need to pee while he was on stakeout, and listened to what Hendrickson had to say without showing any emotion whatsoever. Hendrickson had been a cop, and he was fatae. That crossed a lot of boundaries, and made him useful. That was all that mattered.

The P.I. didn't consult notes, his palms flat down on the table while he spoke. "Your floater's name was Aodink. He was well-known among a certain portion of the community as a hardback with a loud mouth."

"Hardback?" Nick asked. He was seated next to the faun, which was interesting, considering how the pup seesawed on how he felt about the fatae. Ben hoped that

Shune was finally figuring out they were just like humans: some good, some bad, most mostly neither good nor bad because they didn't have that much ambition beyond the next meal and the next screw.

"Physical labor," Hendrickson clarified. "Not as dumb as he looked, but better at taking orders than giving them. Never going to be middle management, that one. Did a lot of contract work for construction companies, off the books, naturally." Most fatae were, unless they could pass for human. Too many questions, otherwise.

"Off the books...and nonunion? Do the fatae even have unions?"

Venec noted that Bonnie looked startled, and then thoughtful, at Pietr's question. She knew something, or had thought of something.

"Not a union as such, no." Danny looked equally thoughtful. "You know the fatae—we're all clannish but not so much with the playing well together. Like lone-jacks. Anyway, our boy Aodink disappeared about a week ago, but he wasn't working, so nobody thought anything about it. His friends aren't, shall we say, the sort to raise any kind of official alarm."

Venec nodded. That would explain why the pups hadn't been able to find anything. In anything that might bring official—meaning either Null or Council—attention on them, fatae were more likely to go to ground, sometimes literally, than talk about it. That meant the gossip would be limited, and unlikely to be shared with humans.

"Any idea who might have wanted him thoroughly dead?" Bonnie was leaning forward across the table now, her entire body engaged in the question, like a cat that had suddenly identified a mouse in the room, whiskers to tail on alert.

"Sorry, no." Hendrickson shook his head. "Nobody admitted to a beef with the guy. He had the usual ratio of drinking buddies and people who'd like to hit him with a two-by-four, but none of it sounded murder-weight."

Bonnie and Sharon were disappointed, like they'd expected more, and Nick was positively crushed, but Ben was grimly pleased. "Thank you. That's helpful."

"It is?" Nick, now looking perplexed. "I mean, yeah, we have a name now, but…"

"Names have power."

That was Bonnie, twigging as fast as he'd expected. "With a name, we can go to the Bippis community and ask specific questions, and they'll answer. Or, at least, not not-answer, the way they were stonewalling us before. Honestly, Nick, I've *told* you to read your fairy tales! Hello, Rumplestiltskin?"

"Oh. Right. You mean, even without a spell, a name can compel someone to tell us the truth? I mean, even though it's not *their* name?"

"Some," Hendrickson said. "Not so much as it used to be, when names were private things. But once you know a fatae's true name, it's like you've got a key to the lock, and everyone assumes you've got a right to what's behind the door. That's why a lot of the fatae have use-names, and unless you're immediate blood-kin, you never know 'em by anything else. Demon do that. And some of them create their own names, invest all they are into those—like nicknames, only more so—and that's where the default power goes."

Ben listened to the explanation, wondering idly if Hendrickson was aware that he referred to the fatae as "they," as though he wasn't half-fatae himself. Not that Ben could say anything about someone else being in denial, or at least trying to distance himself from something. "We're sure that's his true name?"

The faun just nodded, and Ben nodded in return. No need to ask specifics, between the two of them. If Hendrickson said it was so, that was enough.

"Sharon, you and..." He started to say Pietr, but he'd just pulled the pup to work with Lou on the police records for the break-in. "You and Nick take the name, interview the community again, see if anyone will cough up some more information, thinking that we already know enough to be dangerous." He looked at the P.I. then. "Would you be willing to help us? I can authorize a small retainer for your time."

Hendrickson hesitated, but to give him credit, his gaze didn't flicker away. "How small?"

"A hundred dollars, and we don't charge you for the coffee you've already gotten off us."

The P.I. grinned, boyishly cute, dimples and all, and reached out a hard, calloused hand. "You weren't kidding about small, but yeah. Deal."

He could see that Bonnie was annoyed—this was her case, after all, if Pietr wasn't there, and he'd just kicked her off it—but she kept her mouth mulishly shut, and waited while the others gathered up their stuff and left.

Then, before he could say anything to explain, apologize, or defend, she opened her mouth.

"There may not be a union as such," she said, "but the fatae don't want us poking into Aodink's death. It didn't make much sense before, but…I got a visitor on my way back with lunch who had a message for Stosser specifically, to stay the hell out of their business. He didn't give details, but unless Ian's into something we're not being told about…"

If he was, Ben didn't know about it, either. The way Ian had been acting, though, it was possible. "That message come with enough force to tear clothing?"

She looked down at her knee, and her mouth pursed in unhappiness. "Just a love tap," she said. "I get worse in fight practice."

"I'll let Stosser know about the message." He would do no such thing. Ian shrugged things like that off, except when he got annoyed enough to snap people in two, and neither reaction would be useful right now. "Forget about it, otherwise. We keep investigating." She nodded, clearly expecting nothing else. A shove and a buzz-off weren't going to make Torres blink. His girl was tougher than that. "I know you wanted to keep on the case, but I have a side job for you. Stosser's request, before he disappeared again this morning," he added, when she opened her mouth to protest. "Not a job—a favor."

The address Venec Translocated me to—we were in a rush, apparently—was a nice little brick-faced building in the West Village. Nothing spectacular, but clean and well maintained…and a walk-up. The universe was mocking me for not using the elevator in our building, clearly. My knee was starting to ache, and I put a hand on the cap, sending a pulse of current lightly into the abraded skin. You weren't supposed to use current to heal yourself—there was way too much that could go wrong—but making like Bactine and a bandage was fair use, especially if I was going to have to kneel down at some point soon.

The stairwell wasn't much to write home about, but it was clean and recently painted, and unlike too many of the buildings I'd looked at when I was apartment-hunting, it had a weirdly welcoming vibe. Hell of a lot nicer than my place, for certain.

I knocked at the top floor apartment, shifting my kit to my right hand to do so, and I'd barely let my hand drop before a voice came through the door.

"Yes?"

The voice was female, and dubious. "You called for a pup?"

The door opened, and I tried for my best "friendly pro" attitude. "I'm Bonnie."

I could see the woman giving me a once-over, and I wished I'd worn all black today, instead of my favorite bright red blouse, like a miniature fire engine. Not exactly professional. Oh, well. Too late now.

"Come in," the woman said, stepping back enough to let me by.

I went in. Nice apartment, if a little barren—all bland colors and stripped-down decor, like nobody actually lived there. Venec said she'd had a break-in, of the Talented sort. Unlike Sharon's gig, the client was Talent, and certain of the source, so I was there to see if we could recognize any signatures. That meant he—or this woman, anyway—thought it was someone we'd already encountered, because it wasn't like there was a huge database we could cross-reference against. Not yet, anyway. Something about this was a little weird, but mine was not to question why. "So, where's the stink?"

"Kitchen." She waved off to the right. "Think you'll be able to pick anything up?"

Okay, doubt was something I did not like to hear, even if this woman technically wasn't a client. I patted my kit. "If it's there, we can sniff it out. Just give me a little time and space… Oh, man." I stopped and stared into the space. It was less a kitchen than a kitchenette, barely enough room for two people and a fridge, but it had a window at the far end, and was filled with natural light. "Totally retro kitchen. I love it. This entire place is just so totally—are there any other apartments available in this building?"

The woman blinked in surprise. "One, actually. Downstairs."

"Most excellent." I hadn't known how badly I wanted to move out until I walked into this building. "The vibes in this place are…"

"Yeah, I know." The woman finally looked amused, and I took a longer look at her—or tried to, anyway. It was tough to focus on anything beyond average height, average weight, brownish hair, pale-ish skin. It was like trying to find Pietr, only worse, like…

Comprehension hit me like a slap. Oh, sweet fuck. She

was a Retriever. And there was only one Retriever in the region who was female, and that age, and...

Wren Valere.

I tried really hard not to let my sudden penny-drop show on my face. It's one thing to meet a legend, another to act like a dork about it. Damn Venec anyway for not warning me!

Although it was kind of funny: for a legend, The Wren was awfully...unimpressive.

"Right." I put my kit down on the floor and got down on my hands and knees to look around. Stay cool, stay cool, focus on the job.... I sat back and pulled some of my tools out. The undeveloped film was a trick Nick wanted us to try, to see if I could process any images onto the negatives. So far it was an utter loss in the field, but I was willing to give it another try or three. The vials of powdered metal were going to be more useful. I snapped on a pair of latex gloves before I opened those; they were like invisible splinters if they got on your skin, all sticky and sharp.

"Do you mind..." I gestured, indicating that she should get the hell out of my way. I didn't like anyone looming over me while I worked, not even a legend.

"Right." I guess she felt the same about being observed, because she got it right away. "I'll be down the hall."

Left to my own devices, I placed the film on the floor, touching it with just enough current so that—according to Nick's theory, anyway—anything I visualized would impart itself in electromagnetic images on the film.

It was a good theory, anyway. I hadn't even made it

work in controlled runs. Even Lou was better at this than I was, which was sort of embarrassing.

The powders came out, and I brushed them over every available surface like fingerprint powder, swirling the brush to get an even distribution.

Despite Venec's insistence on us "not putting on a damned show," as he said, this worked better if you gave the magic a frame to wrap around. It was a stupid cantrip, but it worked, and that was what mattered, right?

"Anything to show me? Anything to know? If found, twirl and glow."

I worked my way through the kitchen space, repeating the cantrip at regular intervals, and then doubled back, waiting. After a few minutes, there was a whisper of current, and then the air began to whirl and shimmer, as the metal splinters reacted to my spell.

"Oh, baby. Bin-go."

I didn't get a Transloc back, of course. The urgency was getting there, to show The Wren that we respected her time, etc, etc. I could have done it myself but there wasn't any need. The subway slog took me straight uptown, and I made it back to the office just in time to clock out for the night. My luck, I ran into Ian, first off. The office sounded like everyone else had already cleared out, and there was an unpleasant tension in the air that had to be coming from the Big Dog himself. Our fearless leader looked like he could bite the head off a basilisk right then. Thank god Venec said he'd tell Stosser about the warning, because I did not want to be giving him bad news right now.

"Torres."

"Sir?" I hated when I did that, reverted back to eleven years old and formal-around-adults when I was nervous. Thankfully I was pretty sure nobody in the office knew why I did it, and assumed I was either being cautious, or subtly snarky. Stosser appreciated subtle snark. Usually.

"So you've met The Wren."

"Yes, sir." He was standing there, waiting, wearing his demonic candle guise—all black, with his long orange-red hair pulled back in a ponytail—and I just blurted it out. "She doesn't seem very impressive. I mean, even for a Retriever."

His eyes narrowed, just a little. "Don't ever underestimate her, Torres. She holds back, but when pushed…" He seemed thoughtful, suddenly, in a way that prickled the skin on my arms. "When pushed, I suspect that she can be *very* impressive."

Then the weirdness was gone, and so was the odd tension and simmering anger, and he was just Stosser again—Big Dog and all-around scary-brained genius. "And I think the two of you would get along, actually. Cultivate that. It would not hurt for one of us to have an in with her—in case we ever were called in to investigate one of her jobs."

I almost laughed, because the thought was funny: whatever our client up in the Bronx thought, if you got hit by The Wren, you didn't bother having it looked into.

Then I thought again about that apartment, with its incredible vibes of comfort and hominess, and thought maybe I'd follow up on the results, rather than just handing them over to Venec. Not that I would ever befriend someone just to get an inside line on an apartment, but hey, if Stosser thought she and I should become buddies…

"And, Bonnie…"

Oh. Uh-oh. I tensed, expecting finally the other shoe to drop. Either I'd screwed something up, or he was pissed at me for not telling him myself immediately about the warning or… Venec would ream me out for things, but Stosser was the one who would actually do something permanent.

"Is…everything all right? With, I mean…"

I stared at him, trying to parse Stosser actually inquiring into my well-being, either physical or emotional. The Big Dog hired us, used us, occasionally praised us when we met his exacting standards, and I know he bragged on us to outsiders, but Ian Stosser didn't take much interest in us, specifically and personally like this. The skin on my arms prickled again.

Venec, I thought. He knows about this thing between me and Venec.

I don't know why that freaked me out—all right, I knew exactly why it freaked me out. Of all the people you didn't want in your admittedly already unusual personal life, it was Ian damned Stosser. Especially if you worked for him. Especially if the other end of that personal life was his business partner and best friend, and oh, *hell*.

But Ian just stood there, and looked…uncomfortable? Then he shook his head like shooing away a bee, and made a gesture that clearly said "never mind, go away."

I went away. Not just away from him, but out of the office entirely. I'd given the job enough of me, today.

Paranoia lingered even after I left the building: I looked around carefully, just to make sure there wasn't another fatae waiting to pass another message along, or anything that was rubbing its hands and twirling a moustache, or whatever it was mischief imps did. There were a few fatae, yeah, but they were minding their own business, walking like they had places to go, same as everyone else, same as any other day.

The streets were filled with people, actually, enjoying the soft evening air, and normally I would have gotten a mood-lift just being out and hearing other people talking and laughing. But the push this morning had put me on edge more than I'd thought, adding to the uncertainty with The Roblin-threat, and that exchange with Stosser made my nerves jangle worse. I wanted to chew on the case some more—either case, just to have something to show for my nerves, but my avenue of investigation was at a dead end; that was clear from the fact that I'd been sent off to do the pro bono work, and I didn't have anything worth chewing on, with the break-in.

And I knew that if I went home, alone, I'd reach out to Venec. Not meaning to, not wanting to…but the itch was under my skin, the need to pick up the tingle of reassurance that the Merge would give me, that he was there, that I wasn't alone. And the fact that it wasn't real—that it was all the push of some current-based whateveritwas—made me even more confused and distracted and in need of reassurance.

I hated all three of those things.

What I needed, desperately, was to be able to talk it out with someone who could help me untangle what was real and what was fear, without being judgmental or too biased. The only problem was, since I graduated college and started working with the team, all my closest friends were coworkers, too. And while I would trust my pack with my life, I wasn't ready to spill the details of this damned Merge I hadn't asked for and didn't want. Nifty's comment at lunch had confirmed my unease about that.

There was only one person who would understand, and that was the one person I really couldn't talk to—Venec himself. Not right now, the way we'd had to avoid each other to keep things functional. The time we'd walked, close enough our fingers touched, and talked openly about what was between us...that seemed years ago now, not months. Years and miles.

I could, I supposed, yelp to J. Once, I would have. We used to talk about any- and everything, even after I ended my traditional mentorship—there had been very little about us that had ever been traditional, anyway, the retired Council member and the daughter of a ne'er-do-well lonejack carpenter. But since I came to New York, took this job.... Dinner Sunday night had proved, once again, that there were fewer things I could tell him, not without screening what I said.

It was natural, J had assured me more than once. But I could hear the sadness in his voice when he said it, and it made me feel like crap. I wasn't his only mentoree, but I'd been the only one who had lived with him. That changed the dynamic. A lot.

But he wasn't my dad, and he really was not the person I'd want to talk to about this. The thought sent a shuddering laugh through me, drawing a startled glance from a couple walking past me, who sped up, as though to avoid the crazy. Oh, hell, no, I did not want to talk to J about Benjamin Venec, the Merge, or any of it. He'd know a lot, probably, or know who could find things out, things even Venec's mentor, a scholar, didn't know about this ancient and apparently rare current-connection, but the minute he started digging into it, he'd get even more protective, worry even more, and…

I skirted around an impromptu sidewalk café spilling out from a pizza place, and realized I'd walked past my subway station. Apparently I was walking home. Well, it was a nice night, and still light, so fine.

It wasn't a squeamishness about my personal life. J had watched me hit puberty, had taken my curious teenage exploring in stride, had never said a word when I dated a boy, and then a girl, or any combination thereof. So long as I was happy, so long as I didn't get hurt, he was content.

The real problem was that I was pretty sure J would think the Merge was a good thing. He'd be pleased for me, and I wasn't sure I wanted that. I didn't think it was good, or pleasing. And I didn't want to have to justify myself to him, just in order to get useful advice.

Halfway to my apartment, I stopped and changed direction. Hell with getting a good night's sleep; I wasn't going to be able to sleep, anyway, this wound up. There was only one way to deal with this: I was going to go have a drink, flirt with whoever was behind the bar even if I didn't want to take them home, and be a carefree, single twentysomething in the Big Apple, for one. Damn. Night.

The office, the cases, The Roblin, and Venec could all wait until tomorrow.

"Here. Here? Yes, here."

The sense of unease that shivered across the skin of Talent throughout New York City would have worried people if they'd known how far it spread, as though the source was poking its fingers into every office, every apartment, every subway car, looking for something. Across the city, sirens rose and fell in a higher-than-usual number. All day, the incidents of petty mischief and chaos had seemed to increase geometrically, making people irritable and far more likely to use violence. The most high-res of Talent were restless, while current-sensitive Nulls double-checked the locks on their doors and second-guessed their decisions, certain that something wasn't right, and astrologers and New Age folk double-checked to make sure that Mercury hadn't suddenly, unexpectedly, gone retrograde. Even the dullest of Nulls looked over their shoulders, and double-counted their change.

The Roblin was hunting.

"Here." A whisper of satisfaction as it found the source of the potential, the whisper of mischief that had summoned it. The scent of a worthy target.

In the locked and quiet offices of the Private, Unaffiliated Paranormal Investigations team, a single light flicked on, casting gray shadows around the otherwise dark and still space of the break room, although the front door had not opened to let anyone in. There was the quiet sound of soft-soled shoes on carpet, down to the first small office, and then the scrape of wooden file cabinet drawers being opened, the shuffle of papers being riffled, sheets pulled out and then quickly, carelessly reinserted. Information. It needed information, in order to wreak the highest chaos. It had the scent of their magic, but now it needed names....

Occasional muttering filled the air, as though rising from not one throat but several, all at once. The desk was unlocked and more drawers were opened, then that room abandoned and another investigated, the shadows working down the long hallway, checking each room as they passed, heading to the last room in the suite.

A gnarled, crooked hand rose to the door as though to push it open, and let out a deep squeak of shock as current lashed out at the unfamiliar touch, lighting the gray darkness with bursts of hot-orange and neon-green.

"Who are you?" whispered out of the air, a hot voice to match the current-sparks, and the shadow stopped, cocking its head as though considering the question. It had not expected an alarm, but clearly was not bothered by it, either.

"Who are you?" The whisper-voice was louder the second time, less of a question and more of a demand. The sparks intensified in color, as though preparing to attack. A hum, like angry bees, filled the hallway.

The shadow paused, as though judging the whisper and deciding that it was, at the moment, outgunned.

"Gone," The Roblin said. And then it was.

seven

Once upon a time, I'd been a regular at most of the dance clubs in Boston. Since coming back to New York, I'd gotten to know most of the better places, where you could dance and not get hassled or hit on if you weren't in the mood, but the time and energy demands of the job kept me from really doing the rounds. Still, when you have to burn unease out of your system, sweat the uncertainty out of your brain, there's still nothing like a hot, crowded, dark, noisy dance floor.

I didn't stagger home until 3:00 a.m., something I hadn't done since graduation, with the peaceful satisfaction you only get when you've had exactly the right amount of booze and socializing, going home alone because you wanted to, not because you had to. On the dot of 6:00 a.m. I opened my eyes, and practically slithered down from the bed and into the shower, and emerged half an hour later feeling every pore in my body glowing with energy, enthusiasm and health.

Bad behavior, in small doses, could be really good for you.

I rubbed a clear space in the steam-coated mirror, and scrunched my face at the damp, tousled fluff that passed for my hair. Dandelion, yeah. Now that I'd let my hair revert to its natural white-blond coloring, Nicky's pet name for me was really apt. After Venec's scolding over the hair dye, the tousled white-blond mop suddenly bothered me as being too flashy, too visible, nowhere near as serious-looking as Sharon's sleek styling or Lou's classic French braid. Maybe if I toned the color down to brunette...no, I hadn't gone dark since a brief pass at sable my sophomore year, and that had been really unfortunate for my skin tone. Black was effective for gothing, but it made me look older and more tired, and that wasn't what I was looking for, right now.

Professional, the boss wanted. Right. There's no way I could do sleek without also going butch, so I spritzed gel into my curls, shaped them into a slightly neater frame, and abandoned the mirror for the closet. After yesterday's clothing wreck, I felt the need to put my best face—or knee—forward. Black trousers and a pale blue silk shirt, with onyx cuff links I'd borrowed from J about ten years ago and never given back, plus a pair of black half boots, and I felt professional and kickass. Perfect.

I grabbed my kit, and my bag, and a pair of sunglasses, and headed off to do my usual battle with the morning commute.

It was a couple of blocks' walk from my apartment to the nearest subway, which when the weather was nice— like today—was enjoyable. Fresh air, a little morning sunlight, the sidewalks not too crowded yet, this far up-town. Normally I slip into an almost fugue-state, calm and ready, but heading down into the subway station this particular morning, I got a slightly creepy feeling on the back of my neck. Not that that's anything unusual at any given time, with mass transit—when anyone can ride, it stands to reason a percentage will be creepy, if not down-right dangerous. You stay alert, you practice safe subway, and most of the time it never touches you. But this was strong enough—creepy enough—to break through my earlier fabulous feeling, and make me take notice.

I studied the feeling the way I would any bit of evi-dence. It wasn't just the feeling of someone staring, or even leering…it was actual, palpable unease, the sense of a storm about to break, but without the good fizzy feel-ings a massive weather change brings with it.

It wasn't a kenning: I determined that right off. This wasn't that same sort of *certainty.* Just…unease. Creeping, skittering, unhappy-making dis-ease. Normal situation, I'd pay attention to that. After the images that hit me during my scrying? I was hyperalert.

The train came rattling into the station, and as we all shuffled forward, the feeling of being watched fading back to the normal levels. Whatever it was, it seemed to have stayed on the platform. Good.

I wasn't lucky enough to get a seat, and found myself caught between an older guy who smelled of ink and smoke, and two teenage girls who had never heard of personal space, because they were all up in mine. My earlier sense of enthusiasm and health fled, revealing a deeper layer of cranky bitch underneath. When an elbow came too close to my face as one of them extolled the annoyances of her morning class, I gave in to temptation and sent just a tiny zip of current into her foot.

Venec had taught us that. It was safest to tag someone there, farthest away from the heart and any potential medical problems that might be lurking. You only zapped someone in the chest if you were willing to risk killing them.

I was cranky, not murderous. The girl yelped a little under her breath, and shifted onto her other foot, swinging her body away from me subconsciously. I moved into the cleared space, claiming it as my own. The girls glared at me, but moved just enough so that they were the problem of the guy on their other side, instead.

I smirked a little, then froze.

The creepy feeling was back, stronger, like whoever it was had gotten on another car and lost me, back at the station, then followed the origin of my current-spark to this car. Great; with my luck and the way things were going, I'd just gotten myself a Talent-stalker.

Humans were split into two groups: Null, and Talent. But in each group there were gradations. Talent were defined as high-res or low-res, depending on how well they could channel current. Nulls...well, they had splits too, from almost-Talent to utterly Talent-blind, someone who couldn't even see the use of current when it was right in front of them, would look right past the most obvious fatae standing in front of them, stuff like that. Sometimes, a high-functioning Null would develop an almost pathological need to be near someone using Talent. If they didn't know about Talent, and most didn't, they only understood that there was this *need* driving them, to follow some people, stalk them, be as near to them as possible.

Occasionally you got a Talent-stalker who was smart enough to figure it out, who could identify their pathology and how it was triggered. The *Cosa Nostradamus* didn't hide, exactly; we were there for anyone who wanted to see. Once they identified themselves—and most did—it was easy enough to deal with; the local Council stepped in, discreetly, and matched them with a high-res Talent, one of the ones who couldn't even go near major electronics without everything going haywire. Pathology and handicap were both dealt with, making them useful to each other, like symbionts. Most of the cases I'd read about, it worked out surprisingly well.

But sometimes you got mouth-breathers who just knew they had to get up close and personal with the object of their fascination. Those, with no awareness of what they needed or why, could become deeply frustrated, and occasionally dangerous to both the Talent of their affections, and anyone around them.

When we sense a threat, magical or non, a Talent's instinct is to touch the core, to stoke it into readiness, in case you had to do something sudden. In this case, that would also be exactly the wrong move. My self-defense classes in college came back to me: if you're tense, you make a more attractive target, because you're scared and not thinking straight. Relax, show confidence, and the mugger will look for someone they have a better chance of overpowering. Relax...and don't do anything—like gather current—that might drive them to action.

I kept that like a mantra in my head the rest of the trip, until the words merged with the thump-thud beat of the train and got into my pulse. When we hit my stop, I moved with the crowd, walking at exactly the same pace as everyone else, that not rushing yet ground-covering stride New Yorkers excel at.

The sensation followed me off the train, up the steps, and out onto the street. Damn. Despite my best intentions, even as I saw our building down the street, my muscles tensed, and I let myself reach for my core; not quite there, but poised. When someone touched me on the shoulder, I almost screamed, even as I fell into a defensive position, grabbing current and pivoting, turning to—

"Oh." All the air went out of me, and my muscles went limp again. "Bobo."

The Mesheadam looked at me, his normally placid Wookie-face expressing the most concern I'd ever seen him show. "You're being stalked by The Roblin, Bonnie. That's not good."

I stared up at my occasional bodyguard, blinking stupidly. "I'm what?"

Bobo hustled me inside the building, ignoring the occasional odd looks we got—New Yorkers are pretty blasé about most things, but I guess seeing what looked like a muscle-bound Wookie that got shrunk in the wash out in daylight forced some folk to actually acknowledge the weird—and into the office, refusing to explain further until he had the Big Dogs' ears, too. Just us four, in Stosser's office.

"The Roblin has its eye on her. This is not good." Bobo practically radiated worry, and he hadn't taken his paw off me, as though he thought if he did, I'd get swiped out from under his guard.

"The Roblin? The mischief imp?" Stosser looked at me, then Venec. "We should be worried?"

"Yeah. Madame warned me…" I started to say, then stopped.

"Did she now?" I had Venec's undivided attention, now. Uh-oh.

I hadn't meant to tell them, since she hadn't given me anything we didn't already know, and I didn't want to look like I'd been distracted from the case, but that seemed dumb now, and I try not to be dumb. My report went over better than I'd expected, with Stosser only raising one narrow red eyebrow, and Venec just grunting in acknowledgment, then turning the conversation back to Bobo's announcement.

"You saw it?"

Bobo didn't take offense at being questioned. "Nobody ever sees it. We know it is there. It cannot be mistaken for anything else."

I thought about the feeling I'd had, at the back of my neck, and nodded. Oh, hell, yeah. If that was The Roblin, then I'd know if I felt it again.

"Like…?" Venec was looking at both of us, now, but Bobo answered. "Like the feeling that everything not only will, but must go wrong. As though the stars have aligned against you, and it would be best only to stay in bed and even there, you will not be safe from misfortune."

I nodded once, then shook my head. "It didn't feel that bad for me, but it could be because I'm human. It seems like the fatae are the ones who are most freaked out by it."

"We are wiser than humans," Bobo said, his voice deep in his chest like the roll of thunder, impossible to argue with.

I didn't even try.

"You're certain it's stalking her?"

Bobo's neck wasn't really designed for turning, but he managed it, anyway, this time giving Stosser a Look that translated into "I know you're not stupid so why are you acting like you are?" and despite myself I felt an urge to giggle. I risked looking at Venec, who was holding up the wall in Stosser's office as usual, to see if he was amused, too. If he was, he wasn't letting it leak, not in expression or aura.

Ian and I were the only ones sitting—there's no way Bobo could have fit in any of the chairs, and Ben liked to lean-and-lurk. The office, which could fit the entire team with a little squishing, felt about half its normal size just then. I could feel sweat starting to pool under my arms, and my shoes pinched, suddenly. All psychological. I breathed in through my nose, then breathed out, quietly.

"I know what I know," the Mesheadam said. "The Roblin has been in town much of a week. Everyone knows this." Everyone being the fatae, clearly. "You haven't noticed the weirdness it brings?"

"We've been looking, but in this town? How would you notice?"

I suddenly remembered the bird I'd seen, flying backward, and felt like an idiot. We'd been assuming that something big would hit, some obvious, catastrophic chaos, if The Roblin made a move, but maybe we should have been looking closer at the everyday weird, the small, strange things that make people superstitious? J taught me that very little of what we humans historically considered "supernatural" or "magical" actually was…but he might have been wrong.

"We were warned that The Roblin was in town," Venec said, jumping back into the conversation. "A fatae came to tell us, specifically." No more details than that; Big Dog was playing it close to the vest, as usual. "But since there was no further detail given, nor in fact any specifics of what this Roblin might do, we did not see any reason to place it above our open cases in terms of allocating resources." He glared at me, like Madame's information might have made a difference. I stared back, mentally telling him to back off.

"We know that it's a mischief imp," he went on, "but all our research was able to turn up was that the name's a polite nomen, what you use when you don't want to risk offending one of the breeds."

Like "the Good Neighbors" or "Old Scratch."

"Without those specifics, it didn't seem like something we should—or indeed, could—investigate further." I could sense anger inside Venec; at himself, for underestimating the problem, for not responding more strongly to a threat. Then, like he was aware I could feel it—and he probably was—the walls thickened and the sense was gone. "So tell us now, if you would. What the *hell* is going on?"

"The Roblin it is an imp," Bobo said. "But not just any. It is the grandfather of imps, the grandmother of mischief, the child of chaos and boredom."

That was about as eloquent—and incoherent—as I'd ever heard Bobo, considering his usual mode was to slip into "you white man, me play dumb" routine when confronted.

"We gathered that much." Venec had turned on the icy sarcasm. "But why does it worry the Ancients so much? And why is it following one of my people?"

Yeah. I was wondering that last bit, too.

Bobo shrugged his massive, furry shoulders. "I don't know. I saw, and I came to warn. But…" He frowned, which on him was a very odd look. "You investigate paranormal. It causes paranormal. You are opposed to each other, before you even do anything."

Like I said, Bobo only played dumb.

The Big Dogs looked at each other, and there was a humming in the air that wasn't really there, the way it always was when they were doing the not-quite-pinging thing they did. Telepathy was a myth—the closest I'd ever even heard of was the tight-wound connection Venec and I could have when we both let the walls down and reached—but those two weren't even using magic, just years of knowing each other really well.

"Anything that worries both our visitor and Madame worries me," Stosser said finally. "Especially if it is taking a specific interest in one of us. Ben, tell the others, tell them we've officially bumped this from casual observance to high priority. I want them alert for anything even slightly out of whack. No matter if it is in reference to one of our jobs, or life in general—I want to know everything."

"Will you alert the Council?" I couldn't tell, from Venec's voice, if he thought Ian should or not.

"You know I have to."

Like J—like me, technically—Ian Stosser was Council. The rest of our team were lonejack or, more formally, unaffiliated. They didn't understand the obligations even nominal Council membership put on you. Or, actually, they understood just fine, and wanted no part of it.

We—meaning Venec and myself—showed Bobo out. He rested one of his massive paws on my shoulder again, and shook his head at me. "I will be there. Even if you do not see me."

"I know," I said, and touched his hand with mine. J had hired Bobo originally, but he hung around for friendship. That meant a lot to me, even if I sometimes forgot to say so.

The door closed behind him, and it was just me and Venec in the break room. The office was, for once, utterly silent. Everyone else was either running late, or had gotten to work already, and Stosser was likely Translocated to the nearest Council office by now. I knew why he felt obligated, but there was a growing part of me that agreed with the others: the Council repeatedly refused to grant us approved status, meaning their members would not easily or officially come to us with cases, so why should we do anything gratis for them?

"Massive unease?" Venec asked me, referring to my earlier description.

I put aside questions of Council and loyalty, and focused on the more immediate problem. "Unease and discomfort, yeah. Like big test and you didn't study kind of thing."

"But not dread like you realized you studied for the wrong thing?"

That made me laugh, a little. "You did that, too? No, not like that. Venec, a couple of days ago, I saw a pigeon fly by. Backward."

"Uh-huh." He gave me one of Those Looks. "And you didn't think to mention that little detail?"

We had been a little preoccupied with other things at the time. "I figured...okay, fine, all right, I fucked up. If I see something that makes me wonder if I'm hallucinating from lack of sleep, I promise, I'll file an immediate report." I was joking, sort of, but also sort of not. The tension was weirdly thick in the room, and I could feel something almost like it was pushing me forward, like a hand between my shoulder blades.

Taking that one step forward would have put me square inside Ben's personal space.

I'd been that up close and personal once before. Downtown, the night I'd confronted him about this thing between us. We'd been off-hours then, both dressed for the occasion, and I'd danced with him, just long enough to get his attention. I wondered if he was remembering that, now, the way I was. From the way his breathing had gone shallow, and his eyes had gotten heavy-lidded, and the way he suddenly reached up and shoved a lock of hair off his face with way more force than the offending hairs deserved, I was betting he was.

Oddly, what I was remembering, even more than those few seconds of body contact, was the way he had, unconsciously, taken my hand when we walked, and the way his scent had lingered on my skin, after.

The sound of someone in the hallway outside broke the moment, thank god, before either of us did anything stupid. By the time Sharon and Nick came into the office, we were standing a respectable distance apart, and talking about the developments regarding The Roblin like there was nothing else on our minds.

"Hi, sorry we're late, got held up on the subway," Nick said in greeting, seeing Venec standing there like the Fount of Doom.

"People, listen up," Venec said it loud enough that doors down the hallway opened, and Nift, Pietr, and Lou popped their heads out to see what was up. He waved them down, and waited while everyone gathered.

"We're taking the situation with The Roblin to active status. There's reason to believe that he may be looking at us, specifically."

"Meaning what?" Sharon narrowed her eyes, trying to figure out what he wasn't saying.

"Meaning I want all of you to keep your eyes out. Anything even the slightest shade off, be it winning the lottery, polar bears in your bathroom or—" he shot me a glare "—pigeons flying backward, I want to know about, and I want to know the instant you see it."

"And?" Nick looked poised to be given some new, more exciting task.

"And that's it. Don't change your lives, keep your focus on the two cases we already have."

The message was clear: no matter what warning we might get, mischief—no matter the source—was not our priority.

Somehow, from the look in his eyes, the way he watched me for a long minute before excusing himself, I didn't think Venec was going to let go of it that easily, himself.

Everyone scattered again, and I went to get my delayed coffee, swearing under my breath when the only milk in the fridge was chunky. No time to go buy fresh: the meeting was about to start.

A few months ago, we—meaning the pups, not the Big Dogs—had started holding Wednesday morning meetings in the midsize conference room, as opposed to the largest one where we did brainstorming sessions with the whole team. We'd gotten rid of the table that came with the lease, and brought in a bunch of padded benches and armless chairs. It wasn't as comfortable as the break room, and didn't have instant access to the kitchenette, but it was quiet, and more private for brainstorming. Venec and Stosser stayed out, unless specifically invited in.

It was a pretty somber group that eventually gathered, once everyone'd had a chance to digest the news. In an obvious change of agenda, our first item was sharing any information we had found on The Roblin's proclivities since last week. I started out, reluctantly, by telling them about Bobo's warning. I'd gotten enough shit from certain coworkers previously for having a fatae bodyguard,

I didn't want to bring it up again, but for once, Nicky kept his mouth shut.

Everyone had seen things that were, in retrospect, weird, but other than my creepy-crawly sensation, nobody had noticed anything that really tipped the scales. Mostly it was small stuff, pranks rather than what you'd expect from an imp with The Roblin's reputation: traffic signals flashing "better run" instead of "walk," PETA protesters finding bacon in their tofu sandwiches during a protest outing—which had Sharon audibly wishing she'd thought of it—to every TLC meter in the city spinning wildly out of control, resulting either in negative cab fares, or tabs of $100 to go crosstown. The resulting fistfights that inevitably broke out from that were bad, but the cops handled it. It wasn't anything that should be calling for our attention. We weren't sure, in light of the most recent events, if that was good, or bad.

The pigeons flying backward thing had the potential to freak tourists out, and it seemed like that was a pretty widespread occurrence, but when Pietr checked with a birder he knew, we discovered that the falcons that lived in the skyscraper cliffs had caught on quickly, and had no trouble catching an awkwardly flying, and therefore slower than usual, lunch.

"The problem is, in a city this size, with this many of the *Cosa?* Weird is sort of the default mode. How do we know what's The Roblin's fault, and what's just, y'know, Life in New York?"

Like most of Lou's questions, it was a damn good one, and echoed what I had been thinking, earlier.

"When things start to go right, that's when you know

it's weird," Sharon said, with the voice of experience. "I know that's no help whatsoever but it's the truth."

Yeah. Default mode in any large city was to assume that everything that could go wrong, would. You left early because you assumed traffic or transit delays. You left an extra pair of shoes under your desk because you assumed a heel would break. You carried extra cash and a spare MetroCard somewhere other than your wallet, assuming you might get mugged. It wasn't paranoia, just planning.

But I'd been specifically targeted, according to Bobo.

"So we should be looking for sudden outbreaks of peace, joy, and happiness?" Pietr suggested.

"Well, that *would* be weird," Nick said.

"No, your protector said chaos, right?" Lou had an inward-turning look on her face that made her black eyes seem even larger. If I'd taken after my dad instead of my mom, I might have gotten eyes like those.

"He's not my…" All right, maybe he was, technically. "Yeah. Chaos and mischief. Which isn't wrongness, not exactly. We're looking at it from a human viewpoint. The Roblin's not human." Things started clicking in my head, loud enough I'd swear the others could hear it. "Okay, logical thinking here, which sets us apart from those poor schlubs who don't get paid to investigate. What's the one thing all the stories say consistently about the fatae?"

"That they lie?" Nick.

"Other than that."

"That they have rules," Nifty listed, ticking things off on his fingers. "They like things tidy and organized.

They like to count things to make sure, sometimes, or sort through things to make sure it's all there...."

Yeah. Dragons didn't actually count their treasure for value, but to ensure nothing had gone missing. I knew that one firsthand.

"So we look for rules and regs being broken, and that's our imp?" Lou nodded. "Okay. Makes as much logic as anything else. And then what?"

Sharon made a hands-up gesture she'd gotten from me, to indicate "damned-if-I-know." "And then we throw a net over it? Hell if I know. We tell Venec and Stosser and they come up with something brilliant. Can anyone come up with something more immediately useful?"

No one could.

"We done?"

Apparently, we were.

Sharon kept the floor as we moved into preexisting business. "Okay, so what's the status on the floater?"

Everyone looked at me and Pietr, but it was Lou who claimed the floor.

"I took the files you had been going through, earlier," she said, "and sorted through them according to breed characteristics, narrowing down to the ones who might have been able to take down our vic."

"And?" Nifty said.

Lou pulled three files out of thin air—a bit of showing off I didn't begrudge her—with the air of a woman who has cleaned the damned Augean stables after Hercules failed. "And we now have a database of over seventy-five different breeds currently known to be residing within the city limits, broken down into harmless, mostly harmless, and potentially harmful." God, I loved that woman, in a purely platonic but undying fashion. She might be useless in the field, but to sort through that much paperwork and come up with answers was an awesome kind of magic of its own.

"You are a goddess, and totally rock my world," I told her with utter honesty. "Tell Stosser I said you deserve a raise."

"Hah." The sharp bark of laughter was all that comment deserved. We had a surprisingly decent benefits package—health care not something the Big Dogs took lightly, considering the number of times we'd been put in harm's way already—but our paychecks were barely enough to get by.

Nick took the files out of her hand, passing two of them around. Sharon got one, Pietr the other. He flipped his open, and scanned the contents.

"The red-tagged folder," Lou said, directing their attention. "Those are the top candidates."

"If we go by the timeline you put together for the body-drop," Sharon said, "—and yes, I'm going by your timeline, don't give me that look!—then our perp had to be a day-mover."

Lou gave her a withering look Venec would have been proud to claim. "Already sorted," she said. "Anyone who would have problems moving under any kind of sunlight was filtered out, likewise any breed that would be too noticeable to pass without comment."

"We have fatae who are that noticeable?" I was surprised.

"One. Literally—there's reports of a Nriksha up near the Cloisters."

"A what?" I'd never heard of that.

"Flesh-eater. Decent enough creature, according to those who didn't get eaten, but the aroma is...unmistakable."

Suddenly my egg-and-cheese breakfast sandwich wasn't so appetizing anymore.

"According to Pietr's exam notes, there were two sets of bruise-marks on the body," Nick said. "So that rules out one perp.... Or if there was one, he has four hands."

"No four-handed fatae currently residing within the city limits," Lou said. "Although god knows what's out in the 'burbs."

"I doubt they'd haul in here to dump a body in our river when they've got better spots for it there," Nick said.

"They couldn't be imported bone-breakers?" I hadn't thought of that before—mostly we're territorial, and you don't bring in outsiders to do your own dirty work, because outsiders can't be trusted to keep their mouths shut—but we'd already encountered a Talent killer-for-hire, so it was a possibility. "Our vic worked construction... Hey, you think the Mob's gotten in with the fatae?"

There was a moment of silence, and then Nick laughed, and Lou shook her head, and we went back to the realistic possibilities.

Nifty slapped the table with one oversize palm. "Nick, give me a checklist. What *do* we know?"

"We know that it wasn't a domestic thing—the vic

lived alone, didn't seem to be interested in anyone of any breed, and only owed the usual amount of money."

"And that someone wanted it dead enough to use a significant amount of force...and wanted to make sure the body was found," Lou added. "There are places to dump the body where you won't ever find it again, even for Nulls. You think the fatae are any less creative?"

Damn it. She seriously deserved that raise. We were so caught up in how the DB was offed, we forgot to wonder about the whys of the dumping. And that was important.

"Someone wanted to send a message. But if not the Mafia, and we've already ruled out any kind of union goon squad...do the fatae have their own goodfellas?"

"Like a union, that would require them organizing," I said dryly. "They're even worse at it than lonejacks." Not to mention that the different breeds only played well with each other when they were playing against humans. But that gave me an idea. "Maybe we're looking at this wrong." I thought it through out loud, listening to how the logic sounded. "We were warned off from investigating by a fatae, right? And the killing was probably done by a fatae, so we've been assuming, based on the available evidence, that it was an intrabreed thing."

There hadn't been any warnings since my pushy visitor, but it had only been a few days, and maybe they were waiting to see how hard we pushed back. Or maybe we had read the situation wrong.

"Huh. Maybe it's not a fatae thing at all. Or, at least, not entirely."

I looked around the room, and saw that I had everyone's attention.

"My dad was a carpenter," I said, the words coming almost as fast as I was thinking. "A damned good one, and he got called in on a lot of jobs out of the city because people talked about his work, passed his name along. There's a—hell, call it a brotherhood, why not—of people who do finer work like that. They share job leads, information, news about who pays well and who stiffs or treats their workers like shit."

"But not a union?"

"Not a union. No dues, no leadership, no organization except as how they felt like it at that moment. All totally under the radar."

"And?" Lou asked, waiting.

Pietr was thinking along my brain tracks. "And you think that it's this brotherhood, or something like that, that offed him? Because…what?"

That was as far as my thinking had thought out. "I don't know. But it makes as much sense—more—than looking for an individual with a grudge, or some breed-on-breed hostility that nobody else is whispering about." Especially after recent events, when human-fatae relations had taken a seriously negative turn. We'd heard buckets about that. "You said that he didn't owe enough money to get killed over. That means he was working regularly…but he doesn't seem to have been on a job when he died. We need to find out what he was doing the days before he took his swim. I'll bet you next round of drinks that someone says something that points us toward the reason he was killed, and once we have the reason…"

"We have the killer," Nick finished.

★ ★ ★

Ian Stosser knew that the pups were having their weekly meeting, no bosses invited, so he wasn't too worried about them poking their noses in at the wrong moment when he took the phone call, already knowing who was on the other end.

"I want to see you. Alone."

The meaningful emphasis in Aden's voice made it clear who she meant: no pups. Particularly, no Benjamin Venec.

His sister hadn't always hated his best friend, had she? Ian pinched the bridge of his nose, and shook his head. "We have nothing to talk about, Addy. The Council is deliberating my most recent proposal. Go politic at them—leave me alone."

There was a pause, the click of china cup against saucer, and then she spoke again. "This isn't about that."

Her voice was still the cold, dry tone she had used with him ever since he had first gone up against their home Council, years ago. But Ian remembered the little sister who had clung to his leg when he was a teenager, who had called him every Thursday night when she went away to college to ask his advice about classes, and dating, and talk about what books she had just read.

Across the office, Ben frowned, but didn't say anything, aware that on speakerphone she would be able to hear him as clearly as he heard her. Ian didn't need to ping his partner to know what he was thinking. Ben didn't trust Aden not to have something else up her ever-fashionable sleeve. That was wise, probably. Aden was not to be trusted any more than he, Ian, was to be trusted.

Not when it came to the survival of this office, or of the idea behind it, that no Talent could escape accountability for their actions.

Aden truly believed that rank had privileges, and one of those was being accountable only to others of that same rank. Or, in the case of Talent, of equal or greater ability.

She was also his little sister.

"My choice of time and place," he told her.

"Agreed."

Ben looked startled, and then covered it up behind his usual stone-faced exterior. For Aden to agree so readily, either she was plotting something interesting, or she genuinely needed to talk to him about something other than their ongoing disagreement. Ian wasn't sure which one worried him more.

"Half an hour. The old diner, down in Philly. You know the one?" Ian would have had her come here, but she was still under Council ban from entering New York City limits, and even his direct invite could not put that aside. And in that short a period of time she would not be able to adapt any schemes to the location, or call in backup. Hopefully.

The click of the phone being hung up on the other end was his only answer.

"This should be...interesting," Ian said, his voice as dry as hers had been.

Ben shoved his hand through his hair, a move that harkened back to when they were teenagers, and scowled. "What do you think she's up to?"

Ian laughed: a real laugh, with real amusement. "This

is Aden we're talking about, Ben. Who the hell knows?"
He shook his head, dismissing the question for another
thirty minutes. "The cops are starting to push for some
kind of answer on the floater. They want to know if they
can bury the report. And the client called this morning,
he's getting pushy about the break-in—he wants to know
what happened to his trinkets. He also wants to know
why his anti-magic protections didn't work."

"Oh, Christ." The cops were a known headache, but
Benjamin Venec had no use for fools, Talented or Null.

"Let's just get this solved, all right? Take them off the
floater if you have to—he's not going anywhere and if no
more bodies have turned up odds are we aren't looking
at the start of a serial killer."

"You're asking us to give priority to a break-in over a
murder?"

"Not priority, no. Just an additional push on that front,
for now."

Ben wasn't happy. Ian understood that. Murder should
always be the first priority. But the dead have patience.
The living did not.

"Right, fine, whatever. I'll tell them soon's their pow-
wow's over." Ben stood up, stretching his arms overhead
until something cracked, then moved his head side to
side, as though loosening knots there, as well.

"Are you getting enough sleep?" The question slipped
out before Ian could stop it.

Ben looked at him as though he'd lost his mind. "Who
are you, my mom? Go worry about your sister, Ian. I'll
whip the puppies into shape. Sleep is for people who don't
have things to do."

The moment the door closed behind Ben, Ian stood, as well, moving to the bare corner of the room. Technically you could Translocate from anywhere, so long as you knew that your destination was clear, but it was less of a current-drain if you left from a familiar place, so that your mind and body both knew what to do, instinctively.

He closed his eyes, visualized the booth in the diner that was always left empty in case a Council member wanted to have a meeting in that city, without fuss or formality. Technically he no longer had the right to use the booth…but the deli's present owners were old friends of his from college, and would not tell anyone.

More, they would not give Aden any succor, should this be a trap.

Drawing in his current, Stosser dropped down into fugue-state, and disappeared.

In the hallway, Venec felt the gentle movement of current that indicated a Translocation, and shook his head. He wouldn't trust Aden Stosser to pet a dog without there being trouble for the dog, but it wasn't his call to make.

There were raised voices coming from the conference room, indicating that the door had been unlocked and the bosses-out portion of the meeting was over, so he headed in that direction.

"Mafia!" Nick, gleeful in a way that meant he was intentionally trying to goad someone.

"There is no *Cosa* mafia." Sharon, still patient, so no bloodshed was imminent.

"You know the name was a joke, right?" Lou, amused.

"Sort of a joke." Bonnie. "Okay, not really a joke. But that would require way too much structure. So would a trade union. We don't enforce, that's always been the problem."

"Someone wants to change that, looks like." Nifty, the somber note.

"Yah." Nick, less gleeful now.

He paused before opening the door, listening to their voices layering over each other, barely space to breathe in between. He didn't have to hear her voice to know Bonnie was there, and that she was excited about something. They all were, even Nifty: the pack had gotten a clear scent, and were baying as they tracked it down.

He thought about leaving them to it, and remembered Ian's words, and pushed the door all the way open.

"Hey, boss." Lou spotted him first, her normally solemn face looking as animated as he could remember it being, since she failed her first field run and had been assigned in-office responsibilities.

"We figured it out." Nick looked equally triumphant, although he was always an easier show. "The dead body. We know who killed him."

"Technically," Bonnie said, and her voice was less readable, although she was practically radiating excitement to his awareness, "we don't know *who,* as in, a person we can point to. But we're pretty sure we know why, and the why will lead to who."

The others in the room were surprisingly quiet, but no less wound-up. Ian's instructions would wait—if they could shut this down and get the NYPD off their backs, so much the better.

He went into the room and pulled out a chair, turning

it around and straddling it, leaning his forearms on the back, and catching each of their gazes in turn. "Tell me."

It was Bonnie's case, even though he'd yanked her off it briefly, so she took the lead. "Before it went splooey, my diorama showed me that the body was probably dumped, not way upstream, like we'd thought, but just a little bit above. Anywhere else, the current would have dumped it somewhere else. So that threw our estimated timing off. For it to reach that spot when it did, the body wasn't dumped in the middle of the night, but early morning."

Ben nodded, indicating he understood.

"So, you have a guy, you want to off him, but even bound hands and feet you don't slit his throat and toss him into the nearest trash heap. Instead they toss him into the river, right there, at that exact spot. Why? You want to drown the schmuck, okay. Nasty way to kill someone, but why there instead of tossing him off the pier, or dumping the corpse in the landfill, or any of the many many ways there are to dispose of a body? The only reason you'd toss him into the river there is if you wanted the body to be easily found, because if you really want to hide something, you don't toss it right into the nets. Right?"

Her logic was convoluted, but sound.

"They might not have known about the net," Nifty said, clearly playing devil's advocate, a role Sharon normally took.

Lou jumped in, there. "Even if they couldn't see, or read the signs warning boaters, the net system was on the news two nights before the murder. The city was thinking about cutting the budget and pulling some of the nets, and every network rehashed old stories about stuff that's been caught in there, over the years."

"All right, so if our killer watched the news, he knew. And?" Venec waited; they wouldn't be this excited if they hadn't already reached near endgame.

"The DB worked construction, off-radar, right?" Fatae, except in specific, unusual cases, were all off-the-books. "The off-books construction gig is a tight one," Bonnie went on. "A few months in the game, and you know pretty much everyone who's any good, and the ones who are really bad, too. Our DB, being in the freelance construction business, was good...but he hadn't been working lately."

Bonnie's father had been in construction, Ben remembered. Clearly she had kept some contacts, even after Zaki Torres died. "Because?"

"Mainly because, according to one of my dad's old compadres whom I just checked with..."

He'd been right, and Bonnie had that canary-aperitif grin just waiting to burst out.

"Our vic was in the middle of a squabble with several of the folk who slipped him money under that freelance table, about money he says they owe, and they say they don't."

"I thought the report said he didn't owe..." Venec stopped, feeling the grins break out across the room, even though they were all mostly work-sober, waiting for him to twig in. "He doesn't owe. They owe him. Or so he claims...but I bet nobody will back up his accusation?"

Nick confirmed it. "Because if they do, if they piss

off the hiring guys, and then they lose work, too. Yeah. That's how we're seeing it."

"Was he agitating against these hiring guys?"

Bonnie nodded, a subtle dip of the chin. "So my dad's old buddy implied, yeah."

"And you think, suddenly, these hiring guys had someone shut him up?"

"Nope." And the grin came out in full force, totally inappropriate but infectious nonetheless. "We think his fellow freelancers did."

Aden slid into the booth exactly twenty-nine minutes after Ian arrived. She was wearing jeans and a college-logo sweatshirt, and her red hair, darker than his own, was tousled, her face clean of any obvious makeup.

She barely looked as old as the pups, until he looked into her eyes and saw the utter weariness there. Weariness, and wariness.

"What's wrong?" he asked again, and this time he meant it. She was his sister, damn it. Anything that made her look like that, he had the urge to hunt down and hurt.

She hesitated, her pale fingers twining against each other like a nervous schoolgirl. Ian resisted the urge to put his hand over hers, to warm that chilled-looking flesh. "What's wrong?"

She took a deep breath, and lifted her gaze again to meet his.

"You've been so busy with your…experiment, I don't know how much attention you are paying to the chatter, these days."

By chatter she meant Council gossip, specifically; the constant exchange of information and suggestion that tied the social and political bonds tight. Ian listened in, but not with the finely tuned ear he used to have; too many other things demanding his attention these days, and if it didn't affect PUPI… "You've heard something that upsets you."

"There's…not talk. Not even whispers. Suggestions of whispers. Madame Howe is not content with the status quo."

Madame Howe. Leader of the regional Council of the Eastern seaboard and known—with both fear and respect—as the electric dragon. He visualized her in his mind as he'd seen her at their last meeting: a delicate, older woman who didn't try to hide the spine and balls of steel under the demure and elegant lady-of-an-older-generation exterior. She was a powerhouse of both current and political savvy, with a family history of leadership, both on her own side and through her late husband.

"Not content, how?" Each Council was independent, and strictly forbidden to interfere with the affairs of other regional Councils. That was deliberate, done with the full knowledge of the personalities who might rise to power within the Council, and had held for over two hundred years, almost as long as the *Cosa Nostradamus* itself had been in America. Even the old-world members adhered, mostly, to the Council restrictions, these days, and for much the same reasons.

"She wants to…expand. The whispers say she's already

made outreach to other leaders, offered them…deals." Aden said the last as though the word tasted foul.

Ian almost smiled, despite her obvious distress and the seriousness of what she was saying. His baby sister was a traditionalist to the core—her argument with him had never been about the need for oversight and accountability, merely the idea that someone outside of the Council would be allowed to investigate Council matters. The idea that another Council member—a leader as respected as Howe—would go against tradition in such a manner, so obviously forbidden by the very structure and history of the Council itself…

Ian was older than Aden, and far more cynical, and found the idea of shake-up within the Council less horrifying than intriguing. What new fault lines were developing, in that rarified ground? And how could he use that to forward his cause?

"What do you want me to do, Aden?" The waitress brought him a glass of iced tea, and he sipped it, more to buy time than any desire for the liquid itself.

"You still have standing with the Midwest Council." Standing that, thanks to her recent attempts to shut him down, she had lost. "Talk to them, find out what's going on, find out if it has spread there."

"Investigate, you mean? Use my contacts to find out what she's planning, and stop it?"

Aden didn't even hesitate. "Yes."

The irony was heartbreaking. "I can't."

She glared at him like he had just kicked her puppy. "What do you mean you can't? You have to! Find out what she's doing, and stop it!"

He wanted to. He wanted to do whatever his baby sister asked of him, above and beyond any benefit he or his project might gain from it. But if she was a traditionalist then he acknowledged himself as an idealist, and he could no sooner go against his ideals than she could break tradition.

"Aden, it doesn't work that way. You've bitched so much about PUPI, you should know how we operate. We investigate, yes. But that is all. We remain neutral, only gathering information, not acting on it. And we cannot go into anyone's business, most especially the Council's, without cause. A complaint. A client." Especially right now, when he was so close to finally gaining their approval.

There was only one way he could justify poking his nose into this, right now. "Are you hiring us, Aden?"

She glared at him, and Translocated out in a sulk.

The waitress reappeared, not at all surprised by one of her customers disappearing. "So, you're not going to be wanting to order, then, hon?"

"Short stack of applejacks, extra syrup, and another iced tea, please."

He couldn't investigate, not the way Aden wanted. But he could ask around. If the electric dragon was planning a power grab, he wanted to be well aware of it *before* the shitstorm broke.

This was his town now, too. He'd be damned if he let her ruin his plans.

eight

It was one thing to gather intel and come up with what we thought was a brilliant deduction. It was another, entirely, to lay it out in front of Venec, and wait for his reaction. We didn't have to wait long. The moment I finished, he exhaled heavily, the kind of surprised-pleased-thinking exhale, and leaned back a little. You could practically see the thought process racing through his neurons like current.

"Lawrence. How's the itching?"

"Totally gone," Nifty replied, although I'd seen him scratching his elbow against the chair arm not five minutes before. Either Venec had missed that—unlikely—or he was willing to pretend it hadn't happened, because he nodded. "You and Pietr go track down the coworkers last seen with our corpse. Ask them a few pointed questions about their feelings about his relations—or lack thereof—with their employers, and how it was affecting them. Don't be coy. If Bonnie's info is right, these guys are not going to understand subtle. You may have to lean a little."

Well, that explained why he was sending Nifty, who outmassed all of us put together, practically. I guessed Pietr was going along to provide the potential good cop in that scenario?

"But—" And Venec held up a hand as the guys stood up from the table, clearly anticipating a nice day out of the office trying to intimidate witnesses. "Any questioning you do, make sure it's in full view of at least two others, not involved. Do not go with them anywhere, no matter how good an idea it might seem."

Pietr really didn't need the reminder, but Nifty tended to think with his bulk, and while that was fine when facing down humans, against fatae who could maybe, if we were right, restrain a Bippis, maybe less so. From the annoyed "do you think we're idiots?" expression on their faces, I suspected that the fact that they were being sent to question suspected murderers hadn't quite filtered into their awareness. But they nodded seriously, and went off to do their dirty work with probably more enthusiasm than was healthy.

I don't know why I'd expected more from Pietr— smart guys were still guys, sometimes.

"All right, that's being dealt with. Where do we stand on the break-in?" Venec asked, turning his attention to those of us left in the room. I hrrmmmmed and errrred a bit, not having any idea. Thankfully, Nick and Sharon— whose case it had been, originally—had more clue.

"We finally got a report of what was missing," Nick said, and from his expression I was guessing that "we" meant "him." "And confirmed what the owner claimed, that for all the damage that was done, there were only two objects taken—a silver pocket watch, ordinary, and a glass dagger, which looked like an ordinary paperweight, but was actually a memory-glass."

A memory-glass was a Talent-trinket. Nulls get to use digital frames and downloads, we store images and voices a different way. They were low-res, incredibly basic so anyone could use it, even Nulls, and it probably wasn't all that surprising that the client—who had fallen for the "magical defense" line—had one. It was odd that anyone had stolen it, though. They're not lockable, so odds were he hadn't hidden any blackmailable memories in there, even assuming he trusted a Talent enough to share it in the first place, for storing....

But they were taken, so that had to mean something.

"What was stored in the glass?" Venec asked, probably matching my thoughts exactly.

Sharon picked up the narrative. "Nothing sensitive according to the client. Some memories that he didn't want to forget, family trips, things about his wife, that sort of whatnot. Sentimental value, nothing more. Ditto the watch. Pretty, but not particularly valuable or unique. He didn't even have photos taken for insurance purposes, never saw the need, which for this guy means he really didn't think it was valuable—he had photo, acquisition cost and market value on every other thing that was broken.

"Client is convinced that someone stole them in order to put a hex on him, and before you ask, yeah, he's got the usual string of 'nice guy, fair businessman' testimonials that could have come from a playbook, they're so generic. If he has enemies they're playing it cool."

She paused. "I couldn't tell if he was lying or not, but I'm pretty sure he was telling the truth that they were only sentimental memories, not anything worth stealing. And since he wasn't the one who installed the memories...I'm not sure anyone could actually use it for a hex, at least not on him. Could they?"

Lou shook her head. "The only thing to latch onto would be the signature of the Talent who made it. Anyway, anyone who could do this wouldn't bother with a hex, if they wanted to hurt the guy. There are more direct, more impressive ways to do damage."

Venec frowned, leaning forward again. "Wife's dead?"

Nick picked up this time. "Cancer. Kid disappeared soon after, packed a bag and gone. Cops investigated—husband filed a missing persons report—kid had run away before. There were no known enemies, no domestic complaints, so... Guy's had a crap life, for all the money—wife's dead, kid gone a year later, I guess it makes sense he'll pull out all the stops, even magic, to reclaim stuff that holds good memories, even without fear of a hex."

Venec had a look on his face I couldn't quite decipher. The temptation nibbled, to lower my walls and see if I could read his emotions, but I didn't. Wasn't kosher, and, anyway, if I did that he'd be able to read me even easier, and that wasn't kosher, either.

"What was this guy's name again?"

"Wells."

"Huh. Okay, no." Whatever it was that niggled him,

he wasn't sharing. "So we have a guy whose very nice little mansion was ransacked and trashed—"

"Portions of it were trashed," Sharon clarified. "Only the two rooms downstairs, the office and the...call it a library, I guess. Nothing upstairs, the kitchen and front parlor were left alone."

"Right, two rooms taken apart. Specifically, the two rooms where someone might store something valuable, either physical or electronics, not just current-based memory-keepers. Magical thieves do not mean only a magical theft, people."

I hadn't even thought about that, and from the lack of notes, neither had Sharon or Nick. Damn it, that was sloppy. The client was a Null, so we should have thought about digital records. We weren't allowed blind spots like that.

Venec didn't stop for us to beat ourselves up. "So our violence-prone intruder was possibly looking for something specific, either business or personal, but all they took were trinkets? And our client has no known enemies, no business rivals, nobody who'd get a thrill out of seeing him get taken down a few notches?"

"Seven names on the list," Lou said, touching the pad of paper in front of her. "Three of them are totally Null, so it's almost improbable they'd have been able to hire anyone from within the fatae community."

It was a weird tick to Nulls—the more current-blind they were, the more they managed to float through life without even a glancing interaction with the *Cosa Nostradamus*, at least within a magical range of interaction. Not only were they not going to hire supernaturals, they wouldn't hire anyone who would then hire supernaturals. J said there was some kind of physics explanation to it, but I'd never cared enough to look it up.

I pulled out my own pad and made a note to myself: it was time to do some reading about that. If that Null aversion field was a way to eliminate suspects, we needed to know. While I had the pad out, I wrote "electronic files as motive" and underlined it. Twice. Next time, we wouldn't forget to consider it.

"I was hoping that one of the rivals would turn out to be useful," Nick said. "Rumor was he'd had an affair with the dead wife, years ago, and blamed our client when the kid went missing, but the guy, Isaacs, came up clean, and—"

"What?"

Venec's voice didn't rise, and his body didn't move—in fact, if anything, his tone dropped and he went incredibly still, exactly like the air before a tornado hit.

"Ah, he came up clean?"

"The name."

"Isaacs. Jerry Isaacs."

Venec moved then, his hand snatching out to grab the file from in front of poor Nick. "Damn it."

That simple, heartfelt swearword was more chilling than any invective he might have unleashed, because it brought a storm I hadn't felt coming, slamming against my walls in a wave of emotion I was pretty sure he hadn't meant to unleash.

Anger. Annoyance. And...guilt. Overwhelming, agonizing guilt. The hell?

"Boss?" Lou had picked up something, too, while Nick was flicking his gaze from the file in Venec's hand, up to his face, then back again.

The wave of emotions stopped, his wall slamming back up, and I discovered that my heart was pounding and my body was wobbly, like I'd just dashed up all seven flights of stairs in record time, during a fire alarm.

When Venec spoke again, it was as though nothing had ever harshed his calm. "An interesting development. Possibly of importance, possibly merely coincidence." He paused to consider his words. "Or possibly not coincidence, but inevitability."

Whatever he was about to say, I didn't think we were going to like it.

"I was employed, years ago, by the now-dead wife. Christine."

Before PUPI, Venec had been a PUI on his own, that was why he taught us, handled the day-to-day stuff. But he'd been based down in Atlanta, or somewhere, not New York. So how…

Venec's voice was low and soft, like he was talking to himself. "Christine was referred to me. Her son had gone missing while he was in college, down my way. She wanted me to find him. That was my specialization, finding people who had jumped the track. Usually people who had skipped out on a bond, but runaways, too. She had used that guy's name, though. Isaacs. That's why I didn't recognize this…and Isaacs, he had come with her, I thought he was her husband."

Okay, the boring break-in case had suddenly gotten

a hell of a lot more interesting. I didn't think that was a good thing.

From the feeling I got off Venec, neither did he.

Venec left them to rechecking their information with a focus on Isaacs—in their business you couldn't discount someone just because he was dead—and headed for the garage on the East Side where he kept his bike. It was a fast ride uptown from there, up the Henry Hudson and into the Bronx, and the private community of Fieldston. The house looked the same as Ben remembered it. It had been full summer, then, with everything in bloom, under a lazy heat that had felt cool to him, having flown out of the Atlanta airport that morning. He had been there to examine the boy's room personally and see if there was any clue the parents and the cops had missed.

There hadn't been. The room had been utterly, completely normal, for the only child of a well-off family. Ben had wondered, then, if he'd missed anything important. He knew he had, now. He just didn't know what.

Dismissing old memories, he drove past the house, not even bothering to look for parking on the street; in this neighborhood, that was a good way to get a ticket for not having a resident sticker. His bike took the corner easily, down the street and out of the elite neighborhood, to the more blue-collar areas where a motorcycle parked on the street wouldn't raise an eyebrow from anyone, or gather notice from an overzealous private security force.

He left his helmet with the bike, running his hands through his hair to smooth it out, and tugged at his hip-length leather coat to make sure it was hanging properly.

He might not be as appearance-savvy as Ian, but he knew the importance of looking the part.

He walked back, observing the neighborhood from foot. A wide range of house styles, but they all had the same thing in common: distance from the street, and from each other. Privacy was important to these people... and that meant there wasn't going to be anyone to confirm or deny the owner's report other than his own staff, who couldn't be trusted.

He didn't fault Sharon or Nick for not second-guessing Wells. They were sharp, but they still had an innate hope that humans would do the right thing. Even Sharon, with her truth-sense, still had hope.

He wasn't going to beat that out of them. Life would do it soon enough. Life, and this job.

He had found the son a few weeks after his visit, living in a group house in New Orleans. He'd told the boy his mother was looking for him, asked for permission to give her his current address. The boy had resisted, at first, but the longing and loneliness had won out. The boy had been maybe fifteen; healthy and clean. Whatever else might have been going on in that house, he'd loved his mother a great deal, and she had loved him.

The boy had gone back home. According to the dossier Nick and Lou put together, the mother, Christine, died about a year later. A sudden, fast-moving cancer. There was no mention of what had happened to the boy. Probably he had hit the road again, this time for good. If his mother was using another man's name when she searched for him, odds were there wasn't much love between the father and anyone else in the house.

According to the report, Wells had taken residence in his summer home, up in the Catskills, while the repairs to the damaged rooms were being made. The housekeeper remained, to oversee things. He had never met the housekeeper on that first visit, if she was even the same woman, so he wasn't worried about any awkward questions. So far as they knew, he would merely be the supervising investigator, coming out to check on his employees' work.

Assuming the housekeeper saw him at all. He was going to try to avoid that.

There was a gate at the base of the driveway, but nothing surrounding the lawn itself save low shrubbery. He frowned, trying to remember if the gate had been there back then.

It hadn't.

So. Something new the grieving father had installed? Or an insurance requirement? Ben touched the metal briefly with one finger, letting himself reach for anything, electrical or magical, that might be waiting within.

Nothing. For all of Wells's talk of deterrence and alarms, the gates weren't electrified or current-reinforced. They were simply for show? Odd, but not impossible. People with money did strange things.

He walked past the metal gateposts, moving up the driveway toward the house, when he first heard the noise. A low rumbling, as though someone had started up a lawn mower somewhere, or revved an ancient engine, rough and ragged.

He was halfway up to the house when the sound came

again, this time more clearly. Not metallic but organic, wet and angry. And coming closer.

He barely had time to mutter "oh, fuck" before the hellhound was on him.

I'd started to work on restructuring the diorama one more time, after Sharon pointed out—logically, as Sharon was prone to—that we might need it if the guys didn't get a confession from the suspects. I thought she was way overestimating what the diorama might be capable of, but then, we didn't know until we tried, did we?

I knew why I'd resisted: given a choice, I'd rather have been doing almost anything else—setting the base in place again was screwing around with my nerves. The room was still overshielded, so even if the diorama-spell snapped, odds were that I'd be protected from the worst of the blast, but reworking a spell was a tricky thing. Reworking it in the exact same place, using the exact same patterns, meant I was building up even more energy than before, which meant that if anything went wrong, it could snap even harder.

I could smell my own sweat, and the underlay of the lemon-scented cleanser we used on the floor and furniture, and felt my legs cramp from tension, and the pushpins of a headache starting at the back of my skull. Pressure, inside and out.

I suddenly understood why witches and mages in the Old Time went crazy, trying to pull too much magic without understanding it was their own body they were using as the conductor, not knowing how important it was to modulate it, control it. We call that wizzing now, when your body just gets overwhelmed by the pure power you were using, and...

And it didn't do anyone any good to think about it. Control was how you kept control, and the moment you started to doubt, control cracked.

Like Venec, and the Merge. If I let down my guard...

And with that thought, my control totally went out the window, and the structure shattered into annoying sparks and sparkles.

"Damn it..." Even nowhere in sight, the man was a distraction.

"This isn't going to work," I said, trying to dislodge the sense of failure that was dogging me. "I'm overthinking, second-guessing what I saw. Anything I build now is going to be contaminated." Probably. It had been too long, anyway, and there was too much else in my head—not to mention too many people in the room. I worked better alone.

Giving up, I let the base disperse, taking back the current into my core, and turned to look more carefully at the other construct at the other end of the table. Sharon, ignoring my outburst, was still building her own diorama, holding it steady with control that was worth admiring. Nick was watching, adding in a comment or suggestion every now and again in a low voice. Theirs wasn't as detailed as mine; her gleaning skills and memory weren't as strong, yeah, but also a house was more detailed and complicated than the concrete pier, so there were, inevitably, blank spots.

"Nick tried to fill in the details with what he saw," Sharon said, looking up and seeing where my gaze had lingered. "But we couldn't get his gleaning and mine to merge."

The word sent a shiver down my back, but I didn't think any of the others noticed. Or if they did, they didn't say anything. Why would they? The word didn't mean anything to them other than the dictionary definition.

"We'll figure that out, eventually," Nick said with confidence. I wasn't so sure. As a group, we could do it, but not every Talent could work together one-on-one, even when they were friends or relatives. Current sometimes sparked like that. Yeah, we'd done well as a team before, when we tried to glean the emotional evidence from the murder scene in the Reybourne case, and again when we'd seen the confrontation with the ki-rin through Stosser's awareness, but those times had been under Venec's control, his lead. We gave up control to him. Sharing, one-to-one, the way that would be required to build something together, rather than follow in a predetermined route? That was a lot more delicate.

I studied the finished diorama, letting my eyes take in details without actively looking for anything, while my mind chased after that thought. Pietr and I could slip in and out of each other's current-bubble—we'd done it before, to show each other things through mage-sight. But I'd never had to do it with any of the others, didn't know if I would trust them that much, to let them slide into my core, without feeling the need to control the intrusion, trust them not to look, instinctively, where they hadn't been invited.

That might be the next exercise for Venec to run us through, when we had some downtime.

Oddly, that thought didn't give me any flutter of panic, and yet the idea that Venec might be able to do that, slip under my walls at will... Totally different thing.

"These were the only rooms that were disturbed, that we know about. The client didn't let us wander around, so although I think we saw everything, I can't swear to it." Sharon sounded annoyed about that. Considering that Pietr was able to disappear from most peoples' awareness, it would have been a simple matter for him to go anywhere he wanted, if he had been assigned the initial survey of the scene...except it was mainly a defensive reaction, brought about by stress or fear rather than direct control. I was sort of surprised that the Big Dogs hadn't been working with him on that; but then again, maybe they had, and nobody mentioned it to me. No reason they would, after all.

My ego took the hit with reasonable grace and a little relief—I didn't *have* to know everything, even if I sometimes wanted to—and I leaned in to look more closely at their diorama. It was the first time I'd seen Sharon's work, and while the detail wasn't as precise as mine, it was still solidly built. That was harder than it sounded—I was pretty sure neither Nick nor Nifty could have done it as well. Pietr, maybe.

"We think the perp or perps came in through here." Sharon held her finger over the far side of the diorama, indicating the back patio. "There was a set of French doors that led directly to the main room, where most of the damage was done. The doors were damaged from the inside, so we'd assumed it happened during the search, but the fact that we didn't see any damage to the locks on the external side doesn't mean it wasn't there."

Maybe not. We'd all learned how to recognize the signs of old-fashioned lock-picking, but it was still tough, especially when something with claws had been at it.

"Anyway, from there it was a straight shot down the hall to the office, where the objects were taken. For them to do that much damage in that period of time, they had to have grabbed those items pretty fast, probably before they started the wreckage."

"They knew what they were looking for," Nick said. "It wasn't random." The client was right about that, at least.

"Or they were just there to cause damage, and those two items caught their eye for no reason we can fathom," Sharon said, shooting him an ice-blue glare before I could tell him he was making a sloppy assumption. "Or, they couldn't find what they were looking for."

"I like my idea better. If they wanted those items we just have to figure out why and we'll know who. Your theory, we have no way of figuring out who did it."

Nicky-boy had a point.

"All right." Sharon relented, a little. "If they did come in looking for those two objects...why? What is it about them? We know they're not Artifacts—" Artifacts were known magic-shaped objects, with a history if not provenance. They were supposed to be registered, so everyone knew them and what they could do. It was a slow process, though, since most Artifacts were family heirlooms with a dark history, and not every Talent wanted to fess up—

or admit to having access to them, if they even knew what they were. "And the watch is, by the client's claim, just a watch. But could there be something more to the dagger than memories?"

"Guy who allegedly built it doesn't have the skill set to do anything more," Lou said, standing in the doorway. Damn, she was starting to move as quietly as Pietr!

"So he claims," I retorted, more annoyed at being startled than by the comment, and Sharon nodded, but looked hesitant.

"You're thinking something. What?" I tried to mimic the tone Stosser used when he was in high-glamour coaxing mode. It must have worked, because the words spilled out of her, like she wasn't stopping to consider them first; not normal for her.

"The client is moderate-Null. He can charge the dagger—" That was how memory-glass worked; it charged off its owner, the low-level hum of current all but the most Null of humans has naturally. "That would be why he kept it close at hand, to make sure it stayed charged. But wouldn't that make the watch stop?"

A windup pocket watch would survive being near current longer than a digital, but it, too, eventually, would be affected.

"Maybe he wound it every day," Lou said.

"Still." Sharon frowned. "Why keep them both together?"

"He didn't know any better? Whatever he knew about the *Cosa*, it was probably secondhand information, and most of it wrong," Nick said. "There wasn't a damn thing

else in that house that had even a come-hither of magic,
I'd swear to it."

"Not even his magical deterrent system?" I asked.

Nick and Sharon both snorted at that. "Worth about
as much as a wet paper towel," Nick said. "Seriously,
Sharon's right, if there was anything current-based in that
house, we should have felt it, even after it was gone, especially if it had been there for a long time. There wasn't
anything, not even the trace you'd feel if someone was
trying to cover it up. Not even the dagger. Like someone
high-res wiped the slate clear."

"So that means...what?"

"I don't know. Maybe nothing. But it bothers me, and
anything that bothers me—"

"Has to be investigated." We made it a three-way cho-
rus, hitting Venec's inflection perfectly.

"Well, even if you didn't get anything from the client,
Venec will," Lou said. I winced. It was true, yeah, but
showed a level of tactlessness that made even me flinch.
And I still wasn't happy he'd gone off alone, not that I'd
said anything when he signed out. I was neither stupid,
nor crazy.

Besides, odds were he'd picked up my mood, anyway,
even through tight walls.

"If he doesn't get himself kicked out, first," Sharon
said, echoing my own thoughts. "He's going to go in like
a bull in a china shop, probably, and piss the client off."

"Bulls aren't actually..." Nick started to say, then saw
the look on everyone's faces, and shut up.

"Let's do a two-pronged approach, then," Lou said,
coming into the room and sitting down. J would approve

of her posture: she sat with her butt all the way back in the chair, shoulders up, legs crossed neatly at the ankle. It made me want to instinctively sit up straight and put both feet flat on the floor.

I stayed exactly the way I was, one leg curled underneath me, my ankle-length skirt hiked up enough that it didn't catch under the chair's wheels.

"Two-pronged? Us and Venec?"

"Two possible causations," Lou said. "One way, this was random violence. Hooligans or someone looking for drug money, or just someone with an urge to screw with rich people for kicks, and sheer bad luck something magical got nicked, bringing us into the equation. Second, that they came in looking for something specific, either the objects taken or something else, and the damage was to cover it up, maybe distract from the owner realizing anything was missing."

"Except he'd know, immediately," Sharon said. "Believe me, this is not a guy who lost track of anything. If our perps knew that these objects were important, they'd know enough to know that, too."

"So…maybe the objects missing were taken because they knew the owner valued them personally, and that was the distraction, even more than the destruction?"

"But it—" I forgot what I was going to say, as my entire body convulsed, my throat closing up in terror, cutting off air to my lungs. My legs twitched wildly, then my entire body spasmed, knocking me off my chair. I could feel my body thrashing, but all I could focus on was the wave of panic, coming from the fact that I couldn't breathe, a metal band snapped around my chest, compressing at an alarming rate. My pack mates' voices were hollow-sounding, like I was at the bottom of a pool of water, listening to them. They were around me, surrounding me, and I had the hazy sensation that they were touching me, but everything hurt so much I overloaded, unable to distinguish what was real and what was in my brain. I wanted to scream, warn them off, but my throat was locked, my voice silenced, and my body out of control, struggling to breathe, to think clearly, to regain control over myself. I was *Talent,* damn it. I did not lose control.

For that brief flash, the pain cleared enough to hear the voice almost hidden under the pain, wrapped around the pain, driving it toward me, *into* me.

Pain. Teeth. Can't breathe....

And I knew it wasn't me, the pain wasn't mine, but Venec's, and the knowledge was like a solid blow to the gut, clearing my throat enough that I could draw a deep, harsh breath, bringing oxygen back into my lungs, and my brain.

"She's having a seizure!" Sharon's voice, cool and in control. "Lou, hold her head steady. Nick, get my medical kit, now!"

"Mmmmokay," I managed to get out, but since my body was still flailing, and my voice was slurred even to my ears, they ignored me. Sharon tried to stick her fingers in my mouth, I guess to make sure I didn't swallow my tongue, and I bit her.

"Ow!" She glared down at me, indignant through her worry.

"M'okay," I managed again. "It's not me. S'Venec."

She shook her head, not understanding. "Venec!" I managed again, and some control came back as though I was asserting ownership of my body, despite the waves of pain and fear that were still battering my core. Damn it, what was going on?

I ignored Sharon for a moment, now that she had her fingers out of my mouth, and dived down into my core.

Instead of my normally calm, settled mass of current, I landed in the middle of a molten disaster. Swells of electric-bright orange and neon-green made like a roiling vortex; jagged sparking waves and indigo thunder cracking overhead. It was mine, but it terrified me, and for an eternity of an instant I struggled to maintain control.

venec!

The call went unanswered, and the panic swamped me. Impossible. I hadn't realized how much I depended on that immediate response, hadn't understood how much— despite my resisting it—the Merge had, well, merged us. I knew, instinctively, that he should be here, within my core, if I only reached out....

I let down my walls, all my walls, shattering them into crackling dust.

benjamin!

....here...

Faint, weak, hurting, but clear. The relief I felt was run through with the pain he was in, the awareness that he needed help, and he needed it now.

Then, through his ears, I heard sirens, and the sound of human voices snapping orders, similar to the ones Sharon was calling over me, and the fear retreated enough for me to get control back.

hang on I sent him, hoping he was able to hear me, and came back up out of my core, stilling my limbs and regulating my breathing even as I did so, trying to ignore the pain that was still racking my brain and core, if not my actual body.

"Enough," I said. "It's not me." I hesitated, knowing the next words out of my mouth were going to open a major can of worms, and not really caring, at this point. "It's Venec. He's been hurt. He's being taken to Saint Joe's." The information came to me even as I said it, the connection still holding, even though the pain had tamped down to bearable levels. Oh, god, he was in so much pain, why couldn't they do something for his pain?

And then, blessedly, they did, and my body was mine again.

"How do you…" Sharon caught herself. "Never mind. Where's Stosser? Does he know?"

I shook my head. Great, I was going to have to explain this to the boss, too. "Don't know where he is." And then, suddenly, I did.

boss

The ping came back from Stosser, sharp and worried. We didn't ping him, usually, he called us, or had Venec do it.

ben. hospital Less words or emotions than impressions, filtered through me, straight from Ben. I had no idea how we were doing it—I didn't think Ben knew, either. It was enough that we could do it.

The connection cut off, but not before I got a sense of understanding, of being en route already, and…

Gratitude.

Someone cut all the strings holding me together, and I collapsed backward, into Nick's arms, this time with relief. It was being taken care of. Ben was hurt, but he would be okay. Stosser was on the case.

I shuddered, then looked up at the others, steadfastly ignoring the need to go follow, to be there when they brought Ben in. Those weren't our marching orders; we would only be in the way. Colder still: if I was going to refuse the Merge, I had no right to be there. "Boss's on it. We're supposed to get back to work."

"But..." Lou looked like she wanted to argue, probably try to send me to bed with a book and a bowl of her *sopa verde,* which sounded oh my god so tempting, but wasn't possible. Not right now.

"I'm fine." I wasn't, and they all knew that, but they allowed me the fiction, even as I was forcing myself to sit up, unaided. "I'm all right. It was..."

"It was that thing. Between you and Venec."

"What?"

I stared at Nick, blinking stupidly.

"Come on, Bonnie, we're not dumb. That little display a couple of days ago was the most overt, but you two spark at each other every time you're in the same room, and it's not just sexual shit, because I've seen you when you're interested in someone and that's not it. And you're off your game, have been for months."

Ow.

"So what's going on?"

They were all staring at me, expecting an answer. Oh, crap.

I stopped trying to get up off the floor, and just sat up

more comfortably, checking each inch of the way that I wasn't wobbling. I'd underestimated them. How, after more than a year, had I managed to do that?

"We're not sure what's going on." Slight prevarication there: we were sure; we just didn't know what it meant, or how much longer we could keep it at bay. Venec thought forever… I hadn't been so sure, and I was even less sure now. Based on what just happened, it was probably already too late to try. "It's called The Merge. It's…complicated." Probably impossible to explain to anyone who wasn't a pup, who hadn't already gone through the training to work together, that we had.

"Oh, hell. Our current matches. Like puzzle pieces. And the more we're in proximity, the more it wants to, well, merge."

That was the bare bones working version, anyway.

"So you were able to hear him, when we couldn't." Sharon sounded, inevitably, annoyed. She hated being left out of anything, or one-upped on current-skills. I was too tired to try and correct her.

"No." Interestingly, it was Lou who got it, first. "It means he couldn't stop himself from reaching her. And she couldn't shut him out. Like overrush, but coming from someone else."

I wasn't wobbling anymore, but every inch of my body hurt, inside and out. "Yeah. Like that."

When Nicky looked like he wanted to ask more questions, I glared him off, which wasn't easy, sitting on the floor like I was. Time enough to avoid questions about what it all actually meant, later. Much, much later.

nine

"No…"

"Sir, relax. Everything will be fine."

"No…" They were rattling him down out of the ambulance, two young men and an older woman, their faces intent but calm. Normally Venec would have found their competence reassuring. He was fond of competence. But he could feel the thumping of his heart and the hissing of his core, and the taste of the current simmering in the place they were rolling him toward was too dangerous to let him anywhere near it.

"No!" He managed to make his hand reach up and grab the woman's wrist. "No!"

"Sir, we have to…" She tried to, gently, pry his hand off her, but desperation gave him additional strength.

"You can't. Not in there."

They didn't understand, wouldn't listen, trying to place a clear plastic oxygen mask over his face. He could feel the tendrils of his core reaching out, his control almost gone, the blood loss and drain from fighting off the hellhound making him desperately crave the recharge that current offered....

"You can't take me in there!" he told them, his voice muffled, already resigned to what would happen.

"What's going on?" Another man in white, no, he was wearing pale blue scrubs. A doctor? Ben tried to focus on the man's face, willing him to understand.

"Dog savaging victim," one of the paramedics reported. "He's hallucinating, possibly. Disorderly."

The hand holding the oxygen mask hesitated, torn between training and the doctor's interference, and Ben used the distraction to make one more plea. "Don't let me in there. Too dangerous." Talent in emergency rooms were bad in the best of times, their pain and panic causing things to go haywire. As shocky and drained as he was... If his core went down too far, he would pull from the nearest source to protect himself. It would be instinctive, unstoppable except by his death, and without meaning to he could pull so much off that their entire system could fail. People could die.

"Hold up," the doctor said, putting a hand down on the gurney to stop their progress. "Sir?"

Ben tried to focus, again, on his face.

"Sir, are you Talent?"

He almost cried in relief, managing to give a quick, sharp nod of agreement.

The doctor turned to the paramedic trying to affix the oxygen mask and snapped off an order. "Bring him into the overflow room."

"But—"

The other male EMT, either quicker on the uptake or

more experienced in the whims of doctors, slapped his companion on the arm, hard, and nodded in agreement to the doctor. Ben felt the gurney shift slightly, rolling in a different direction, the pace picking up as they went down another hallway, not into the main emergency room but a smaller, quieter space. The same off-white walls, the same smell of disinfectant and urine and sweat filling the air, the same undertone of concerned voices speaking too softly, and then a cry or a shout breaking the tension and causing a flurry of activity....

But the seductive, dangerous hum of high-powered machinery was less, as though the room was wrapped in a protective bubble.

You didn't take a panicked, injured Talent into an emergency room filled with expensive, high-maintenance, highly calibrated electrical life-giving equipment. Not without precautions. Not when other people's lives depended on those machines.

The doctor leaned in closer, his voice now pitched only for Venec to hear. "Do you need a sedative?" In other words, was he still a danger to anyone in the hospital?

Ben managed to shake his head. The urge, the panic, was fading, removed from the direct lure. Whatever they'd done to block out the current in this space, it was effective.

He might not need the sedative, but he wanted it, badly. The lacerations in his throat and arms were agony, and although the drip in his arm was dulling the pain, it didn't do anything for the memory of the beast coming for him, the hot stench of its breath on his face, the acrid burn of its drool....

It hadn't been a full-on purebred hellhound. If it had been, he would be dead. A crossbreed, or maybe even a quarter-breed, something with mastiff or—

His mind went over the details, trying to determine what the beast was, so that he could find out where the client had gotten hold of one—and why—and then go find the breeder and issue a smack-down for letting a Null have a goddamned hellhound, even one that watered down. It was pointless obsessive work, but it kept his mind occupied and away from what they were doing around him, shifting him onto another surface, drawing white curtains around him, switching out the drip in his arm for another and the doctor was there again, his face covered but his eyes dark gray and focused the way a real professional got when they were in the groove, and Ben was able to let go of the last bit of conscious thought and let them do what needed to be done.

When he had first approached Benjamin with the idea—then only a glimmer born out of frustration and anger—for PUPI, Ian Stosser had thought about things like justice, and conscience, and how to win people over to his cause.

Ben Venec had thought about things like training, licensing, and hospital authorizations. Making his signature on the seventh page of tagged forms, Ian was thankful, once again, that his partner had a grasp on the practicalities he sometimes forgot. Trying to reach Ben's family in time...wouldn't have happened.

"Fortunately, he hadn't lost much blood, and there doesn't seem to have been any infection in the wounds.

From the size of the bite marks, I'd say it was a mastiff or some other large breed. We gave him a rabies shot as a precaution, but..."

The doctor's voice trailed off, and he looked at Stosser with a steady gaze. He was young, maybe barely out of residency, but Ian had a suspicion that he'd ended up in the E.R. not by chance but choice. Ex-military, maybe. Calm in crisis and able to think no matter what the shift threw at him. Not a Talent, but he knew what he was about—and had recognized what Ben was. Ian owed him.

"Hellhound."

The doctor's eyes went a little wider, but he only nodded. "So rabies probably not an issue, but better safe than really sorry. It will be taken care of?"

"It has already been dealt with."

You didn't send cops or ASPCA workers in after a hellhound, not even a half-breed. The moment Bonnie had shown him what had happened, Ian had put the call in to the local Council, who had sent a team in to take down the animal. They had found it, bleeding, in a corner of the client's property, and taken it in.

Ian regretted the inevitable ending to this story. It wasn't the hound's fault; crossbred and properly trained by someone who knew what they were doing, a hellhound was an amazing creature. Smart, loyal, fierce... and deadly without the proper ownership and continued handling. The client was damned lucky the animal hadn't turned on him, or one of his staff—if Ben hadn't shown up, and been strong enough to beat it back with current, someone would have died, eventually.

Ian was willing to bet that the client had been told the beast would be a good guard dog, prevent anyone who had come the first time from returning. Same idiot who had sold him the "magic-proofing" alarm system in the first place, probably. If the Council didn't take care of that, too, Ian and Ben would pay the fellow a visit when this was all over, and explain to him that fleecing Nulls was one thing, but endangering them—and anyone else in the damned vicinity—was another entirely.

"Boss."

He wasn't at all surprised to hear Torres's voice behind him. In fact, now that he thought about it, he was surprised she hadn't been at the hospital when he arrived. Whatever was going on between the two of them, it clearly did not allow for indifference.

And that was another thing he was going to look into, now. Ben owed his life to her reaction—but it was clearly something that involved the agency, not just their personal lives. And that meant he, Ian, had to know what the hell was going on.

"Torres. Where's the rest of the pack?"

"Working." She looked past his shoulder once, briefly, then her gaze came back to him. "I drew the short stick, to brief you."

He didn't believe that for a minute. From the look on her face, she didn't expect him to, either. He let it pass. Now was not the time.

"You know why Ben was there," she asked, "the connection between him and the client?"

He did not. "Tell me."

★ ★ ★

I updated Stosser on everything that had happened, standing there in the hallway, hospital staff and patients going past us as though we were nothing more than furniture. Part of my brain wondered at that: normally Stosser commands at least a first look from everyone in the vicinity, his natural charisma is just that damn impressive. But today, he had the mute button taped down, or something.

"There was no reason for the client to connect the P.I. his wife hired, with us," Stosser said, when I was finished. "Ben was acting in a purely Null capacity, then. I don't see why he thought there might be anything suspicious about the connection now."

"Venec thinks there's something suspicious about everything."

That almost got a laugh out of the boss, mainly because it was true. Venec wasn't cynical, or jaded, just really wary.

"I think..." I hesitated, not because I wasn't certain, but because I wasn't sure how to tell a Big Dog what I thought without him asking why I thought that.

"You think, or Ben thinks? And does he know that you know what he thinks?"

Ow. I guess the boss could do direct as well as he did politically indirect, yeah.

"It's called the Merge," I said, just as blunt. "You ever hear of it?"

Stosser blinked, as surprised by my counter serve as I was, and then shook his head no.

"Me, neither. It's rare, and stupid, and it boils down

to we're stuck with each other. Current-wise, I mean."
I should have given him more detail than I'd given the
rest of the team, probably, but I wasn't in the mood for
details, and if he was so damn brilliant, he could figure
it out.

"Your current...merges." He wasn't asking for confirmation; I'd been right, and his scary-brilliant brain had
already leapfrogged over the basics and was going into
the possibilities. And, knowing the boss, his possibilities
had nothing to do with the personal lives or preferences
of either of us, but what it would mean for PUPI.

Considering the sideways looks and uncomfortable
body language I'd left behind in the office, I actually
preferred Stosser's reaction.

"Can you hear him now?" he asked.

"No. They have him drugged too deeply." I could
feel him, this close, and with his walls down under the
drugs' influence; restless fingers fluttering at the edge
of my awareness. If I dipped in, I knew I'd be inside his
morphine-dreams. So I stayed out.

"All right. There's nothing we can do here—they'll
keep him drugged for a few more hours, and he won't
welcome either of us hovering. Come on."

"Where?" But I knew, even as I followed him. The
client had put Ian Stosser's best friend and partner in the
hospital. The boss was going to take a direct hand in the
investigation, now.

Part of me wanted to stay in the hospital, lurking in the
god-awful waiting room, to be there when Venec woke
up, and to hell with what he would or wouldn't welcome.
But I went with Stosser. Boss was brilliant, and way more

high-res than the rest of the office put together...but he had no damned idea what to do on a crime scene, and would probably do more harm than good, if unsupervised.

Besides. I'd know the instant Ben woke up.

We exited the hospital through the main door, and I blinked in the sunlight, relaxing a little now that we were out of direct surround of all that technology.

I figured that we would take a cab back to the site, because there was no way Ian Stosser used mass transit, but I hadn't taken into account the fact that the high-res do things different than us peons. The only warning I got was his hand coming down on my shoulder, and the quick tingle of current, and we'd Translocated.

Most people knew better than to Transloc blind, out of line-of-sight, without prepping the destination, if it wasn't an emergency. Ian Stosser was not most people. I guess he was arrogant enough to assume everyone would get the hell out of his way, somehow.

Apparently he was right, because we hit the street without so much as a bump or stare, mainly because, unlike the crowded avenue outside the hospital, there was nobody on this residential street to bump or stare.

The house looked pretty much exactly the way Sharon had re-created it in the diorama, at least from the street. Ian landed us just inside the shrubbery surround, on the well-trimmed, if muddy lawn. I took two steps toward the house, and almost fell to my knees.

The grass wasn't muddy. It was bloody. Ben's blood. I knew it without even looking, the way the images flooded my brain like my own memories. A wave of woozy nausea hit me, like it was my own blood there, flushed from tears in my own flesh. Oh, god. I'd almost lost him. Oh, god.

"Keep moving."

It was an order, not a suggestion, and my feet kept moving, carrying me forward onto dryer ground. The memory remained, but its hold on me faded enough that I no longer felt it in my own flesh.

I didn't think Stosser noticed anything except his own thoughts. I was wrong. "This Merge-thing. It can be a problem, too."

"Yeah." Boss had that right, and then some.

We were met at the door by the housekeeper. She seemed a little less together than Sharon and Nick had described; I guess a break-in, however damaging, was easier to deal with than a guy almost dying on your front lawn.

"Mr. Wells is not home...."

"We're not here to see him," Stosser said, walking past her as though she'd invited us in. "I want to see the room where the missing objects were kept."

She looked at me, and I gave her my best "I'm just the flunky" look. "Best to give the man what he's asking for," I suggested. "He's kind of cranky about one of his people almost being puppy chow." The flippancy cost me, but it worked. Her lips tightened, but she led us to the office.

We passed by the library, which according to Sharon and Nick was the room that had gotten the most damage, first. Peeking in, I saw that it was covered with sheets, the kind you use when you put a house up for the season, not the kind workers use, so I figured they hadn't gotten the insurance evaluation yet. No matter how rich you were, insurance companies made you wait, I guessed.

The office where m'lady chatelaine brought us was uncovered; most of the damaged furniture had obviously been cleared away, but the space otherwise untouched. If Wells was anything like J in his desk management, the staff was afraid to do anything in here without his express orders.

"The missing objects were kept here."

She stood in the doorway and didn't offer any more information. I wasn't sure if she was being recalcitrant, or she just honestly didn't know anything more. In my experience among J's friends and colleagues, housekeepers knew everydamnthing, especially the stuff they weren't supposed to know, so I was betting on recalcitrant. She was possessive of her boss's privacy, and felt that we were just as bad as the goons who'd broken in originally; maybe even worse, because we hadn't already made the problem go away.

Stosser stepped into the room, and I could swear, even from behind him, I could see his nose twitch.

While he was doing whatever the hell he was doing, I surveyed the room from the doorway, ignoring the housekeeper, who sniffed and retreated, apparently not worried that we would sticky-finger anything left behind.

Deciding I wasn't going to discover anything standing there, I leaned against the doorway, crossed my arms over my chest, and watched the boss do his thing.

"Are you looking for something in particular, or just sniffing in general?" I wasn't being snarky; the only way to learn, Venec constantly reminded us, was to ask when we didn't know something. And I had no damn idea what he was doing, or why we were here.

Well, no, I knew why we were here. We were here because Ben was in the hospital, and Ian Stosser was angry, and worried, and needed to do something, even if there wasn't anything to do. Also, it kept my thoughts off Venec, away from the bite marks I could still feel ghosting on my skin. The hellhound had, obviously, been dealt with, and it wasn't illegal as such to own or hire one, so we couldn't do anything about the owner in that regard…especially since Venec had, in some respects, been trespassing….

My brain was starting to ache, so I shut down that line of thought and waited for Ian to answer me.

"There was something about those objects."

"Yeah," I said, because he seemed to be waiting for a response, even without looking at me. His hair was pulled back and tied at the base of his neck, but even as I watched, the strands quivered, as though touched by a wind nobody else could feel. Current-use rising from his core, so subtle and powerful you couldn't sense it any other way.

Sometimes, the boss scared the hell out of me.

"And what is that something?" I asked, when he didn't offer anything more.

"If we knew, we'd know why someone would take it, and then we'd know who."

"Well, yes." I didn't even think the "duh" because he'd probably pick it up and neither of us needed that right now.

He was waiting for something else from me. It was

like being in fifth grade and having a surprise pop quiz
first thing in the morning, while you were still trying to
wake up and remember what subject you were in.

"And…?" I gave up, baring my throat, figuratively, in
submission.

Stosser sighed. "And that is exactly what the client
doesn't want us to know."

I blinked. "How the hell…" I started to ask, but Stosser
was already moving on farther into the room, inspect-
ing the floorboards with the air of someone who has
answered all the questions he intends to acknowledge.

Working with a genius? Not all that it's cracked up to
be.

I stood and watched him work—or whatever it was
he was doing, and then retraced my steps, back to the
main room, where Nick and Sharon thought the perps
had come in. There were the French doors that had been
boarded up with plywood. It was a decent job, and I left
it in place—I had no desire to bring the wrath of the
housekeeper down on me. They'd already checked for
magic-trace on all the entrances, I knew that from the
report, and ditto the physical lock on the other side, but
it was possible—not probable, but possible—that they'd
missed something.

Stepping back until I was in the middle of the room,
more or less, I slipped into fugue-state with an ease that
I wouldn't have thought possible even six months ago,
when I'd still needed to do the counting-backward thing.
I didn't call up a spell, or even consciously touch my
current the way I normally do, just opened my eyes and
looked at the room.

Mage-sight is sort of like viewing things, not under-water, exactly, but close enough. You can "see" normally but it's wavery and blurred, and there's current flickering everywhere, dipping and flaring with its own natural energy, influenced by and influencing everything around it. Cantrips or spells can focus it, but then you risk missing something that your cantrip didn't take into account.

Sharon and Nick were right: the only major source of current in the room right then was me, and I knew how to identify and tune out my own signature. That left the normal dark-hued streaks in the walls and floors—current ran alongside electricity, which meant that every house had at least some, hanging with the everyday wiring that Nulls took for granted. Normally it was baby-level, tiny threads that wouldn't give you much of a jolt at all. But the threads seemed thicker here, somehow. How had they missed that? Was the room specially wired, maybe the "anti-magic" system the client had been sold? Or…

I moved closer to the wall without thinking, lifting my hand to summon the current to me. If it had been installed by a Talent, their signature might still be linger-ing….

What I got was the magic equivalent of a spluttering raspberry, and the sense of something skittering away. The shock was enough to kick me out of fugue-state, embarrassingly enough.

"What the hell?"

Like that, Stosser was in the room with me. I didn't know how the hell he moved that fast—there had been no inrush to indicate he'd Transloc'd; he must already have been heading down the hallway when he heard me.

"What?"

I was staring at the wall, my shock fading into annoyance at having been caught off guard. "There was something...in the current."

Rather than looking worried, the boss actually laughed, although his eyes were still shadowed, and his body language more tense than amused. "Tiny, scurrying, giving an impression of a lot of eyes and not much sense?"

That was it, exactly. "What...?"

"Elementals."

"Oh." I felt stupid. Of course. Elementals were...well, creatures, I guess, that lived within the current-stream. They weren't really alive, as such, or maybe they were, in some way nobody could quite explain, but they had a certain crude awareness. Usually, unless they were grouped together, you wouldn't even notice them. What I had sensed was definitely a flock. Like pigeons, fluttering and scattering.

"I wonder if that's what they were using as the alarm system," Stosser said. "If so, it was a failure, of course. Anyone with a lick of current could calm them down, even assuming you could train them to react and sound an alarm."

"You really think elementals could remember anything that long?"

One narrow red eyebrow rose over a mocking gaze as he turned to look at me. "It doesn't have to work," he said. "Whoever's selling the alleged security system only has to talk it up as though it does. Not like a Null would know any better."

Boss was feeling better, if he was being snarky. Didn't mean he was wrong, though.

"Pity we can't glean their memories," I said. I parsed that thought, then shook my head. Too scattered, anything I picked up would be fragmented at best. Stosser might be high-res enough to hold them still long enough to get something significant, but he didn't have a clue how to glean. He was management, not tech. I supposed we could teach him....

Still in mage-sight, I watched him prowl around the room, lifting sheets and poking under furniture without a clue where he was stepping or how many delicate tangles of remnant signature he might have been wrecking with the unmoderated swirl of his own core, and shuddered. No. Even now, with the scene already processed, without any trace to pick up, he was doing damage. The thought of him actually trying to work a hot scene...

I squinted, my thoughts interrupted by the glint or glimmer of something. "Boss? Freeze."

Stosser hesitated, his hand halfway to the cloth covering a sofa, and started to turn back toward me.

"Freeze!" I said, far more sharply. "Tamp down your core."

It was newbie instruction, the kind of thing you'd tell a first-year mentoree, and I could see the expressions on his face range from shock to frustration to acceptance. Even as he gained control over his core, the continual sparks and static we had gotten used to around him smoothing into a quieter pool of energy.

"What?"

I ignored him, now that he was no longer interfering with my ability to follow the spike of current.

Tracking trace was a delicate thing. You have to look and not-look at the same time, as though you were trying to spot the picture-within-a-picture, but do it with your mage-sight, which meant that you were open to every other spike of current within range, even the stuff you couldn't see directly. Like patting your head and rubbing your stomach, while roller-skating. Backward.

"There's something in the room. Something we missed." "We" meaning Sharon and Nick, anyway. "Hang on, I'm trying to get a read on it...there." I moved past him, going to the far wall, where the French doors had been boarded up.

"Signature?"

"No. Wait. I don't know." It was current, yes; shaped, which meant that someone had been carrying it around for a while, the way you did when you took it into your core, but it didn't feel like a signature. This was...smudgy, for lack of a better term. Current was hot neon, sharp and sparkly, not smudged. It reminded me, a little, of the dark current we'd found by the memorial sites during the ki-rin case; current that had been touched by the darkest kind of hatred, that verged on madness, but even that darkness had been sharp and neon-bright. This was smooth and...not so much dark as totally without light.

"I don't know what this is," I said, almost to myself. Almost, but not quite. Without thinking, without planning, I reached out with a tendril of current, not toward the smudge, but away, toward my sense of Venec...

And found myself met by a different kind of smudginess: he was unconscious, still drugged into a motionless sleep by the painkillers.

"Damn."

"Torres?"

Stosser was standing where I'd left him, his core still quiet, but his expression did not bode well for that lasting much longer. Big Dog was not the patient sort, unless he was the one with the plan.

"I need to try to glean this," I told him. "And then I'm going to need you to get me back to the office without disturbing it. Okay?"

We'd been practicing flinging—the skill of throwing magical evidence from one person to another—but it wasn't easy or precise, and with this, something I didn't know, didn't understand…better to keep it under wraps, if I could. Who the hell knew what flinging it could wake up.

The fact that I was thinking about current-trace like a live thing was disturbing. I blamed it on being surprised by the elementals a few minutes ago. That didn't change my feeling that I was taking a risk in gleaning this to begin with. No need to mention that, though. Stosser cared about results, not risks, and Venec…

Ben was out of commission. He could yell at me later.

"Ready when you give the word, boss," Stosser said, and for once there was neither arrogance nor irony in his voice. Unfortunately, I was too focused on what I was about to do to really enjoy the moment.

Normally, gleaning a scrap of current is the magical equivalent of removing a splinter from your own thumb—you need to be careful, but it's not particularly difficult. This was like trying to do that in the dark, with a splinter that had a tendency to shimmer and wiggle out of your grip the moment you thought you had it. Like a splinter made of Jell-O.

"Relax." Stosser's voice, but there was an echo of Venec in it, too. "Whatever you're trying to do, you're focusing too hard. Let go of your control a little."

"What?" That made no sense. Control was what let us—

"Trust me. Let go a little, relax, and try again."

Ian Stosser didn't know crap about fieldwork, or the details of forensic magic, but he knew more about the elevated theoretical applications of current than I'd ever understand even if I lived to a hundred. I took a shallow breath and, on the exhale, let my control ease just a fraction.

The fragment of current slowed, as though it were trapped in molasses. I unrolled several strands of my own current, stretching them wide and ruffling them so that they were static-sticky, then rolled the fragment up inside them, containing it best I could.

"Now," I told Stosser, keeping my entire awareness on that fragment, maintaining the isolation between it and me so intently, I was barely aware when Stosser's current rolled over me the same way I'd rolled the fragment, and took us home.

Our arrival made a bit of a flutter in the office, and the rest of the team trailed after us, not asking questions— quelled by Stosser's glare, or my own tense aura, I don't know—but lining up against the wall quietly, watching while I did the hard work.

Scraping the trace out of my holding-space was easier than lifting it, interestingly. It was almost as though it didn't want to stay within the container-of-me. I would have been insulted, if I hadn't been so relieved.

"Y'know, I've scraped up a lot of trace in the past year," I said. "I've poked into a lot of weird places, and talked to a lot of crazy people."

There was a muffled almost-laugh from the wallhangers. Nick, I thought.

"And?" Stosser was standing behind me, lurking like a bored teacher making sure nobody used the wrong pencil, only a lot more intent.

"And that's weird shit."

Stosser had guided me into the smallest conference room, which also happened to be the one without windows, and the one with the best warding on it. Normally we used wardings to make sure that gleanings and signatures remained uncontaminated, like putting something between glass slides. Here, with this? I was thinking that the warding was to keep the trace from getting *out*. I finished what I was doing, and stepped back, shaking my arms out, trying to release the tension that had crept in.

"Although I would normally resist that sort of vague description," Stosser said, stepping forward to put his seal on the current-jar, overlaying my own closure in a notable mark of paranoia, "in this instance, I think it's appropriate."

The seal on the current-jar shimmered, then went dormant, but I could still feel it, holding steady. I could also feel the scrapings contained inside, dark and still but not inert, not by a long shot. Stosser looked at it, then shook his head. "I don't think we should linger here. Everyone, out."

I was all too glad to leave the room, and Lou and Nifty were moving even faster than me, but I noted that Sharon and Nick were both more reluctant. Figured. Sharon was more stubborn than the rest of us put together, and Nick had absolutely no sense of self-preservation whatsoever. Nicky was a current-hacker, one of the rarest of all skill sets, and I was beginning to think they were rare not because the skill was unusual, but because they got themselves overrushed or crispy-killed at a faster-than-normal rate.

Instead of going into the larger room next door, Stosser herded us down to the break room, as far away as you could get without actually leaving the office. Nobody questioned it, if they even realized what he was doing. We settled in as though it was totally normal for Stosser to hold a meeting here, Nifty taking his usual armchair, me and Nick and Sharon on one sofa, Lou and Pietr pulling up the ottoman and perching on that, and Stosser pacing between. The absence of Venec was like a real, palpable hole in the room. For me, anyway. I didn't know if anyone else felt it. Nobody had mentioned him; either they'd gotten an update already, or they were afraid to ask.

I checked, unable to stop myself. Still in morphine-land.

We all watched Stosser pace back and forth a few times, then I rested my head against the back of the sofa, and closed my eyes. Now that I'd actually stopped, or at least paused, I was so very, very tired. And my feet hurt. But I was too tired to bend down and take off my boots.

"Hey, Nick," I said.

"No."

"C'mon, Nick…"

"Why don't you wear something you can just slip off, like normal people?"

Because J never let me wear sneakers except when I was going to the gym, and I wasn't a dress-pump kind of girl, normally. But it was too much effort to say all that, so I just whined a little.

Nick ignored me.

"So, whatever Bonnie found and brought back. What is it?" A year ago, Sharon would have been all bristling and annoyed that I'd found something she'd missed. Now, she just sounded curious.

I could hear Stosser pause in his pacing, off to my left. "Easier to say what it isn't."

"Okay." Lou took the straight role willingly. "What isn't it?"

"It's not human," Sharon said flatly. "We're all agreed on that?"

Quick nods around the room. Everyone had gotten a chance to feel what I'd been unloading. We all were agreed.

"Fatae, then. We suspected that already, from the amount of damage that was done, and the claw marks. This had to come from that, right?" Sharon continued.

There was a silence, the kind that comes when everyone's waiting for someone else to say something first, and nobody does.

"Right?" Nick said, hesitantly.

"It has to be," Nifty agreed.

"There are a lot of different fatae breeds that have claws

that could manage the damage done," Lou said. "I've barely been able to start a file on the known ones, here in the city. There are a whole bunch who are singular, or isolated, but it has to be a fatae."

"It has to be fatae," I agreed, sealing it superstitiously with my thirding, or fourthing, or whatever we were up to. It had to be. Because if it wasn't...

Then it was something else.

There was a little quiet, after all that, and then the arguing began. We were all determined that it wasn't human, and therefore it had to be fatae, but nobody could come up with a suggestion as to what breed, even with Lou's beautifully indexed database, and Stosser's additional knowledge.

"What about a..." Nifty squinted at the name on the page, then shifted the paper so we could all see. "One of those? Serious claws."

"They're arctic-based?"

"Oh." Nifty scowled and turned the page.

"You think it could have been a demon?" I'd only ever seen one, that I knew about—the courier known as PB—but its claws had been scary-looking, even if the demon itself was too short to do this kind of damage. They came in all sizes, though....

"I would have known if it were demon," Stosser said, and that was that.

The discussion went on. And on. And if we were working so hard to keep from worrying about Venec, then nobody said anything.

Or maybe it was just me.

Thanks to Stosser leading us, and not Venec, we

worked right through dinner, and probably would have gone all night if Stosser hadn't gotten pinged by someone, and told us all to take a break until morning.

"And Ben's still out cold," he added, carefully not looking at me, "so stop worrying."

What, us, worry? But, yeah, there was no point checking in; they'd let us know if anything changed, even if I somehow missed it.

At that point, I was running on fumes and muscle memory. By the time I got home it was nearly 10:00 p.m. and I was wiped out, physically, emotionally, and magically. Even the thought of climbing the stairs to my apartment was enough to make me cry, but there was no way in hell I had the energy to Translocate. If I'd been halfway thinking, I would have had someone Transloc me from the office to my bed. God, the commute would be so much easier if we could do that. Why didn't we do that?

Proof that I was exhausted: I knew damn well why we didn't. And it had nothing to do with wasted current or overextending ourselves, of becoming too dependent on magic, or any of the other reasons our mentors hammered into us from the time of our first lesson. It wasn't even because Translocation was damned difficult to do properly. It was because, of all the things that Talent could do, all the things that set us apart, Translocation was one of the few that Nulls couldn't dismiss as a trick of their eye, or a misunderstanding, or some other rational non-magical explanation. And it hadn't been that long ago, by anyone's measure, that the cry of "witch" was more than a Halloween greeting.

Talent wasn't a genetic thing, exactly, but it did gallop in some families, and there wasn't an American Talent who hadn't gotten stories of the Burning Times hammered into their head about the same time they started to get stupid with what they'd learned. Salem was the most publicized, but it wasn't close to the worst.

I sighed, and resigned myself to having to sludge up the stairs like a regular Jane, when there was a commotion, and I looked up to see lights flickering brightly from...

Hey. My apartment. What the hell?

I had the front door opened, the inner security door opened, and was up the stairs to my landing before I was aware I'd taken my keys out of my coat pocket. It might even have been faster than Translocating.

However fast I was, though, the super was faster. He was standing outside my door, glaring at me like it was all my fault. Clearly he had been waiting for me.

"What the hell's been going on?" he greeted me. "All day, all night, noises and thumps, and now you're leaving untended flames when you're out? And locking the door so I can't get in? I was about to call the fire department, have them bust down the door."

I stared at him, totally lost. "I haven't been home all day," I said. "I've been at work."

"This has been going on too long," he said. "I'm tired of hearing the complaints about your parties which were bad enough, but this..."

I moved past him, putting my keys into the lock, intent on proving him wrong, that I hadn't left any flames burning, tended or otherwise. At the same time, the memory of the flickering lights in my window taunted me. What the hell?

I opened the door—and it opened easily, with the standard key he had, too—into a reassuring darkness. Reaching out to flip the light switch, so I could see the super's face when I told him off, was a mistake, though. The entire apartment was a disaster, furniture shoved utterly out of place, the mattress down on the floor, the sheets piled up in the center of the room like a giant nest.

And my mosaic, my beautiful, delicate, shimmering rainbow glass mosaic, was in a hundred thousand pieces on the floor.

It was too much, on top of the worry about Venec, and the sheer exhaustion of everything else. I almost cried.

"Enough," the super said, not seeming to care that whatever flames we'd both seen were not only gone, but were never there. "You seemed like a nice kid, but this is enough. There are too many complaints already, this is just the last straw. Building management's got cause to cancel your lease, for this."

I heard him, but it barely registered, staring at the disaster of my once-beautiful apartment. The utter chaos…

Chaos. Causing trouble.

My eyes narrowed, even as my brain started to work again. The Roblin. It had to be. Damn it, what did I ever do to that damned imp?

ten

I suppose I should have, as per orders, reported in immediately. The thought, though, of facing everyone, of dealing with more questions and what-ifs…it was too much. It was all just too much and I needed the quiet to just not-think, for once.

Also, if The Roblin was following me, targeting me, I wanted to be somewhere well-warded to even discuss it.

So instead I spent the rest of the night cleaning up the shards of the mosaic, and putting things back to order, best I could. Current was surprisingly crap at moving physical objects—you needed more energy than it took to move it physically—and I didn't want to risk even more pissed-off complaints from my neighbors, so mostly I left the heavy stuff where it was for now, and focused on getting my mattress and sheets back up onto the loft platform where they were supposed to be. I'd hoped that the activity would wear me out enough so that I'd be able to fall asleep and not think or dream about either Venec or the weird trace we'd found or The Roblin, sniffing at my heels.

No such luck. The adrenaline rush finally wore off, but my brain was way too revved up to shut down enough to sleep. Unfortunately, it was also too exhausted to do any real thinking. So I ended up sitting on the off-skew sofa, wrapped in a blanket and clutching a mug of cocoa heavily dosed with peppermint schnapps, trying very very hard not to reach out to the sense of Benjamin Venec, in a hospital bed several miles to the north. My trying not to do something, though, apparently had the exact opposite effect, because there was a sliver into my awareness, as though responding to a ping I hadn't sent.

sleep?

yes, baby I responded without thinking. *sleep*

Benjamin Venec, drugged to the gills, had a soft, almost little boy feel to his thoughts, and I wasn't strong enough to resist the urge to brush against it, the emotional equivalent to patting someone's hair until they settled down again. I needed the comfort, and he wasn't going to remember anything, come morning and sobriety.

I hoped.

something wrong

Damn. He was more alert than I thought. There was an instant when I was going to lie to him, and the instant passed. Drugged or not, this was Venec, and this was me. We'd never lied to each other, not before, not in all the crap that we'd already been through, and sure as hell not now.

*case stuff * True enough, if I counted The Roblin as

a case. *worried about you* Also true. It wasn't words I sent him, any more than he was forming them in his drug-sleepy mind. It was…like water flowing from one container to another, if one was colored blue and the other gold. If that made any sense, which it did to me.

i'll sleep if you will

And because I never lied to him, the moment I got his water-flow assent, I put the mug down on the table, snuggled myself into the blanket, and went to sleep.

If I dreamed anything, I didn't remember it in the morning.

The next morning guilt and responsibility trumped my disinclination to have anyone poking at my personal life, and I geared myself to tell all. Well, mostly all.

For once, though, Nick and I were the only ones in the office at 8:00 a.m. He took one look at my face, and handed me a doughnut, fresh out of the box.

We had made a serious dent in the box before I finished.

"Sounds like The Roblin, yeah," Nick said. "I mean, not that I'd know, particularly, but the circumstances had way too much going on for it to be sheer coincidence. How come you got so lucky, Dandelion?"

"No damned idea. First it stalks, and then it splats my apartment, and what's next? Is it going to chase me across the city, hound me for the rest of my life?" On waking up I'd found a note from the super under my door, confirming that they were going to claim I was in violation of my lease for noise issues. That hadn't helped my mood any, either.

All right, I'd taken the apartment out of a panic to get

out of the hotel I'd been staying in—on J's dime—and now that I'd been working, and didn't expect to be fired, probably…I could afford something a little nicer, in a better part of town. But still, it was a pain and a hassle.

On the third hand, this would give me a reason to get in touch with The Wren again, like Stosser had strongly suggested would be a good idea. "Hi, just checking in to see if there's an apartment coming open in the building, like we'd talked about…" That had been an awesome building, in a perfect location—okay, I wouldn't be able to walk to work on nice days anymore, and the commute would take longer, but it would be a straight shot up the 1….

"I wonder if anyone else had trouble last night. Would explain why everyone's late. Hey, you think The Roblin had anything to do with Venec…"

"No." That came out more sharply than I intended, but the thought unnerved me too much to consider. Mischief, all right. But that attack had nearly been fatal.

"How much damage could a mischief imp do, assuming a mischief imp did do damage?" Nick stumbled over the last few words, and pursed his lips as though trying to limber them up. He looked like a demented goldfish.

"What damage did it do?"

Stosser, with Sharon in tow, came in through the front door. The almost-frantic Ian Stosser of yesterday had been wiped clean, leaving behind the usual smooth-faced, dapper-dressed Big Dog, his hair slicked back and his nicely tailored Euro-style suit hanging without a wrinkle. Half the time he dressed like a color-blind granola-cruncher, and the other half he could have posed for *GQ*.

I'd learned to read Stosser-sign, a little: granola was his downtime, when he was trying to be Just Another Guy. He really wasn't very good at it, and it kind of, honestly, freaked me out a little. Seeing him in a suit was like having the sun rise on the proper side of the city: you didn't know what kind of day it would be, but at least it wasn't starting with a pre-apocalyptic warning.

"We think The Roblin made its first real move last night," I said, before Nick could tell my story. I gave them a quick rundown, ending, "Something tore up my place—moved furniture, loudly, tossed my linen closet, broke a piece of glass-art—" damn it, I was still weepy about that "—and made everyone in the building believe that there were open flames in my apartment. I'm just lucky I got home when I did, or they would have called the fire department and maybe hacked down my door to get in."

Which might have been funny, seeing my super trying to explain to the fire department...but no, thanks.

"You saw The Roblin?" Stosser went on alert.

"No." Seriously? I would have told him that, instead of sitting here bitching. "The place was empty when I got there. The windows were all locked, the door secured.... I guess imps can Translocate."

"Or walk through walls."

"Comforting thought, that," Sharon said dryly. "So it's gone from following you to fucking with you. Why you?"

"It was here."

"What?" We all looked at Stosser at that revelation.

"A few nights ago. I have an alarm set up, similar to

the spell Ben has on the front door that recognizes us, and challenges anyone it doesn't recognize. It went off, but by the time I got here—twenty minutes, tops—the place was empty. And also a mess. Whoever it was, it had been going through our personnel files. Based on the timing of it first stalking Torres, and the tossing of her place, I think that it is a reasonable assumption that it was The Roblin, looking for…whatever it was looking for. Your address, one supposes."

"Great. So flattered." What the hell made me such irresistible imp-bait?

Stosser looked at the other two. "Have either of you had anything odd happen? Not just the general weirdness we've been seeing, anything out of the usual at all?"

Sharon shook her head, but Nick looked thoughtful. "Maybe. I didn't think anything of it, or, at least, I figured it was just under the 'shit happens' category. But yesterday morning I was tweaking my netbook—" And that still freaked me out, that Nick could use a personal computer. Most of us, a heavily warded desktop was the best we could do, and even then we had to be careful, but the rules were different for current-hackers. "—And something surged."

"Surged." Ian had a look on his face that meant he knew what Nick was talking about. "You're all right?"

"Yeah, I was more surprised than anything else."

"You should have told me."

"Yah, well, I was going to mention it to Venec, and…" Nick's voice trailed off. "How is he, anyway?"

And, damn it, he looked at me when he asked that, not Stosser. Damn it…I gave back a blank face like I didn't know anything. Which I didn't, other than the fact that I hadn't gotten any Merge-inspired alarms, so he was probably doing fine and either still sedated or had his walls up tight.

"They are releasing him later this morning," Stosser said. "Knowing Ben, he'll be here as soon as he finds his clothing and hails a cab."

"You let him check out alone?" Sharon turned on Stosser, probably as pissed as she got. Sharon was a prima donna and a pain in the neck, but she was also in a lot of ways the mom of the group, her and Pietr, and apparently moms did not let people check out of hospitals alone.

"If I'd shown up, I would have told him to go home, not come here, and we would have gotten into an argument," Stosser said calmly. "This way, we avoid the fight, which I would have lost, anyway."

When the hell did Stosser develop a sense of humor? He wasn't wrong, though. That would have been Ben all over.

Big Dog turned to me, then. "Your apartment's okay?"

"For now," I said. I really didn't want to get into the details, not until I had a new place lined up.

"All right. Nick, I want you to work with the netbook, here, where we're properly warded, so we can determine if it's infested."

"Infected," Nick said, correcting his terminology.

Boss scowled at him. "With a mischief imp, *infested* might be the better word. Go. Sharon, when Lou and Pietr get here, do a full sweep of the office, and double the wardings. And then do the same in everyone's apartments. I don't like this, not at all."

"And me, boss?" Be damned if I was going to sit here while everyone else got to work.

Ian turned and looked at me. "You stay here until Venec arrives. Lawrence and Cholis came back with new information on the body dump case, and I want you three to close it today. If we're being targeted by a mischief imp as powerful as the Old Man thinks, I don't want any dangling threads left it can possibly yank."

Given our marching orders, we marched. Or Nick did, anyway. I'd helped him a time or two with his hacker-magic, and was just as glad not to be anywhere near when he did his thing. It made me feel like I was going to throw up, and I hated throwing up.

"You really think The Roblin's after us? I mean, not just you but all of us?" Sharon asked, sitting on the sofa next to me.

I lifted my hands palm-up, to show my utter ignorance and frustration. "Don't know. Makes sense, doesn't it? The warning, the break-in here, the break-in at my apart-ment…we're a natural focus." Bobo had said as much, when he warned us. We investigate chaos. The Roblin causes it. Peanut butter and jelly.

"But why you, and Nick specifically?"

Why not her, was what she wasn't asking. How was The Roblin picking its victims.

"Damned if I know," I said. "Just be glad, if you're not on the short list, not insulted."

"I'm not. I'm just curious. Like Venec always says, if we know why, then we can figure out the rest of it. Nick's skill set is unusual, so maybe that's it, but you're not…" She stopped, aware she'd been about to go somewhere seriously not-complimentary.

"Not unusual? Not special? Not exceptionally strong?" I kept my tone mild. I was moderately high-res, as the general population went, but not in this crowd, no.

"You're practically perfect in every way," she said, and I thwapped her on the arm, laughing for the first time in what felt like days. Maybe even weeks. Since we'd gone to the Devil for drinks, maybe. That felt like a month ago, with everything that had happened.

"You think the attack on Venec was…" She trailed off, as though not wanting to follow that train of thought. I sobered, turning the suggestion over in my mind in a way I hadn't been able to, when Nick suggested it.

"No. It doesn't feel right. The Roblin is about confusion and chaos, the more people involved the better, probably. Even my apartment, he got the entire building in an uproar. A single attack, and the cause easily put down? Anyway, the client had just hired the dog a few days after you cleared the site," I said. "Stosser said the trainer was recommended by a friend of a friend, the same idiot who suggested the mage-alarm. The housekeeper was so terrified of the thing when it showed up, she refused to go near it, so it was prowling the grounds on its own. Sheer bad luck."

"Oh, lovely," Sharon said, in the tone of voice that was very much not-lovely. "Do we have a line on the trainer?"

"Stosser said that it was taken care of." The look on the boss's face had told me that the trainer was a name he knew, which meant either high-placed Council, or low-down scummy. Stosser might be useless on the scene, but he was the best we had at getting high-level people to sit up and listen.

Venec was the one who handled the lowdown. With Ben in the hospital—

Like my thoughts conjured him, I *felt* Venec come through the main door downstairs, like a trickle of warm air against my skin.

"There've been so many complaints about hellhound breeders, you'd think somebody would have tried regulating them, or something," Sharon said.

"They tried to ban them entirely, about a hundred years ago," I said absently. "Huge yowl of complaints, said true hellhounds were so rare, anyway, they were doing a service by continuing the breed." Like anything that was supposed to harry the souls of the damned was going to make a cuddly pet for junior.

"How could the housekeeper just let it run around like that? If she was so scared of it, why not shut it up somewhere?"

"Seriously? You wanted her to do something about a hound? She was probably afraid to do anything beyond coexist. It was introduced to her, so it knew she was allowed on and off the property, but I doubt she trusted it beyond that," I said, listening without trying to be obvious for the sound of someone coming down the hallway. "And it wouldn't go beyond the lines of the property, so she didn't have to watch it. That's why they're so in-demand—smarter than any mortal dog, even quarter-bred, and most human guards, too. Plus, they're vicious."

The door opened, and proof of that viciousness walked in.

I thought I was prepared—Stosser said that the doctor

had to do some serious stitching—but he'd been released, right? So it couldn't have been that bad?

I hadn't thought about the fact that this was Benjamin Venec, and his release was almost certainly AMA— against medical advice.

I think Sharon started to say something; I couldn't hear it. My entire focus was not on the thick white bandage covering his neck, or the arm in a cloth sling, or even the blue-and-purple stippling of bruises on his face that looked like they'd been made by a giant paw, or the tiny stitched scar by his left eye, too painfully close.

My entire awareness was taken up by the look in that eye; pupils pinpointed way too much for the casual overhead lighting. He looked at us, blinked, and the pupil remained narrowed.

Benjamin Venec, Mr. Control, was stoned on painkillers. That would explain the utter lack of discomfort I felt coming off him; in fact, he was remarkably muffled. I'd thought it was because he had his wall up again but... nope.

And Ian wanted us to take him out in the field? Oh, hell, no.

"I'm fine, Bonnie." His voice sounded solid, almost amused, and he moved into the office with his normal graceful prowl. "A lot of stitches, and some lectures on what to look for, infectionwise, and I'll have to go for a follow-up to make sure everything's healing all right. But it was just a bite."

"It almost tore your throat out," Sharon said, but in a much calmer voice than I would have managed. I don't think—even with all the worrying—that had really sunk in, for any of us.

When it did, I needed to be ready for a meltdown. Hopefully somewhere private.

"*Almost* doesn't count," he said, with a dismissive air that made me want to shake him—or tie him back down to a hospital bed. I did neither. "Where's everyone else?"

"Stosser's got us all off and running. You and I are supposed to go help Nifty close the body-dump case. The break-in gets all our attention, after that." I decided not to say anything about The Roblin, right now, and hoped Sharon had the same thought.

She did.

"All right." He sat next to me, maybe just a bit too close, and I should have moved away. I didn't. The smell and the fear of the hospital came back to me, and the urge was to do something totally and wholly inappropriate, especially in the office, with Sharon watching us with far too much lively curiosity.

"All right?" I blinked at him, his words finally making it through my brain.

"You were expecting argument?"

Actually, I was. Even with the muted, mellowed-out feel, this was still Benjamin Venec, hard-ass and Big Dog.

He smiled: barely a lift of his lips, like it hurt too much to use most of his lower face, but a definite smile. "Believe me, I have no desire to tear open these stitches, or do anything likewise idiotic. Nifty will do any required heavy lifting, and you will do the lighter lifting, and I will stand back and glower as required, with these wounds undoubtedly adding to the impression of a team too tough to tangle with. Ian is annoying but no fool."

And that, actually, was pretty much what we did. When Nifty came in, we headed out, following up on the name they'd gotten as a possible Person of Interest, one Nico Kaufman, a freelance dockworker who'd had a sketchy alibi for the hours our DB went missing, and— more relevant to our interests—had been working for the same company that stiffed the DB financially.

And if I stayed a little too close to Venec's side, was too aware of his every move, trying very hard not to flinch every time he was jostled by someone, neither he nor Nifty commented on it.

The building—a four-story walk-up down in Alphabet City—was, in a word, dingy. In two words, run-down. The moment we knocked on the door of Kaufman's apartment, I was really glad Nifty and Venec were with me. The info we'd gathered had neglected to mention that our suspect was a minotaur.

"We come in?" The way Nifty said it, it wasn't a question, or even a request. The bull-headed fatae glared at him, but took a step back, and made a gesture with his thickly muscled arm that translated into "yeah, whatever."

The apartment was bare and barren, matching the building, and pretty much the way you'd expect a minotaur to live. There were beautiful photos on the wall, though, of sweeping blue seas and clear skies.

Greece. J and I had been there once, when he was still working on expanding my horizons. I wondered if this guy was an immigrant, or if he just longed for the ancestral home.

We'd discussed our plan of attack in the cab ride down—with the Big Dog along, injured, we weren't worried about having to justify the expense report—and now it fell into place like we'd had time to rehearse.

"You worked with Aodink," Nifty said without lead-in or introductions.

"Yeah. What's it to you?"

No accent, beyond the basic stereotypical Noo Yawkah I'd learned to recognize as actually being from Queens. Local boy, then. Dreaming of a better time and place?

He took the only seat in the apartment, a sofa that looked like it had been retrofitted to support his mass. Minotaur weren't actually that large—no bigger than your average pro wrestler—but they massed something fierce. Venec leaned against the wall, as usual. With his arms folded against his chest—the sling having lasted halfway through the cab ride, before he took it off with a muttered swear and shoved it into my kit—and the white bandage stark against his black jeans and sweater, he really did look the part of annoyed and potentially violent hard-ass.

Nifty, to contrast, perched himself on the edge of the wood table and leaned forward to talk to our suspect, his body language going for the big-man-to-big-man thing. I leaned against the now-closed door, my arms loose by my side, and looked at the minotaur, trying to channel Stosser's best "I know something you don't want me to know" expression, which mainly involved a perfectly emotionless face that still managed to smirk. The smirk

was easier than holding my arms loose. Now I understood why Venec crossed his arms when he leaned; it
helped you balance.

"He's dead."

No surprise. No reaction at all. Not that it was easy to
tell, on that bull head, but not even his ears twitched.

"You and he had some words. You wanted him to stop
bitching about the company that wasn't paying him, Elliot Packing."

The bull shrugged, and on him the gesture looked less
like, in J's words, "an inelegant expression of uselessness,"
and more of a threat. "Wasn't just me wanted him to
shut up. He opened his mouth, and work dried up. They
didn't know one beast from another, so they stopped hiring us all."

"And you put an end to that."

"You're the pups, you tell me."

Interesting. We hadn't identified ourselves. I felt a
pulse of interest and—amusement?—coming from Venec,
while Nifty frowned. This was changing the plan a little.
I reached down and pulled up some extra current, playing the neon-bright strands between my mental fingers,
remembering Nicky's cat's cradle, keeping the current
cool but limber, ready for anything.

Fatae were magic, could sense magic, they didn't *use*
magic. I kept repeating that to myself, even as Nifty
picked up the change in direction and ran with it.

"How did you get him into the river?"

The minotaur looked at Nifty like he was insane. "I
threw him."

Venec laughed. "Ask a stupid beast, get a stupid answer."

That wasn't to the script, either; Ben was trying to rile the minotaur, get it to attack him, so we'd have an excuse to take it down. My guys all had death wishes.

"You're admitting that you killed Aodink?" Nifty asked, pulling the bull's attention back to him.

"I ain't admitting nothing. Threw him in the river, is all."

"Yeah, well, you're not smart enough to figure out that if you shut Aodink up, the work would start to flow again," Nifty said. "So who gave you the orders?"

That wasn't going to work; I could tell already. The minotaur wasn't ashamed of being bottom of the brain-pile; that was just the way the breed was; strong but not built for cognitive functions. And it wasn't intimidated by current, either. We weren't going to get an admission of the actual killing, and he wasn't going to attack us, either; he was dumb but not a fool.

"You were used," I said, totally breaking the plan. I was supposed to watch, not talk. "You were used and then set up to take the fall, just like your ancestor. And for nothing. The jobs aren't coming back, cousin. Elliot Packing has already moved on, hired other people to do their work. Bought machinery that can go 24/7, without being fed, without giving back talk. Machinery that humans will work—legal, licensed humans, not fatae."

I was using everything I'd heard from Danny and Bobo, playing into the worst fears of the fatae underground; of being replaced not with others of their kind, but humans, the majority population, with legal papers and legal standing. I did it, knew I was doing it, hated myself for doing it, and did it, anyway.

"They said..." the minotaur blurted, and then stopped. But Nifty caught whatever it was he wasn't saying.

"They said if you took one for the team, it would all go back to the way it was before? Do this for them, and they'd take care of you? All one team, working for the same goal, and everyone has a specific job…."

"All I had to do was take him down and throw him in," the minotaur said, like he was complaining. "That was all. Then they'd hire us all back."

It was so sad I was almost angry. At the fatae for believing, at the humans who had manipulated them, at the world where fatae had to work in the shadows, taking this kind of crap, killing their own just to survive.

"But they didn't," Nifty said.

"They didn't call. It's been days, and they haven't called." The minotaur sounded aggrieved.

Venec glanced at me, and I nodded. My ability to run cool with my current was paying off; I had the minotaur's voice down on tape, the small recorder hidden in the leg pocket of my pants. It wouldn't hold up in a Null court of law, but it didn't have to. We were hired to find out the truth of an event, without worrying about right or wrong. It wasn't a perfect system, but it was better than what used to exist, where even if someone asked who-what-why, they couldn't get an answer because too many people were invested in Talent being above the law. Like my dad's killer, still walking around, unpunished.

I had a more-than-suspicion that Stosser's grand plan involved actual courts of enforcement, someday. But that wasn't my headache.

Right now, my headache was in front of me, starting to radiate faint tremors of pain. The drugs were wearing off. We had what we needed; now it was time to go.

enough I sent to Nifty, a sense of finality and a tinge of urgency, with the flavoring of Venec. I wasn't sure how much of that he actually picked up, but it was enough.

"Don't go anywhere," Nifty told the minotaur, standing up, looking down at the fatae. He didn't use current, not even a gleam of a spark, but he managed to project a sense of Official Doom. "If you do, we're going to be really unhappy with you."

We left the bull sitting on his sofa, moaning about how life wasn't fair, and walked down to the street level in silence—me acutely aware of the fact that Venec's pain meds were starting to fade, and he was holding that injured arm close to his chest. We made it as far as the curb, looking for a cab to flag down, before Nifty put his hand out, asking for the tape recorder.

"Hell, no," I said. "You touch it, it will go up in sparks." I took a few steps away from him. "In fact, get the hell away from me."

Venec shouldered Nifty aside neatly with his good arm, giving me room to walk unmolested.

"Bonnie, the tape?"

Because he asked politely, I pulled the mini-corder out of my pocket and showed it to him, hitting the play button just enough that we could hear the minotaur's voice rumbling, low but intelligible. I really didn't think there was any danger; it took a couple of days of steady core-contact to kill something that low-tech, and we'd managed to get through the confrontation without active use of current. But shit happened, and even dumb tech like a tape recorder could get fried by a sudden defensive twitch.

Fortunately, I ran cool, which meant...

I stopped dead on the corner. "That's it."

"What?"

"The Roblin. It didn't go after the stronger ones—it went after the weirder ones. I run cool, and Nick—oh, shit, Nick!"

I was surrounded by stronger Talent, and carefully not being active. Nick, on the other hand, was probably nose-forward right this fucking moment into tricky, weird, prone-to-chaos-anyway magic. He'd be like a carnival target to something like The Roblin.

My ping was instinctive: not to Nick, for fear of distracting him at a bad moment, but Stosser, who might be within reach—and had the power and the control to risk getting between a hacker-mage and a mischief imp.

"I need to get back," Ben said suddenly, a faraway look in his eyes. "Bonnie...."

I felt the same sharp urgency he did, filtered through his connection to Stosser. "We'll take the subway," I said. "Go."

eleven

Either intentionally or not, Venec left that faint connection open, so by the time Nifty and I made it to the office, I already knew that Nick was mostly all right, his computer was utterly fried, and while the rest of the team was nervous and edgy, and Stosser was annoyed, Venec was *furious*.

Not at Nicky, not even at the imp. He was furious at Ian, who had, as Nifty would say, sidelined him from the game, telling him that his injuries were serious enough to keep him on office-duty, same as Nifty had been. I walked into an office that was practically simmering with frustration and resentment.

Part of me wanted to avoid the entire thing, make like the others in obliviousness, just go directly to Nick, make sure he was okay, and then get my orders with the rest of the team.

I'd been raised to deal with my responsibilities, though, even when I was the only one who knew what they were.

And the first responsibility, like it or not, want it or not, was getting Ian and Ben back on track.

I just wasn't quite sure, even as I walked into the Big Dogs' lair, how I was going to do that.

The two of them were sitting in chairs at opposite ends of the small office, glaring at each other. "Shune's fine," Ian said as I walked in, not even bothering to look at me. "The Roblin singed his fingers and fried his hair a bit, that's all."

Being a Talent means, by definition, that you can handle a load of current—and electricity—running through your body. Something that singed Nick's fingers might have killed a Null. Stosser wouldn't have thought of that, probably.

I knew that Venec had.

"I think our original guess was right. If The Roblin's here to make mischief, its biggest challenge would be the ones who investigate mischief. So long as it's targeting us, it's not harassing others," I said, addressing Ben's worry first. "If we can keep it focused on us, nobody else will get hurt."

Except maybe us. Still. Did a mischief imp, even the grandmother of imps, intend to kill? Then I thought about what some fatae considered harmless pranks, historically, and reconsidered.

"We can't have it interfering with the ongoing investigation," Stosser said. "You've probably wrapped up the body dump, and that was good work, but this break-in has already caused too much trouble. The client lied to us, hid details of the story, and nearly got Ben killed. I want to know exactly what is going on."

"It goes for the unique," I said, following my earlier thought. "I think that's the trigger. That's why me, and Nick." I'd had time to think it through, on the subway ride back, lay it out into a semblance of a formal report. "We're not the strongest of the pack, but our skills are unusual—I run cool so I bet that it was trying to make me angry, breaking all my stuff and getting me kicked out of my building, to see what I could do, what trouble it could cause. But Nick's—" I paused; even among ourselves we didn't often vocalize Nick's skill "—Nick's a challenge it wasn't going to get many other places. So he's going to be the real target.... But it might get bored, anyway. We need to find something…"

A thought struck me, and the way Ben's head lifted, his dark eyes looking even more shadowed with exhaustion and pain, I could see the thought reached him in that exact instant.

I said it first. "If it wants something unique, something different to play with…"

"No." Venec-voice. Boss-voice.

I didn't let that stop me. "It makes sense. And if it's already here, there's no way to avoid it. We need to make it work for us, not against us."

"Bonnie, no." And then, suddenly, it wasn't boss-voice anymore. "It's too dangerous, especially without knowing how far it will go to get its jollies."

Stosser was looking between us, his expression caught between knowing we had a juicy bone, and frustration that he didn't have a chunk of it himself, and knowing that if he was patient, we'd work it out and then present it to him.

"If we're ready for it, we'll be okay." Probably.

Venec was still shaking his head, even as I could tell he was running through how it might work. "We would have to…"

"I know." It would require that we open the very doors we'd shut, take down the walls we'd built. Make a target of ourselves, and use the Merge as a trap.

And neither of us knew if it was a trap that we would be able to escape, if we'd be able to rebuild those walls, once The Roblin was dealt with.

The idea terrified me.

"This thing we have," I said to Stosser, before Venec could say, absolutely, that he wouldn't do it. "The Merge. It's unique enough to attract The Roblin's attention, distract it from anything or anyone else. Even more than Nick." And Venec was higher-res than Nick and me both; he'd be better able to handle anything The Roblin might try. I'd be the weak link here, but I was willing to take the risk. Okay, not willing, but I didn't see any other choice.

"Trick the Trickster?"

"Exactly. And when we have it caught, then we can figure out how to make it go away," I finished, keeping one eye on Stosser to see how he would react, and the other on Venec, to see if he was going to try to stop me from pitching the plan. There was always a way to banish imps, either through magic or bribery. We just had to get the upper hand, somehow.

I expected Ben to be angry that Ian knew, since he'd been as much about keeping it quiet, for his own reasons, as I had, but he just looked resigned, which was how I felt about it—resigned, and glad it was out in the open, sort of.

"You think it would be enough?" Stosser asked, considering what I'd suggested.

"I think it's a crap idea." Ben's voice was flat, low, not at all growly. I hated the sound of it, hated being the one who took the growl out of his voice, but I honestly didn't know what else to do. The Roblin was focused on us right now, but what happened if it got distracted? How ADD were mischief imps? What happened if someone less-grounded, unaware of what was happening, was its next target? Madame was wary of The Roblin. The other Ancient had come to the office to warn us, specifically. And the unease from my scrying was still riding between my shoulders like an imp itself, telling me trouble was in the neighborhood. Not good, not good, and not good. We couldn't look away. Not us, not now.

"You have anything less crappy?" I asked Venec, letting him *see* where my thoughts were leading.

He glared at me, then deflated, shaking his head. "No."

Stosser intervened, then. "She's right. It's the best plan we've got, and allows the others freedom to continue the investigation of the ongoing cases." I got the feeling that Stosser really didn't give a damn about the imp—it was an annoyance to him, not a problem. Keeping our solve rate up, that was the problem.

"Yeah. Oh. And here." I pulled the recorder out of my pocket, popped the tape and handed it to Stosser. "You might want to go play this for whoever it is needs to hear it. Incriminates the company, and our minotaur friend."

He took the tape, his long fingers cool against mine. I swear, the guy really did have ice water in his veins. "I have no idea how this one will play out," he admitted. "The NYPD has no authority over the fatae, and the Council will deem it a matter between the business and their employees, and no concern of theirs."

The Council was kind of bloodless that way, no matter what region you went to, yeah.

"Don't take it to the Council," Venec said, and there was a faint growl back in his voice. "Take it to the local unions. Dockworkers, garbage haulers, anyone you can find."

"Null unions?" I was surprised; Stosser looked utterly shocked.

Venec reached up to touch the bandage around his throat, and almost smiled, but it was the smile of a dog that knew it had you cornered. "My dad used to tell me that the unions were all that stood between the working schlub and indentured servitude, not out of the goodness of their heart, but because they wanted the power of those working schlubs organized to *their* direction, not someone else's. Let's see if their desire to swell the membership rolls trumps fataephobia."

Oh. That was twisty, so very twisty. Appeal not to someone's desire to see justice done, but to prevent anyone else from taking advantage of someone they could make mutual advantage from. I forgot, most of the time, that straight-shooter no bullshit Benjamin Venec had a brain as devious as my mentor's, and utterly lacked most of J's ingrained social graces.

"It might not work," Stosser said, tapping a finger

against the back of his other hand, like a metronome for his thoughts. "But it's definitely worth a try. If nothing else, it will bring Elliot Packing to the attention of others—and once they start looking for violations of objectionable practices, change might come."

And that, really was why we did this gig, holding the actions of the *Cosa* up to the light. People—whatever their species—did shitty things to each other, for a whole range of reasons and justifications. We weren't going to change human—or fatae—nature, but if there were consequences to those actions, then maybe it would stop them from happening again. Maybe.

Stosser stood up, my tape in his hand, and walked out of the office without another word, leaving Ben and me trying hard not to look at each other, but not able to look away.

Wow. Talk about an elephant in the room.

"You know I'm right. If this is as rare as you say it is, and we already know how much trouble it can cause, it will be like waving a red flag in front of a bull. The Roblin won't be able to resist."

"Bulls are color-blind, you know."

I didn't even bother to glare, instead reaching inside to slowly, carefully, dismantle the wall I'd built, one brick of control at a time. I wasn't going to take it down all the way; I wasn't quite willing to do that, not even to stop The Roblin, but enough. I could feel the pressure brushing against me, shifting against the exterior of my core, like…I couldn't describe it; there were no words in my experience. Like waves rolling over each other, separate to the eye but not really, not in composition, water drops from one merging into the other, and then reforming....

That wasn't right, either, but it was the visual that stuck with me, even as I could feel Ben unbuilding his own wall, coming down less like bricks than a melting sheet of ice.

The image of two lovers undressing for the first time? Really not far off the mark. That thought didn't help my nerves any.

I couldn't say when it happened. I'm not sure it actually did happen, that there was a moment of Before and then After, or if things that always had been were suddenly surfacing. I didn't feel any different, didn't think any different; all the things I'd quietly, subconsciously worried about not happening, at least as far as I could tell.

I was me, still. Ben was Ben. I wasn't overwhelmed, or undercut. Just...

Aware.

Really, really Aware.

weird

His voice, my thoughts, or the other way around. A sense of wonder and oddness and agreement and not a little awe.

And a sense, from both of us, of "this far, no further." The Merge pushed; like a living thing: it wanted more. We resisted, and it subsided again, taking what it could get.

A moment passed, then another, and the sense of oddness faded.

Still aware, though. Like breathing for two, or... I had

no frame of reference, and from the look on Ben's face, neither did he.

"Now what?" Ben asked. "Here, Roblin, Roblin, Roblin?"

I had no idea.

"Well, while you figure it out, we still have an investigation to handle." He walked past me to get to the door, and I reached out, almost instinctively, and touched his hip. The cloth of his slacks felt rough, abrasive under suddenly oversensitive fingertips, and he paused, as though I'd grabbed at him.

I could hear him swallow, without even looking, and felt guilty for the pain that must have caused his throat.

"I'm all right," he said immediately. "It's like having a bad sore throat, mostly, only on the outside. You can't tell?"

"I didn't try."

That seemed to reassure him, and he nodded, heading out the door.

I let him go; he was the boss, he got to give the orders. But I mentally followed him down the hallway, anyway, the echo of his movements in my head, almost but not quite like hearing, or seeing, or smelling something familiar.

There weren't any words to describe it. I wondered if, over time, I'd figure it out. I wondered if we'd get the chance to figure it out.

I didn't wonder, any longer, if I *wanted* that chance.

"Here Roblin, Roblin, Roblin," I said. "You want something that's going to mess up my life, make me pissed off? Come try and rearrange the furniture *here*."

I waited, but there was no indication that I'd been

heard, no evil chuckle or high-pitched giggle or even a passing whiff of sulfur, or whatever presaged the appearance of an imp.

I waited another few minutes, then got up and went to join the rest of the team.

"We already know that the trace isn't anything any of us have seen before," Sharon was saying when I came in. It took me a minute to catch up with what she was talking about, my brain so filled with The Roblin, and Venec, and how much more trouble I'd just gotten myself into.

Right. The trace I'd picked up in the house. The thing locked in a warded jar, hopefully inert.

"We've been trying to come up with some way to test it, if we can figure out where it comes from, but there's barely enough to poke at, and..." She hesitated. "And it makes me feel queasy just being in the room with it. That's not normal."

Yeah. It had made all of us feel uneasy, hadn't it, the moment we were aware of it. Why? Something stirred in my awareness; not me, but Venec. I glanced sideways at him, but nothing showed on his expression or body language, and the stirring faded, as though he hadn't been able to get a grip on it, either.

Sharon hadn't been comfortable with the guy from the start, certain he was lying but unable to prove it. Venec had investigated a missing kid, and now both kid and wife were gone, the wife dead, the kid missing-presumed-dead...and now this.

Could all be coincidence, the end run of some really bad luck on the part of Mr. Wells.

Or maybe not.

"So without knowing who broke in, or why they wanted those objects, or why they were so pissed off at the client, we've got nothing. No clues, no witnesses…"

"We do have witnesses," Pietr said, suddenly. "The house itself. The things that were broken, you said they were still there?"

"Yeah," I said, sliding into a chair and waiting to see where he was going with that. "But how do you ask—oh."

The Merge had nothing on a well-run pack when it came to sharing thoughts. No sooner had Pietr raised the idea than the rest of us were running with it.

"What about the simple scoop?"

Pietr was talking about a spell we'd been working on earlier, the one that was supposed to simplify the re-creation process. The one that had blown up in Nifty's face.

"What about it?" Sharon asked, not following his logic. Neither was I, to be honest.

"The scoop. It pulls everything from a scene, like a photograph, right? I mean, ideally. But what if we turn it into a mirror? To reflect what happened?"

"It wasn't designed to do that," Nifty said, his expression doubtful. Like Sharon, Nift was a damn good field op, and definitely tops in the decision-making, judgment-calling area, but they were crap at developmental magic. I was already feeling out the possible threads, and so was Lou, from the expression on her face.

"We designed it…we can redesign it," Lou said, pulling out her notebook and flipping to a spot midway through. She studied that page, and nodded. "Yeah. Okay, maybe.

Bonnie, we have the impetus of the spell aimed at retaining information—that's why it kept imploding on us, because it couldn't hold it the way a human brain can. What if we switched that to reflect, not retain?"

"Make it shiny instead of sticky?" My brain had already kicked into high gear. I'm a decent field op and crap at management, but when it comes to developmental magic…well, Pietr had the chops, and Lou might someday be as good, but honestly and with all due modesty, I doubted it.

"What exactly do we want it to do?" I asked the rest of the team. "Clarity is important, if we want the cleanest result. I mean, do we want a reflection, or a re-creation, or…"

"We need the evidence to talk," Nick said. "Literally, we have to be able to pose questions to it—'what happened here?' and have it answer."

I glared at the notebook, biting the inside of my lip while I thought. "No." I hated to say it but, "No. You can't make things act against their nature, Nick. Reflecting what happened around them is one thing, that's basic science." For Talent iterations of science, anyway. "Asking an inanimate object to react and respond? This isn't Disney. We don't do talking teacups."

There was grumbling and an overall letdown in the mood of the room, as we tried to reshuffle our thoughts, and pick up another lead. I took out my own notebook and started jotting notes down, starting with a box in the middle labeled "evidence" and then drawing lines out in radiating spokes, trying to draw my brain out the same way, to give me an answer.

As though it were being poked, as well, my core shifted slightly, swirling warmth alerting me to something....

Ben?

No, it wasn't the Merge, but he was alert, too; I could feel him come to a higher awareness, even though his physical attention was on the conversation he was having with Nifty and Lou.

Something had just poked at us.

ignore it The thought was deeper than a ping, fuzzy and muted like a morning whisper.

The Roblin? Maybe. I took Ben's advice and went back to my notes, intensely aware of the connection shimmering between us, silent but real, luring the imp out to play.

"There was no magic trace in that house," I said out loud, thinking my way through. "Nothing except the one bit we found, that we can't identify." Sludge, I decided. Icky sludge. "We haven't been able to identify the source of the claw marks."

"We haven't even been able to confirm they were claw marks," Nick said. "There wasn't any residue in any of the grooves, to test. I don't know if they were calcium based, or metal, or..."

"They had to be of a specific hardness to dig into that wood," Lou said. "I've been able to eliminate some breeds based on that, but...it still leaves too many to be useful."

"So without a known enemy, or trace to work from, all we have are the objects that were taken...a glass dagger, and a pocket watch." Nifty got up and paced. "Why them? Was it for their sentimental value, or something else?"

"You think the dagger is more than a memory-glass?" Sharon frowned, then shook her head. Her blond chignon was starting to come loose, and she had stuck a pencil in it at some point, and forgotten about it. It was unlike her, but cute. I decided against mentioning that to her. Right now, anyway. "But there was no trace of anything more powerful. I mean, not even a hint of a smidge, anywhere in the house."

"Not all magical items are obvious," Nifty said. "Some of them don't even register as magical, because they don't actually do anything. They just *are*. Like the fatae."

I nodded, underscoring the center box in my drawing. "Exactly. By their very nature they won't call attention to themselves, unless you know what you're looking for." Like trying to pick a fatae out of a crowded subway car. Unless it had a particularly unusual physical appearance— a rack of antlers, or flames instead of a face—mostly they blended, your eye slipping right over them. It took knowing that they were there, and actively looking for them, to pick one out.

"My mentor called it inert magic, present but not ac-counted for." Nifty was nodding, and Lou's eyes were bright with thought, but Sharon, Nick, and Pietr ei-ther hadn't had the same style of training we did, or just weren't seeing it yet.

Right, Sharon's mentor had been of the "have but don't use" school, whatever it was called, so theoretical magic probably wasn't on the agenda.

"Look, all current has a…a presence, call it. Right? We can channel and manipulate it. So it leaves an impression in the world, no matter how slight, even if our human senses can't quite see it." It sounded like I was talking out of my ass but there was something there, if I could just keep talking long enough to grab it.

"So we can't see it, but that doesn't mean it wasn't there. And if it was there and now it isn't, can we see its absence?"

"Negative space," Nifty said. "You're talking about negative space. That's insane, and possibly brilliant."

"So you think that the objects themselves can tell why they were taken, even though the objects aren't actually there now?" Nick looked like his brain hurt.

"Well...yeah." It sounded more stupid than brilliant, put that way. But I had the feeling that it would work, and I'd gotten a lot done over the years, listening to my instincts. Only one way to find out.... I was nodding even as my pencil flew over the page, everyone's comments blending into an idea being constructed under my fingers. Lou leaned over to watch, and Pietr ghosted to my side, but I barely noticed.

"Empty space impressions," he said. "The current-weight of what isn't there." Pietr was almost classically handsome, with a jawline and nose that would make a Roman sculpture cry in envy, but right then he reminded me of nothing so much as a jowly, rheumy-eyed bloodhound, lifting his head and preparing to bay to the world that he'd caught the scent.

"Yeah." Lou sounded pleased and satisfied. "I think we can do that, push energy into the blanks, let it sift around.... We just need someone with a really light touch."

That would emphatically not be her. Or Nifty, for that matter.

"Bonnie, you're the one who came up with it, you should do it," Sharon said, like she was gifting me with something.

"I can't."

"What?"

I paused, and looked up at Venec, trying to figure out what to tell them.

"Bonnie and I are bait for The Roblin."

Oh, okay. Blunt was how we were going to tell them, then.

"Bait? How bait?"

"If it is targeting us, taking the mischief to the investigators, the way we'd thought, then it's going to look for ways in which to cause the most mischief. The situation we have, Bonnie and I, the ability to communicate directly the way we do, is…ripe for mischief."

That was a mouthful. It also managed to skirt the fact that we knew damn well what was causing the connection, not to mention the physical and emotional affects and effects, and how much more than just communication it was enhancing. It also avoided any possible hurt feeling that could come up from our theory on why Nick and I had been targeted earlier, so long as Nifty kept his mouth shut, for now. And he would; nobody wants to be told that, even high-res, they're still commonplace. Of course, I'd rather not be told I was odd, either. But there it was.

"So, either Sharon or Pietr…or Stosser?"

"Not Stosser," I said without thinking, and everyone looked at me. I threw up my hands in a gesture of disgust and helplessness. "I saw him on-site, guys. The boss is brilliant, yeah, and way high-res, and he doesn't have clue one what to do with evidence."

Nifty snickered, and swallowed it almost immediately, but even Venec looked amused—and not surprised. "Ian doesn't like situations where he can't manipulate the results."

Being born with plus-ten charisma and a mind that made both Venec and J look about as subtle as a rock... yeah, I could see where Stosser got used to being able to finagle scenes. But you couldn't do that to evidence, not and keep it usable, and the boss knew it, and he must have found it howl-inducingly frustrating.

I almost felt bad for him. Almost.

"Sharon," Pietr said. "She's got the truth-sensing mojo working, so it makes sense for her to try, first."

"I think Pietr should do it," I said. Pietr faded from sight when stressed, the same protective invisibility that Retrievers specialized in. In fact, I probably could never have come up with this idea, if I didn't know Pietr so well, how he felt when he faded, and how to find him again once he did. Huh. That was interesting, and worth mulling over—later.

"Both of you go," Venec said. "Two attempts will give us a better chance of success."

Fair enough; Lou, Nick, and Nifty would keep following up on our other leads, like the guy who had been with the missus, before he died, and our yet unidentified memory-glass maker.

"All right," I said, pushing my paperwork toward them, so they could see better. "This is what I think you need to do. Instead of directing the current at the surfaces of what's there? I want you to go into what's not there."

"What?" Sharon was our logical thinker, and I had a feeling the b-ass-ackward way this spell had to work was going to confuse her. Pietr got it, though. The spell was probably going to be almost intuitive for him, since we were looking for something that wasn't there anymore.

There wasn't any time to do a test run, not with The Roblin lurking around waiting for the chance to screw things up for its own entertainment. Also, odds were that the client had realized by now that we had figured out that there was something hinky about his missing objects, maybe even realized that Venec had worked for his dead wife and knew dirt on his past. Rich people very much did not like people investigating outside the lines, and they liked even less when we had dirt on them to fuel the investigation. Even when they were, nominally, our client.

Unlike Danny, who would do whatever it took to satisfy the client's needs, we worked for the evidence, not the individual. They knew that when they hired us, but most of them didn't really understand what that meant. Once Wells figured it out, he would kick us off the case, shut down our access to protect whatever he was hiding, whatever had drawn the housebreakers to him.

We would still investigate—once you set the pups on something, *we* decided when the case was closed—but it would be harder to run tests, or get anything resembling a straight answer.

Venec tapped on the table, getting everyone's attention. "Pietr, Sharon, are you confident that you can handle this?"

My pack mates nodded, because what else could they

say? They had a good hold of the original identification spell I'd riffed on, and this wasn't really all that different, but nothing remained the same once it was implemented; your own personal current adapted to it, so everyone ended up with a slightly different result—ideally within a set range, but not always.

"Yeah. We got it," Sharon said.

"So, go," Venec told them, waving a hand in dismissal.

Pietr held up my notebook, asking permission, and I nodded. I'm not sure that I would have let anyone else take my notebook—we put down all our working thoughts there, almost like a traditional grimoire, now that I thought of it—but this was Pietr. I'd had sex with the guy—more, I'd *slept* with him. I trusted him at my back—or inside my notebook.

I felt a twitch of unease; what happened if the spell backfired? What if...

No. Not me. That prickly, poking swirl was back, a little harder than before, and it was difficult to ignore it. Acting on impulse, I *leaned* toward Ben—not physically, not even with current, exactly, but with an awareness that was something else, as though seeking reassurance or comfort.

The swirl caught at that movement, swarmed it, and I swore I could feel a hundred tiny little teeth latch on, like being nibbled on by itty-bitty alligators. It took effort not to flinch, not to let it know we'd felt it, were luring it further in.

I saw the edge of Ben's mouth turn up, barely a move-ment, but a definite smirk.

Our imp had taken the bait. Now, to wait and see what the little bastard did with it.

"Nick, give me your notes, too," Sharon said. "If we're going to be doing this negative space thing, maybe I can tell if anything's changed since the first visit."

"You want me to come?" he asked, even as he removed a section of pages and handed them to her. "If nothing else, to watch your backs?"

"Thanks, but I think we'll be okay."

Although nobody had said anything, it was inevitable that we were all a little leery of that house, now. The hellhound had been dealt with, one presumed, and the client wasn't going to be idiot enough to hire another—we hoped—but who knew what else a scared Null with a penchant for magical security devices would get up to?

"Where is he getting this stuff, anyway?" I wondered, after Pietr and Sharon left. "The dagger—okay, that's easy enough for someone to craft, it could be anyone in the damn *Cosa*, but the rest of it? Is there a storefront somewhere, hawking magical protections, or are they working out of someone's kitchen? Shouldn't that shit be licensed?"

"Selling protections is a time-honored profession," Venec said idly, sounding more like J than I really felt comfortable with. "A hedgewitch or village wizard specialized in that sort of thing, especially against the wee folk as went boojum in the night."

"Yeah, three hundred years ago," Nifty said.

"Not hardly," Lou corrected him, a little more snappishly than usual. Venec looked sideways at her, and she bit her lip, but he didn't say anything and she didn't apologize. The Roblin, even without doing something, was already doing its thing: everyone was on edge, waiting for something, anything to happen.

Having a theoretical discussion was one of the better ways to keep occupied, without actually doing anything important. Also, Venec always said that we came up with our better ideas when we argued things off-topic. So...

"There are still hedgewitches," I said, trying to keep the peace. "They might not call themselves that, but everything but the name's the same. Off the grid, low-res and small workings, but savvy enough to know the deal and how to deal with it." I'd run into more than a few when I was traveling with J, and not always in the places you'd expect. "There was a Talent who had a little storefront in Florence. She sold religious relics and love spells over the same counter."

"Were her love spells any good?" Nick asked, his face a mix of real curiosity and mischief.

"Probably better than the relics. My point is, she did a good business there, and not just from the tourists, but it was small, handmade stuff, like the memory-glass. What Wells is getting his hands on...current-run security system? Hellhound rentals? That takes more skill, more res. A lot more money involved. And probably not so much a one-person gig."

"Spell Rentals R Us," Nifty said. "Nice sideline. You think Stosser would go for it?"

"No."

The opinion on that was pretty much universal.

We batted around a few more ideas, most of them just arguing for argument's sake. I tuned out a little, and went down inside, dropping into my core the way you might a hot tub, slowly, with muscle easing as you sank. I'd been eating regularly, and making sure to recharge my core—mostly—but that didn't explain the incredible feeling of well-being. I let a tendril wander off, not directing it anywhere in particular, and wasn't at all surprised to feel it make its way, like it was following a ley line, to where Venec sat, sliding into his aura and disappearing...but not disconnecting.

A sense like a sigh, and a faint touch, and a reassurance, then he pushed me away, not dismissively, but almost playfully.

And the sense of being watched, of being pricked at with a hair-thin needle, came back.

My good mood faded a little: we were putting on a show for the imp; that was all.

we're here

The ping came from Pietr; I recognized the mental flavor immediately, and also that the ping was directed to me, not broadcast to anyone else in the room. The impression I got was that they'd run into slight but non-violent resistance, but persevered.

"I don't think the housekeeper is too fond of any of us right now," I said into the room. "But they're in the house."

"How come they reported to you, and not Venec?" Nifty looked like he'd been the one insulted. I guess, after fighting so hard for lead pup spot, he would be offended by someone not following the organizational flow chart. Still, it annoyed me that he was annoyed.

"Pietr and I partner a lot—it's probably easier for him to reach me." I didn't say a damn thing about sleeping with Pietr—if Nifty hadn't realized that by now, it was none of his damn business, and he'd probably get a bug up his nose because he assumed I was sleeping with Venec, too. They all did, even Stosser; you could tell from the things they weren't saying, the way they weren't talking about it even to joke about it anymore, like we were doing something wrong.

The fact that we'd not done anything more suggestive than hold hands—and that, almost by accident—wasn't going to fly with anyone. They just assumed....

careful The thought came low and soft along the connection, and I touched it, took reassurance from it. Reassurance, and clarity: the anger I was feeling wasn't mine, or Venec's. It was the imp coming back, trying to push us, manipulate us. Cause mischief among the pack.

"So that's how we're playing it, are we?" I said softly.

Nifty heard me, and misunderstood. Of course.

"Playing it? Only one here playing is you, seems…" He stood up, and then stopped, as though surprised to find himself standing. I looked up, remembering again, suddenly, how damn *big* Nifty was; not only way taller than my five foot six but twice as wide in the shoulders, with bulk to match. Anyone else, I might have been worried.

Anyone else, anyone other than a pack mate, and I wouldn't have seen surprise, and then a slow dawn of understanding cross his face. Nifty was a big guy; he used to hit people as part of his sport. He perfected control even better than most of us, out of necessity, and he knew that the anger, the frustration he suddenly felt wasn't real, wasn't his.

The Roblin was used to manipulating Nulls, and civilian Talent. It had never taken on pups before.

Before Nifty could retract his words, though, Venec stood up, facing him down. Bulk for bulk it wasn't a contest, but this wasn't about bulk but alpha dominance.

Nifty might want to be top dog, but Venec was a Big Dog. Nifty automatically began to back down, physically, then Venec grabbed him by the shoulder, shaking his head in warning even as the words came out of his mouth.

"You have something to say, mister? You want to get it off your overinflated chest?"

Nick gaped, and looked at me. I spared him the briefest smile before looking back to the pseudo-confrontation. Lou looked concerned but not really worried; I wasn't sure if she understood what was going on. I could only hope that Nifty did.

★?★

Pietr's query came through the swirl, and I hesitated, not sure if I could risk taking my attention away from what was going on.

"Yeah, I got something to say, all right." Nifty's voice was loud, but his expression was almost panicked, like he was trying to remember lines he didn't know he was supposed to have memorized. "You playing favorites now, *boss?*"

"I always liked some of you more than others," Venec said. His tone was cold, but his body language relaxed just a hint, the hand holding Nifty's arm not gripping so tightly. You had to look for the signs, though. Like finding a fatae, you had to know what you were looking for—and what it looked like. If you didn't know the incredible control Venec had, the discipline Nifty embraced as a matter of a lifetime's training; if you hadn't seen them training together, before, you might think those two were about to go head-to-head, possibly with violence.

⋆?⋆

⋆imp⋆ I tossed back to Pietr, hoping it would be enough to explain.

Apparently it was, because there were no more pings.

"Yeah, well, for a guy who was dumb enough to walk onto a live site without any backup, you're maybe talking a little too loudly...."

"He pays our salary," Lou said. She didn't get up, and, in fact, she looked almost bored, but her tone was pitched just right to be someone sucking up to the boss. Nick was staring at the three of them, barely daring to breathe, then looked at me for some kind of reality check. I shook my head, just a little. Neither of us were worth a hard shit at dissembling; he'd overplay it, and I'd be an utter flop; when I get angry I get angry, but when I'm not... well, I don't fake anything well, that's all.

"Careful what you say, *boy*."

My eyes went round at that. Just the wrong inflection, and Nifty's shoulders shook as though he was forcibly restraining himself from attacking Venec. I tensed in reaction, my instinctive reaction to scoop current and shape it into readiness. The sharp poking swirl came back, pricking the skin against my back and up my scalp, like it was trying to find a way in, and I held on to the fear and worry, even as I realized that Nifty's body language wasn't rage at the implied insult, but the result of hard-held laughter, trying to escape.

"Hold it..." I murmured, a double meaning in the

words, and they stood there, tensed and fierce, until the prickling sensation ebbed, the imp maybe realizing it was being too obvious, and sliding away again.

"All right."

The letdown in tension was immediate, and I could feel the change in Venec's core, sliding from a tight, hard knot into a softer coiling. My own, almost frozen, thawed a little. But not entirely. I could still feel that pricking awareness on my skin, and I knew that the imp had only retreated, not gone away for good.

"Well. That was fun," Nick said, leaning back and breathing again. "Next time warn me before we go all reality show showdown, okay?"

Lou hit him, hard, before I could.

pietr? I risked pinging him, just to let him know that the situation was on hold for the moment, and got back a flash of excitement and concern and…something else, I wasn't quite understanding. It flooded over me, and then was gone, the way pings did. Damn it. Already I was getting spoiled by how much deeper the communication between me and Venec was; the annoyance and fear of being always-connected that I'd been fretting over seemed a long way away, right then.

I blinked, coming back to the moment, and looked around the room. The others had settled back down after that bit of excitement: Nifty and Venec in a tight little tête-à-tête that looked to be some serious dog-to-pup reassurances, while Lou was scribbling something in her notebook, and Nick busied himself pouring coffee out of the carafe in the middle of the table, trying very hard not to eavesdrop on the other two guys.

I studied Nifty and Venec for a moment, trying to be less obvious than Nick. Funny; Nifty was always so confident, so assured, that you forgot that he spent most of his life following a coach's direction, one way or another. But Venec never forgot.

Even now, his attention on one pup, I'd swear I could feel this roving lighthouse spotlight sense coming from him, swooping around the room to touch on each of us in a constant, passive loop. It should have felt awkward, or annoying, but...it wasn't anything I hadn't already suspected he did, only now I knew he did it. More, because he was *letting* me see it.

No walls. No barriers. The only secrets we were keeping were the ones we let the other keep; a gentleman's agreement not to look. It was a level of trust I'd never really imagined, even in my most open relationship, and I don't think Venec ever believed it existed. I was pretty sure he didn't think it was healthy.

He might be right. I remembered the feeling of not being able to lie from the ki-rin case, when Sharon had used me as a test case for her truth-spell. It had driven me into a near panic. I don't think people are meant to share that much, that openly, without the option to say no. It goes against all our self-protective instincts, that loss of choice, and having to trust someone else to keep those private places safe.

And yet, even with all that, those thoughts going through my head, I couldn't find any upset at the sense of Ben so close, so...intimate.

I tried to remind myself not to get used to it, that it wasn't real any more than The Roblin's manipulated emotions, just the Merge, and the moment The Roblin was caught—or got bored—we'd be back to walls and distances.

Assuming we could. The thought caught at me like a fishhook into flesh, and the more I tried to ignore it, the deeper it settled into my brain. Would we be able to rebuild those walls? Just sitting here, not even trying, I could feel his presence like flesh to flesh, sense the gentle patience at war with his frustration—not directed at Nifty, but the world in general, and his bandage specifically. It was chafing him.

A lot of the world chafed him.

I didn't want to know that about him, but I did. Without looking, without trying to look, I also knew that his sweater had an emotional memory attached to it, which was why he wore it so often, and that he was worried about Sharon and Pietr, and that he knew where Stosser was and what he was doing, and was deliberately not thinking about it.

And that he was as hyperaware of me as I was of him.

That realization got me up and out of the room, muttering an excuse I forgot the moment it left my mouth, feeling the need to hyperventilate charging against my breastbone.

And Venec knew that, too. And I felt him letting me go, not because he wasn't worried but because he knew I needed to deal with whatever was bothering me elsewhere, and he had other things to do, and at that point I had no choice but to put up the frailest, flimsiest wall, just so I could breathe.

In the hallway, I found myself heading for the smallest conference room, my decision both unconscious and unhesitating. Wrapped up in not thinking about the thing between me and Venec, it took me the length of the hallway to remember that the small conference room was where the scraping we'd taken from the house was locked away.

I really, really didn't want to go in there, especially not alone, but what were my options? No matter my feelings, there was work to be done and it wasn't as though fleeing the office would help. It was either make myself useful here, or hang out in the break room and feel useless and spend, inevitably, too much time thinking about the things I didn't want to think about. At least if I was doing something proactive, I'd maybe feel less exposed, waiting for The Roblin to come back and take another shot at us? It was as good a theory as any.

I let myself into the room and reset the warding behind me, then sat at the table. The box—a purely current-based construct—rested in front of me, glinting balefully, dark reds and a particularly ugly neon-yellow, like a filthy fast-food restaurant's decor.

I studied the box, not reaching for my own current, not slipping into a working fugue-state, doing nothing that might alert the trace within that it was being watched because, all common sense be damned, I was pretty sure it would know.

Use more than magic, Venec instructed us, over and over. We're more than the sum of our skills, and the physical world is just as useful as the magic one—and covers a lot more territory. So: what did my basic senses tell me?

Once upon a time, that time being a year ago, I went through most of my day without drawing on current. It wasn't that I didn't enjoy using it, I just…didn't. Most Talent are like that; magic is the something extra, not so much used in the day to day. Now? Now it was an effort to not default to current, not to reach for it instinctively, even if only to make sure I was prepared.

I wasn't sure I liked that. Now, though, wasn't the time to stress about it: whoever I'd become, she was needed.

I'd already covered sight. My nose didn't smell anything different. Sometimes even a Null could pick up a whiff of a spell, like burnt ozone after a storm, but not here. My ears…was there a hum, low in the background? No; I was putting it there because I thought there should be. No noise at all, other than the usual old-building, multi-tenant grumbles and thumps that you ignored after the first couple of days.

Taste… I made a scrunched-up face. There was no way I was so much as licking that thing without a direct order from the boss.

Touch I already knew: it was slick and smooth and vibrated slightly under my fingertips, what was inside reaching directly to my core of current, making it curl in on itself in unease. No need to touch it again.

That thought struck me harder than it should have, and I turned my head slightly, instinctively, looking at it again. That last thought hadn't been mine. I know the feel of my own head, and that wasn't me. The feeling wasn't the now-identifiable static swirl of the imp, but heavier, slower.

Don't look, it whispered. Go away.

I so very much dislike being manipulated. It wanted me to stay away? I'd touch it.

And yeah, I knew that was dumb. I wasn't going to mock horror-movie heroines anymore.

There was a faint, familiar touch against my awareness, coming up against the gossamer-thin wall I'd put up and stopping there, asking if everything was all right. Irrationally, that touch made me even more determined to poke the box, as though dealing with the trace inside the lockbox was preferable to dealing with Venec.

"You're classic, totally textbook avoidance," I muttered to myself, even as my hand lifted, and touched the top of the box.

It was…a box of current. Not motionless—current itself was never motionless by its very nature—but not doing anything, either. Normally you could feel a tracebox working, the steady, staticky not-quite-noise of current set in an ongoing spell. That's all a tracebox was: current shaped by the controlling influence of more current—a spell—into a solid form. Okay, a mostly solid form.

Now, I not only didn't feel the box working, I didn't feel the trace inside it, although the glow told me that it was still there. I had a sudden panicked thought that, while we were distracted, it had escaped, somehow—that The Roblin had let it out, leaving a decoy behind, and it was roaming the hallways even now, the two of them, plotting some terrible, dire trick.

"You're getting paranoid," I said in disgust. "Half an hour's exposure to Venec, and you're totally paranoid."

The box sat there on the table, glimmering and glowering with current-light, and I could swear it was taunting me, like there wasn't anything I could do or think up that would crack the mystery of what was in there, and why I couldn't feel it, now.

The only thing I hate more than being manipulated was being told I wasn't capable of doing something. The combination? Oh, that just pissed me off. Knowing it was dumb, knowing I was being played, I slipped down into fugue-state, and "lifted" the lid of the box.

It was still there, settled at the bottom of the box like a handful of ashes, lacy and harmless-looking.

"Who are you?" I asked it. Not what—who. The part of my brain that wasn't busy being incredibly stupid noted that for later.

It answered me. A hiss of current slithered back at me, heavy and dark, and filled with echoes a thousand miles deeper than anything I could reach, licked from below by the flames of something that might have been the devil's laugh.

That laugh froze me in place while those flames crawled all over the skin of my hands, tried to reach deeper inside, gunning for my core, wanting to eat me, down to the last glittering drop of Me. I panicked, slammed the lid down and threw an extra layer of current into the lock, praying that would do the job, even as I was screaming along the Merge-connection for help.

VENEC!

The spell wasn't a complicated one; Pietr had the suspicion that was probably why the others had trouble with it. They applied too much force, and when you forced current, it lashed back at you. The trick was to be gentle, almost not asking anything of it even as you invoked the words. Negative space needed negative force. He thought about trying to explain that to the intent-looking blonde to his left, and almost laughed. Sharon was more of a blunt force object. No, this was a spell only Bonnie, with her ability to see multiple layers of gray in every shadow, could have thought of…and he was probably the only one who could do it properly, existing as he did so often in those shadows.

"Anything?"

"Not yet."

The two areas that had been the most trashed in the client's office were the desk and the bookcase behind the desk. So they had focused there; anything that might have been on the surface would have been found when Sharon and Nick cased the place originally, and by the time Stosser and Bonnie arrived, anything but the most obvious or persistent trace would have been obliterated.

Except, of course, for what wasn't there.

He had the notebook in his jacket pocket, but the words were easy to remember.

"Shadow of air and weight of light, make clear what now is not."

Even as he spoke the words, he reached into his core and, with gentle spectral fingers, lifted a handful of sparkling threads of current, letting them run through their range of colors before shading toward a peaceful, calm blue that let itself be drawn up by the words of the spell, spinning out into a thick, darkly neon-blue vapor that settled into one…two…three different spots where the bookcase had rested.

"Three?" His gaze flicked from one to the other and then to the third, his face still with concentration. "What did we miss?"

Sharon, standing off to the side and not able to see the results of his spell, said nothing, understanding that he wasn't actually asking her.

"Talk to me," Pietr said. It wasn't a command, wasn't even a spell, just a request. "Please," he added, to be polite. When something was unknown, his mentor had told him a hundred and ten times, be polite. It cost nothing, and could save your unworthy life.

Something shimmered, and Pietr slid deeper into fugue-state, letting the shimmer form more clearly in his awareness.

And that was the last thing he remembered, before blacking out.

Ever hear someone describe an anthill that's been overturned? That was what the office reminded me of, thirty seconds after I realized what we'd got trapped in that box. I got yanked—there's no other word for it—*yanked* out of the conference room by the scruff of my shirt, not by Venec but Nifty, who had a manic gleam in his eye that would have scared me if I didn't think there was a similar wild-eyed look in my own. The door slammed shut behind us, and I slammed my hand on it, engaging the wards and adding another layer of my own, wishing I'd had time to study that elemental thing the client had—I might be able to make it work.

"Come on," Nifty said, dragging me away before I'd barely had time to finish the lock.

"Hey, there's—"

Nifty barely slowed. "Is it gonna blow up or bite someone in the next five minutes?"

I had to think about that. "No."

"Then it can wait. We got bigger problems."

I doubted that. A lot. But I let him drag me back to the break room, where the furniture had been shoved to the side in obvious haste, and Sharon and Venec were both on their knees beside—

"Pietr!" I broke from Nifty's hold and pushed through, almost but not quite displacing Sharon, who was doing CPR.

Or rather, she was doing *Cosa*-style CPR, which involved less thumping, and more gentle current-shocks direct to the heart while Venec did the breathing thing.

I counted off in my head, helpless to do anything, knowing any distraction could be fatal, my chest clenched tight in agony until Venec sat back and Pietr's chest fell and rose on its own. He turned his head to the side and hiccuped painfully, and I turned on Sharon so I didn't have to deal with how I felt right then.

"What the hell happened?"

She sat back on her heels, her hair totally fallen out of its chignon, her makeup still perfect. "I don't know. I was trying to keep the housekeeper off our backs while he went into working fugue, and the next thing I know we've got current ricocheting all over the place, everyone's ducking, and he's out on the floor, not breathing." Sharon wasn't hysterical—it wasn't in her nature any more than it was any pups, but her voice was tight and high and she looked like she wanted to hit something. I could relate. A lot.

"People."

"What?"

We all turned to look at Pietr, who was, with Venec's help, slowly sitting up. His pale skin looked parchment-thin, and I'd swear he'd aged since I saw him last, only a few hours ago. I wanted to cuddle him, and I wanted to shake him to get an answer, all in one really complicated, crazy moment.

"They're people." He shook his head, a violent shuddering, and grabbed at Venec's hand where it was holding his other arm, directing his words to the boss. "The dagger, and yeah, the watch, too. The client lied to us. They're not magic, they were *magicked*."

twelve

I think we all heard the words, but couldn't process them, as though they weren't in English, or they were, but we'd suddenly lost the ability to translate it in our own brains.

"People," Pietr said again, seeing that we weren't getting it, his voice rising in frustration. "They're people!"

"In the objects?" Sharon frowned, trying to imagine how.

"They *are* the objects." A growl, low and dangerous.

Venec got it first. I stared at him, hearing what he'd just said but shaking my head.

"That's not possible," Nick said.

"Yeah, it is." The words were drawn out of me reluctantly, like someone else was talking with my mouth. "Or it could be." Everyone turned to look at me, then. I suspected I didn't look much better than Pietr did, honestly. I felt about the same level of shocky-cold and dizzy. It was all starting to make an ugly kind of sense, all the bits we'd seen and not recognized. "The sample we took, from the house? I think Pietr... I think the spell he used woke up more of it, and it slapped back at him."

"Woke it up? How, it's not—"

Venec lifted a hand, cutting Sharon off mid-word.

I swallowed. I didn't want to say it, but...I knew what I knew. "It's Old."

"You mean it was there before the crime, or...?"

"I mean it's Old," I repeated, trying to put enough emphasis on the word that they'd hear the capitalization, so I wouldn't have to actually spell it out.

"Old... Impossible." But Nick didn't sound convinced, and Sharon, who always knew if someone was lying, was staring at my face, her own expression stricken.

"An Old One was there? In the house? Connected to the client? But he's a Null!"

"It makes sense," Pietr said, although he didn't look happy about it. "That's the only thing that would be able to...do that."

Old Ones were legend. No, not legend, because we knew that they were real. They were just...old. Older than the Ancients, like dragons and klassvaaks. Ancient was a courtesy title, the way you used a call-name like The Roblin. Old Ones? You didn't talk about them, not even with reverence and certainly not with affection; they had no use at all for humans, every story was quite clear on that. They were few and dying, and good riddance to a bad age....

Except that, apparently, not all of them were quite gone. And maybe, and we were so very fucked, one was paying attention to human affairs. Through an intermediary, because we would have *known* if an Old One was around, but... Even once removed, the thought made us all obviously uneasy.

We had thought that The Roblin was our biggest problem?

I was suddenly all too aware of how fragile my physical and magical selves actually were, how damned... breakable we all were.

gently

I wanted to cling to that mental touch, but it was gone, casting its lighthouse-touch on us all, in turn, and then Venec turned to Pietr, focusing on that almost-more-reasonable side of the case, first. "People. One male, one female?"

"Yeah." Pietr looked stunned, as much that Venec believed him as the gender guess. Then realization hit him. "Oh, fuck. That bastard."

I got the gut-sick feeling that had to come from Venec, because it was his knowledge that drove it. The wife. And the son. Not dead, not missing. Transformed.

From the expressions of my pack mates, they were thinking the same thing.

"Wait, why are we assuming he's the bastard?" Nifty said. "I mean, he...maybe they were transformed, and he was protecting them, and..."

"I've never heard of anything even remotely like this." We all turned to find Stosser standing behind us, his expression as close to Zeus on a tear as I ever want to see. Before, he'd been worried and upset. This...this was fury.

He knew everything we knew; Venec must have told him, somehow, in the way the two of them had. Or maybe he just put two and two together and came up with seventeen. How the hell did I know what scary-brilliant brains could do?

"Magic of that sort cannot be hushed, not on a human level. If it were an accident or a threat, if he had ever tried to seek help, or find an answer, it would have been whispered about, and those whispers would have reached the Council."

"Or it would have gotten into the lonejack under-ground," Venec said, and then glared right back at Stosser. "Don't give me that, Ian. Lonejacks know as much or more than the highest Council wonk. They just don't always give a damn."

That was true, and Stosser just shook his head, the thunderbolts and static shimmering around him not di-minishing at all.

"So he knew, and kept them like that, and didn't try to change them back. He kept them on a shelf, in his office, so he could see them like that, every single damned day. Even if he didn't arrange for it, he's a bastard." Sharon summed it up neatly, still kneeling on the floor where Pietr had been. She reached up and gathered her hair back into its knot, securing it with a silver pin that looked like it could do damage in a fight. "So this robbery wasn't a theft but a kidnapping? Did they mean to rescue them? Or hurt Wells by taking them away?"

"And how did the Old One play into this? If it had been there, taken them…"

"There wouldn't be a house standing," Venec said dryly. "No, I think it's safe for us to assume that whoever was there merely left the trace of its master. Accidentally or as a warning, yet unknown."

"But that means…"

"That an Old One is somehow connected to all this. Yeah." Venec sounded about as unhappy about that as I felt.

"So what the hell do we do now?" Pietr asked, not unreasonably. We'd taken on some heavy hitters before, but this…

"We go ask the client a few pointed questions," Stosser said, in a tone that made me very glad I wasn't going to be anywhere near that questioning. Only his tight control kept every electronic device in the office from shorting out. The client had lied to us—which we were kind of getting used to, at this point—and landed Venec in the emergency room, and now we discover he was using magic to abuse his family. Stosser was all out of forgiveness, charity, or compassion.

The office got really quiet, once the Big Dogs left—Stosser bitching because there was no reason for Venec to come along, still looking like something the dog tried to drag out, and Venec grim and stubborn all the way out, refusing to let Stosser do this alone.

It was doubtful, considering the "magical defenses" crap that the client had fallen for, and how little he seemed to know about the *Cosa Nostradamus,* that he would be a real threat. The hellhound was gone, and Venec and Stosser were both forewarned and alert. Unless the client brought out the Old One itself…and Ben was right, if he did, he'd most likely be the first to go down in a bloody puddle.

But Venec wasn't taking chances, and we were glad they were both gone.

Except I really didn't want to let Venec out of my sight. Or be out of his, one or the other. It took all my self-control not to reach out and make sure that the connection between us was still there—I knew it was, the instinct was the same that drove me to dig mental hands into my own core, stroking and soothing the strands of current resting there. A security blanket, a reassurance that I wasn't undefended, or alone.

The urge annoyed the hell out of me, and quashing it felt good. For about thirty seconds.

"So what now?" Nick asked, voicing what we'd all been sort of tap-dancing around. "What the hell do *we* do now?"

"Now we wait," Sharon said grimly, getting up and stretching her legs out, toes pointed like a dancer, her sensible and yet stylish pumps badly scuffed from recent events.

She was right, unfortunately. The body-dump case was closed, to all intents and purposes, and the break-in case had morphed into something totally other. We could muck about with what we had, see if anything else got stirred up and gave us new evidence, but we had no evidence to process except the gleaning, and there wasn't enough money in the world to get me to go in there again. Everyone else seemed to feel the same way.

At the same time...nobody wanted to leave, either. I joked about the pups being a pack, but we really do tend to huddle, tail-to-nose, when the weather gets rough. I glanced at the coffee machine, and sighed when I saw that the light was out. It had gotten fried at some point during the ruckus, probably when they were working on Pietr. The fridge was probably dead too, then. They were simple machines, and usually proof against current, but...

Coffee was probably a bad idea, anyway.

"I'm going to go over the police reports again," Sharon said. "Maybe there's something in there about the dead guy, the one Venec met with the wife."

"Yeah." It was make-work, at this point, but being occupied was better than sitting here biting our cuticles until they bled, or sniping at each other.

Pietr, who I already knew had a "sleep whenever possible" mentality, took over the sofa; within ten minutes he was sound asleep and snoring lightly. Sharon picked up the case-file and settled in on the chair opposite him.

I shook my head and slipped off his shoes, and he tucked his legs underneath him like a little kid. He was probably still shocky from the effects of the spell going haywire. I studied him closely, to make sure he wasn't showing any signs of distress; he might shrug it off, but getting hit by the backlash couldn't have been pretty. I knew the spell, how it worked, and shock aside, I suspected he had gotten more than just the knowledge of what he was looking at.

Had he felt their emotions? Heard their voices? I could ask, but I wouldn't. Not unless Pietr indicated he wanted to talk about it, and I didn't think he would. Not until we had the objects back safe, and found a way to restore them to their proper, human forms.

Bored by the quiet, Nick and Nifty disappeared down the hall; I could hear voices, the sound of heavy objects being moved, and then some soft thumps that made me think they were practicing defensive moves in the large conference room.

Left to myself, I took over Stosser's office, closed the door behind me, and picked up the phone.

"Bonita. What's wrong?"

Trust a mentor to always know. I bit back a laugh that was totally inappropriate, and put my feet up on Stosser's expensive wooden desk, admiring the dull sheen of my boots. "Nothing. Okay, everything, but nothing urgent and nothing you can do anything about. I just... we haven't talked in a while, and I wanted to say hi. Did you hear we have a mischief imp in town?"

I managed to skirt over the details, making it sound more amusing than it had felt, and didn't say a damn thing about the Merge, or The Roblin, and especially not how Venec and I had set ourselves up as bait. Dancing around J always took some doing, since he was smarter than the average smart bear especially where I was concerned, and focused my mind nicely. Exactly what I'd wanted, when I called him.

When my mentor was reassured—and had wrangled a promise from me that I'd head up to Boston and have dinner with him, as soon as our cases were wrapped—I hung up the phone, and then stared at it again, the moment of quiet letting me consider lesser emergencies.

"Oh, what the hell." Taking a card out of my pocket, I dialed the number, practically holding my breath.

A man's voice answered. "Didier Gallery, how may we help you?"

"Yes. I would like to leave a message for Wren Valere, please."

There was a pause, as though the speaker was holding the phone away from his ear, and then I was clicked
through to another voice, also male, who took my message and repeated it back to me to ensure he had it right.
I thought he sounded amused. He also didn't promise
that she would get back to me.

I hoped she would. If I had to move again, The Wren's
building had felt...comfortable. And the idea of living in
the same building as one of my generation's most notable
Retrievers amused me.

I needed amusement, badly.

That done, I contemplated going out to find today's
newspaper, to look through the apartment rental ads, but
the disinclination to leave hung over me still, and instead
I fetched my notebook back from Pietr's case and went
back to Stosser's office. I wasn't sure why I went there—
there were more comfortable places to do research—but
the chair was comfortable, and nobody would be wandering by unless something urgent happened, so it seemed
as good a place as any.

The fact that Ben's usual chair was directly opposite the
desk had nothing whatsoever to do with it. What was I,
a moonstruck twelve-year-old?

I was working through my notes, notebook open in
my lap, pen clenched in my teeth, and totally lost to the
outside world, when the air in my head filled with the
heavy weight of one word.

ass

It wasn't a ping; more like a muted thought that came
from me, except I didn't think it. More like an echo,
the emotion so thick and layered that it couldn't be con-

tained. Ben was annoyed, but not angry. I was curious, but not enough to inquire. I flipped my notebook closed, though, and waited to see if anything more came along.

About five minutes later: *incoming*

That *was* a ping, and it was directed at me, as though he knew I was in the office—he probably did. I had just enough time to get my feet off the desk and my ass out of the chair before the Big Dogs Translocated into the office.

They looked...tired. Stosser's hair was staticky again, like he was barely holding his core quiet, and Venec—

I didn't think; I don't think I could think. I moved around the desk and slipped my arms around him, resting my head against his chest, feeling his heart beating, slow and hard.

I'm not a caretaker, damn it; I was raised to be self-sufficient, and I expect everyone else to be, too. But the pain in his eyes was more than I could bear.

There was a hesitation, and then his arms came up around me, resting loosely across my shoulders. It wasn't a hug, but he wasn't rejecting the comfort, either. We leaned against each other, not saying anything, just breathing.

Whatever they had done, whatever they had heard, I knew I didn't want to know. But the job was about knowing. We were the investigators, the witnesses-after-the-fact. The ones who didn't look away.

Thankfully, both Big Dogs seemed willing to just let it be, for a moment. I let Benjamin's warmth under my hands soothe me, and tried to send it back into him, knowing that he was blocking me, holding his walls firm, and The Roblin be damned. He didn't want me to see what he had done.

The fact that Venec could be a badass wasn't news to me. If he had done something that was hard by his standards...it was only what was needful and necessary. But I'd be just as thankful not having it in my own brain, yeah.

"He had them transmuted." Stosser's voice, like it was coming from far away, through a stone tunnel. "The watch, his son. The dagger..."

"His wife. Christine." Ben's voice was hard and ragged, like a cold wind. The moment he spoke I could feel the anger and the frustration in him, held tight against his spine like it was all that was holding him upright. He had no regret for the way he'd gotten the news out of our former client—and he was a *former* client, I knew that instantly.

Even without the Merge, I understood why Ben was reacting the way he was. Years ago, he had worked for the woman. He had met her, taken responsibility for finding her son. He was thinking that if he'd been better at his job, been able to do what was needed, seen the danger she was in, they'd both still be human, be free, right now.

Being Venec, there was no way he could be thinking anything else.

I wanted to reassure him, to tell him that he'd done the job he was hired to do, that he'd had no idea the danger the woman and her son were really in. Thankfully, the Merge didn't make me stupid. He knew all that, and he still felt responsible. I didn't understand it, but I understood him, if that made any sense.

Whatever had happened between then and now, if Wells had always been batshit insane or something had caused him to totally lose his shit and dabble in things even the most high-res Talent would blanch at, it didn't matter. I'd hoped... I don't know what I'd hoped. That the objects had been his parents, maybe, gone willingly into another form rather than die of old age. That they'd been volunteers, trapped in an experiment gone wrong, and the client was safeguarding them. Anything but this.

Because however Wells had managed to do this, whatever price he had paid, it was a crime worse than any I'd ever heard of, one of the prime and undeniable crimes of the *Cosa Nostradamus:* to remove free will from another. Talent or Null, it didn't matter.

And how it had been done—all the evidence we had suggested that he had done it by bargaining with an Old One, or an agent of an Old One. God. Of all the arrogant, oblivious stupidity... And had he found it, or had it found him? I wasn't sure which thought was more distressing.

No, wait: I knew.

The hard beat of Venec's heart was slowing to a softer thump, and I slid away from him as discreetly as I could, before he suddenly realized what he'd allowed and pulled back first. I'd offered; I wanted to be the one to control when it ended.

Stosser, thankfully, didn't say anything, or even look at us; he might be staring at the far wall, but his attention was somewhere else entirely.

"You think the...whoever cast the spells, came to take them back?" I had to ask.

"We know so." Stosser again. Now that the tableau had been broken, he moved, as well, sitting behind his desk like a guy twenty years older. I'd only ever seen the boss so beat-down once before, when a teenager died in our building, because of something his little sister did. "Apparently, a few years back, Wells had been browsing for someone to help him with a domestic problem."

"The problem of a wife who wanted to leave him, and a son who didn't want to listen to dear old dad," Venec interjected, his voice still low and bitter.

"And he found an Old One?" Most people, Talent or Null, who ran across one of the old races, would have backed away as fast and as quiet as they could, and prayed that it didn't follow. But it was better than an Old One actively trolling for humans.

"Wells has no idea who the source of the original spell was," Stosser went on. "He only spoke with a magician."

In other words, Wells was an idiot. But if nothing else, we knew now who had sold Wells his so-called magical protections. "Magician" was a damning phrase, in the *Cosa*. It meant someone who was still using old magics more than current, relying on tricks, and supplementing their own natural core by deals with the fatae, just like the old tales. A magician couldn't shape or form a transformation spell; it was totally beyond their capabilities. Had he made a deal with an Old One for power? Wow, talk about a classic Bad Idea. And then to turn around and deal with Nulls, who had no idea what they were doing or getting into? Lovely.

"The spells were maintained on a regular basis, with a payment due every season-change." Traditional old magics ritual bullshit. "Wells...defaulted on the payments. Several of them, in fact."

I went still. I'd once had passing contact with a cave dragon, the loan sharks of the *Cosa Nostradamus*. It had been a misunderstanding, and he'd been only pleasant to me, all things considered, but just the memory of that glare directed at me was enough to make me pay my bills on time even now. Cave dragons were short-tempered when it came to breaking your bond. How much worse...

"What happened?"

"What do you think?" Ben's voice was way too calm. "The magician came, with what sounds like a hell spawn pet, jaws like a sabertooth, and demanded payment. Wells refused—he felt that he had paid long enough."

Wells was damn lucky he was still intact and breathing. The *Cosa Nostradamus* wasn't exactly invisible—we were part of the day-to-day world, and enough people knew about us, interacted with us on a daily basis, so I guess I'd gotten used to them knowing enough to stay out of trouble. It wasn't difficult. Like I'd told Nick more than a year ago—read your fairy tales; everything you need to know to stay clean is right there.

Nobody ever read Wells fairy tales when he was a kid, clearly.

"I assume the goon was what tore the place up." You did not fuck with hell spawn. Ever. They were the bad-ass creatures hellhounds had been bred down—way down—from.

"The magician...?" I let the question trail off, not sure how to phrase it.

Venec answered me. "The name went to an empty storefront. Whoever and wherever our guy might have been, he's in the wind, now."

Or gone, in a more permanent fashion. No loss whatsoever to the world. And whoever, or whatever he had been working for would now be impossible to find; that went without saying. I wasn't sure even Stosser was angry enough to go after an Old One, no matter how many claws it had in the modern world. If we didn't bother it, maybe it would go bother someone else.

Even the Big Dogs knew there was only so much we could bite off at a time.

I tried not to think about the scrapings in the conference room, and refocused on what we could handle. "And Wells called us to investigate, when he already knew damn well what had happened?"

"He's used to being in control," Stosser said dryly. "He thought he could still control the game, get his toys back without admitting anything, and without having to pay the fees, in the future."

Venec's dark eyes looked at the far wall, his face expressionless. "Yeah. He knows better now."

I was surprised and a little alarmed by the surge of vicious satisfaction I felt at those words, until I realized that it was coming from Venec, not me. All right. My Dog was a fierce bastard. I knew that.

And yeah, I knew what I'd just thought, and how possessive it sounded, and I'd deal with that later, when the walls were all the way up and we had time to breathe. If the barn door was open and the horse was gone…well, neither Zaki nor J had raised a dummy. I'd deal with it then.

"So what now?" I asked.

Venec looked at me like he couldn't believe I'd actually asked that question.

"Now, we get them back."

Oh. Right. Of course.

thirteen

"It's too dangerous." Nifty crossed his arms and looked… well, like a large dark wall of muscle, which was what he was. "I get what our job is, and I get what our obligations are, but what the *hell* do you think we're going to be able to do against an Old One? Seriously. You're damn good, Ian, ain't nobody denying that. All of us together, we've got a decent level of firepower. We're a damn good team—at investigating and discovering. That isn't going to mean crap, here."

"We don't even know the level of Old One," Sharon said, not quite so outwardly defiant, but clearly set against the plan, such as it was. The alphas of the pack, facing off against the Big Dogs. It was fascinating, if not exactly what I wanted to be dealing with, right now. "No idea as to how much power it actually holds, what its intentions are. The last time an Old One was actually involved in human affairs was, what, 1917?"

"It was 1924, actually."

Sharon accepted my correction with a tip of her chin,

indicating—rightfully—that the difference in years didn't mean squat. "Our information about them is hearsay and hundred-year-old history. If this is an Old One…"

"After a hundred years, what's the real chance that it is?" Lou asked, tapping her pen thoughtfully against the table. The noise was soft, but annoying. "I mean, I know what Bonnie and Pietr felt, but all we know is that it's powerful enough to transmutate…."

"That's not a Talent skill set," Pietr said. "Not s'far as I've ever heard or read, anyway. All the alchemists in the world never tipped to the secret."

"Rumpelstiltskin," I said quietly. Straw into gold. Borrow a fatae's ability and you could do things humans only dreamed of. You made your promise and you paid your price. If you kept to the bargain, all ended well. But humans seemed almost incapable of keeping their bargains.

"So it might be a fatae?"

"What do you think Old Ones are, Nick?" I asked, and was proud of the fact that I neither rolled my eyes nor let anything other than matter-of-factness into my voice. Seriously, was I the only one with a mentor who taught them anything?

It was closing in on midnight, we'd been at this all night, and I felt unutterably weary, as though the entire week of stress was catching up with me all at once, and wanted nothing more than to ditch this scene for a nice long soak in a power plant. That wasn't going to happen anytime soon, though. Someday the lectures Venec kept giving about topping off our cores was going to sink in with me, so I didn't get caught short like this.

"But fatae don't use magic."

Fatae didn't use magic; they were magic. That was why they were able to disappear, to change form, to fly, to create glamour, and live far longer than we frail mortals. But those were all things they did of themselves, not projecting onto others, or even creating something separate. The fatae needed humans—Talent—to actually work magic, to control and shape current. It took something more, to do this. The miller's beautiful daughter had made a bargain with an Old One, who worked straw into gold…and then she reneged on the deal, refusing to give up her infant when the Old One came to claim it.

Read the story today, and she was clever enough to come out on top. That was where stories were different than real life: you could rewrite the ending, over the years, until it came out happy.

Stosser took up the lecture-voice. "Old Ones are like the fatae we know like…dinosaurs are like chickens."

"Old ones old ones beware the really really old ones," the refrain to one of the stories went, and it was true. They were the fatae who had been around since forever, since when humans were learning how to save fire, and most of the other breeds were hiding in trees or lurking in bogs, waiting for something edible to come along. We'd grown up since then, but we were no match for the masters of old, their memories dark and filled with resentment. All we could do was hope that they left us alone, that the worst we ever saw were the Ancients, who mostly held no malice toward us.

There was something there, in that thought, and part of me wanted to follow after it, but the conversation was moving on and I needed to focus there. I tucked the story behind my ear, and brought myself back to the table.

Apparently, they'd all come to terms with the fact that it was an Old One of some sort—no shit, guys—and now the argument was raging over what the hell we were supposed to do about it.

Which was pretty much where we'd been all night.

"Seriously," Nifty repeated again. "How are we going to make…anything that powerful cough up two objects it probably thinks it reclaimed in fair terms? We just don't have that kind of juice, and anyone who did…we'd have to convince them to do it out of the, what, goodness of their own hearts?"

"Or the guilt in them," Stosser said, like Nifty had just given him an idea.

Venec shot him a look that went from curious to annoyed to worried, like the strobe of a flashing light, 1-2-3. "Ian, no."

"It will work."

"It's insane." Venec was using the tone of voice that normally ended discussions, all dark and jagged, like lava rock that might not be entirely cooled. "Also, incredibly stupid."

Stosser leaned back, tugged at the end of his long flame-colored ponytail, and lifted his elegant eyebrows at his partner with exaggerated curiosity. His voice, by contrast, was mild, almost disinterested. "You have another idea? Other than charging in there on your own, like a time-delayed White Knight to put right what you think you should have solved before it happened?"

Oh, boy. Usually the Big Dogs took their squabbles

private. This one was out in full display. I wanted to kick Stosser for being such an ass—guilt over a failed sense of responsibility had gotten Venec's throat nearly torn out, for chrissakes...you had to add onto it? But I kept my mouth shut and my fingers curled into the arm of my chair. Not my fight.

"Ah..." Nifty shut his mouth with a snap—someone had kicked him under the table to tell him to shut up.

"You want this done?" Stosser didn't even look at Nifty, probably hadn't even heard him. "Then that's how it will get done. Lawrence is right...we don't have enough firepower to compel, and there's no time for me to build a consensus. Isn't that the argument you would make? Do it now, not wait, and mumble our way through protocol?"

It felt like a direct quote, and from the way Venec's eyes stormed up, I knew it was his, used against him.

"Let me go with you, then."

"No." Stosser might have considered the idea, but if so it was only for a second, then he shook his head. "You two in the same room makes things worse, not better."

"Oh, fuck," Nick said, not quite under his breath, and I echoed that, more quietly. There was only one person I could think of who was a powerful Talent, whom Stosser could influence that quickly, and whom Venec hated— and hated him in return.

Aden Stosser, Ian's sister.

The way Ben accepted Ian's words, I knew I was right. "You still shouldn't go alone."

Whatever their plan was, I already knew I didn't like it. Not if it involved Aden Stosser. From the look on everyone else's faces, they were of like mind. Nifty, though, unfolded his arms and nodded. "Take Pietr with you. He's unobtrusive, but sneaky. If you need backup, he'll do, without setting her off."

I figured Stosser would brush off the suggestion, but he looked at Venec, who gave a tight little nod. "He's decent with his protections, and can double-up a Translocation. Any help you need, it's not going to involve bulk or muscle."

The slur on Pietr's build went unanswered; I knew full well Pietr had a deceptive strength, and Stosser—who had worked with us all, closely—knew the same, if for different reasons. I refused to believe that Ben was jealous; we'd agreed he had no cause or right to be jealous, but…it sure felt like jealousy, to me.

It wasn't funny, nothing about any of this was funny; but when I looked up, Pietr had a warm humor in his eyes that meant he was amused, even if I wasn't.

I scowled at him, and he laughed. It was totally inappropriate, and stupid, and lightened the mood in the entire room, just a little.

"Don't feel left out, Torres." Venec pointed at me, then at Nick, and there was a look in his eye that was all Big Dog. "I have a job for you two, too."

Aden Stosser's apartment had a view that would have cost a fortune, if she were actually paying for it. Ian recognized the view immediately, having spent much of his childhood visiting his mother's sister, a long-term seated member of the Midwest Council. Pietr gawked for a full ten seconds after arrival, then brought himself back to business. In a crisis situation, that might have been enough to get him killed.

Ian declined to rebuke him for it; this was neither the time nor the place, and nobody was going to open fire on them. Probably.

"This is unexpected."

Aden had just walked out of the kitchen, holding a mug of something in her hands, and looking completely unsurprised. The two of them had never been able to sneak up on each other, despite countless attempts during their youth. Their parents had encouraged that behavior; had encouraged all their competition. That might be why, Ian thought not for the first time, they had instead become so close.

"We need your help." He saw her open her mouth to start their usual bickering, and overrode whatever she was going to say. "This isn't negotiable, and it's not in exchange for anything else down the road."

"And I'm going to agree, why?" Aden lifted the mug to her mouth and took a deliberate sip, projecting a mood of utter unconcern.

"Because I'm asking you. And because you won't be able to resist."

Beside him, Pietr drew in his breath: if they were going to have to do anything, this was when.

Current surged in the room, filling the air with a dry crackle, and Pietr found himself categorizing it almost automatically: Stosser's signature, clearly defined and recognizable, plus another, less recognizable but equal in strength and showing definite similarities in patterns.

"Look at that," Pietr said, almost to himself. "If I could

map it, build a proof that would establish familial—or at
least lines of mentoring—similarities…"

Ian almost laughed, but never took his eyes off his
sister, a more delicate, darker-flame mirror of his own
lanky build. "Research later."

"Assuming I agree," Aden said, "what exactly do you
need me for, that I will find so…fascinating?"

Ian matched her dry, casual tone. "We're going to hi-
jack an Old One."

Pietr really, really did not like the way Aden Stosser's
expression lit up at her brother's words.

"You have my utmost, and fascinated, attention," she
said.

An hour later, they had cleared the main living room
area by dint of shoving the furniture back, and drawn
the proper design on the gleaming hardwood floors with
liquid detergent.

"Aunt Madeline is going to kill us," Aden said with
satisfaction, looking at the chemicals marring the finish.

"That's assuming the Old One doesn't kill us first. In
which case, she can deal with getting rid of it when she
comes home and finds it in residence instead of you."

"Oh, that's a lovely thought." Aden's smile was decid-
edly cold.

Pietr just shook his head, trying to stay low and useful, finishing the design. It looked, at first glance, like a
pentagram, but if you switched into mage-sight it glim-
mered almost like a 3-D projection, displaying a deeper
outline of a six-pointed star underneath, and below that,
an eight-pointed one. Around it, there was a larger circle,
which they hoped would be protection enough to keep

The Roblin, if it followed them hoping to cause more trouble, from being able to interfere.

In theory.

"All right. This is either going to work, or it isn't. Pietr, go stand by the door. In the archway. Just in case."

"If something goes wrong and we're sucked into the mythical vortex, that's not going to save him," Aden said, clearly enjoying herself.

"Doorways have their own protection. It might give him enough time to Translocate back to the office." Stosser was so matter of fact, you might have thought they were discussing running out of staples. Pietr shook his head, and went to stand the proscribed distance away.

"Fine. Let's do this. If we don't get killed, I have theater plans tonight."

Most modern magic had little ceremony; the effort went into shaping your current, not impressing the neighbors. Stosser's plan involved mixing a dash of old stories with a large dose of improvisation, and hoping it would work. The siblings sat in the center of the markings, hands resting on their knees, and slipped into fugue-state.

The room was filled with a deep red glow, as though they were underwater, under strobe lights. Aden's expression was peaceful, but there was a small smile on the corner of her lips that someone who didn't know her well might think was innocent excitement.

Stosser gave Pietr one last look, which the pup returned with a single nod of his head—don't worry about me, boss, I'm good—and settled into the ritual.

"We bring a question you hold the answer to, oh eldest of the cousins."

Aden picked up the chant, her voice an octave above Ian's, but the inflection and cadence otherwise identical. "We are respectful of your worth, oh eldest of the cousins, and ask that you favor us with your attention, for this brief instant of time."

Then, both voices together: "Forgive us our need, oh eldest of cousins, and remember the delicate thread that binds us all."

The red-tinged air shivered slightly, like a heat mirage, then thickened, becoming more of a fog. They could still see each other, across the distance of the ritual markings, but not well enough to determine expressions or make out details beyond—the room outside of the markings might as well have disappeared.

For all they knew, it had.

"We bring you a question, oh eldest of the cousins," Ian repeated, softening each word so that it blurred as it left his mouth, inviting visitation, even as he kept a hard control over his core; if the Old One tried anything, he would be ready and able to defend himself, even though it would inevitably be futile.

All they could do was hope that the binding within the markings and the spell itself restrained it, and that Pietr would be able to escape, unscathed.

YES.

The voice filled the space, although none of them would swear that the word had actually been spoken out loud or been whispered inside their heads. It was neither male nor female, high or low, but pervasive, and slightly metallic.

Ian touched his core, bringing up the glamour that

made him such a persuasive speaker, at the same time careful to let the Old One know what he was doing, offering no secrets, no attempts to beguile, and in doing so, flattering the Old One—or amusing it—into doing what he wanted.

Ideally.

"We would speak to you of the human named Wells, and the objects that your minions took from his dwelling place…."

Crickets were loud, in the middle of the night, but surprisingly soothing.

Although I'd been annoyed at what sounded like a crap assignment, it was better than sitting in the office worrying about what was going on wherever Stosser and Pietr had gone off to, or trying to convince Venec to go away and rest, the way the doctor had told him to. And it wasn't too bad, actually. We were sitting on the front porch of the little country house Wells was using as a base of business operations while the workers were repairing the damage to the place in the city; it was a large cottage, really, but the amenities, while rustic, were still first-class. And apparently, despite the Big Dog's interrogation, he had no idea we were on to him yet, because he accepted Venec's story that we were there as added protection, and didn't seem to suspect we were actually his jailers.

I suppose that kind of arrogance had to go with the personality that thought nothing of locking away his wife and son like damned keepsakes, and then calling us in to find them when they were stolen.

After a period of polite chitchat to the backdrop of the

crickets, he stood up, all boardroom grace and manners. "You'll excuse me? I have a conference call to Japan that I need to make."

"Sure, go ahead," Nick said. The porch was far enough away from the office on the second floor that even if we had to pull up a sudden surge of current, it probably wouldn't disrupt his call. Probably. And I really doubted we'd have to do anything magical at all: The cottage was set back from the road, with a clear view in either direction thanks to the sloping lawn, and the back of the house was set against a stone hill that went straight up about forty feet. If anyone came our way, we'd grab Wells and run like hell, Translocating only if needful. Wells already knew too damn much about Talent for a guy without any visible moral grounding, and he was the sort to lust after the ability to Translocate in a really unhealthy way.

I listened to the sound of his feet going up the carpeted stair—a not-terribly-expensive Berber weave that was just the right tone of wealthy-casual for a cottage—and then turned back to my partner. "You think we should be listening in on him?"

Nick leaned back in his chair, his feet up on the footstool. "Already bugged the place, while you were checking the perimeter."

I nodded, satisfied. When he said bugged he meant literally—a lovely bit of set-magic that cost a small fortune, but were difficult even for Talent to find, if they weren't looking specifically for it. If they heard a significant phrase or series of words, they'd let Nick know. I thought they were creepy as hell, myself, but you made do with what you had. Someday I'd come up with a more elegant solution. Someday. I was starting to get a really long "someday" list.

"So." Nick looked down at his coffee mug and then back at me. When I'd first met him, his short build and placid brown eyes had almost fooled me into not taking him seriously, the same way I'd pegged Nifty for a muscle-bound goon. I knew better, the moment they opened their mouths, and now not even trained dissembling could hide the sharp brain behind those eyes. "You and Venec."

My instinctive reaction was "what me and Venec?" But it was a little—a lot—too late for that now.

There was the instinctive—and annoying—reach for Venec; the walls were there, but thin, and then they dropped suddenly on his part, and I recoiled a little from the unexpectedness of it, like thinking the shower was warm when the water was actually ice-cold. What the hell?

No time to worry what the Big Dog was up to; Nick was looking at me, waiting for an answer.

"Yeah." I'd known this was coming since we got sent off together, the first chance Nick's had to corner me, and he wasn't the type to waste opportunity.

We'd been friends from the first day, but we'd never been more than friends and coworkers, never would be, even though he'd flirted like crazy at first. He wasn't a confidant, the way Pietr was, but he might be my best friend in the office, and I'd been treating him like shit the past few months, while Venec and I danced around all this, figuring our deal out…. And now he was going to ask what was up, and I had no idea what to tell him.

Nick had obviously taken lessons from Sharon, because he went in with a scalpel. "You sleeping with him?"

"No."

"You going to?"

That was the tough question, wasn't it? Me, who never had to take long to decide one way or the other... "I don't know. It's...complicated."

"Sleeping with the boss is kinda tacky."

"Yeah. Only it's not just that. There's stuff we need to deal with."

"Cause of that Merge thing."

"Yeah." Understatement of the year. We'd told them a little, not everything, but my pack mates would have done their own research, and pooled notes.

Nick scrunched his face at me, and for a minute I saw the terrible ten-year-old he must have been. "You...don't want it?"

I widened my eyes back at his expression, channeling my own not-so-inner ten-year-old for a moment. "Would you?"

"I..." Nick played the dumb bunny sometimes, but he wasn't, not by a long shot. He stopped to think about his answer. "No. Not really. Talk about awkward. Does it work between two guys? I mean, straight guys?"

I laughed, the way he'd probably meant me to. "I don't know. No reason why it would. Or wouldn't. It's about magic..." My voice trailed off. It was about magic, and passing that magic along, maybe. That was Venec's theory, from what his mentor told him. Current looking to ground along the bloodlines. Genetics. There was still a big hullaballoo over if Talent was genetic or not; it ran in families, but not always, and could go dormant for generations, or appear out of nowhere, and nobody'd ever found a gene that identified current-use, although there'd been a lot of quietly funded studies done, according to J. Even before they knew what genes were, there were always people who wanted to know the origins of power.

If people found out, beyond the pack…there would be a line of folk wanting to pick us apart. And even more who would want to make me into a broodmare.

I loved kids. I just hadn't been planning on even thinking about having any for…a long time, yet.

Nick, though, had moved on to another question. "How long have you known about this?"

That question was a hell of a lot easier to answer. "Since the ki-rin case."

Nick leaned back and whistled between his teeth, softly. That had been more than a few months. I wondered if he was putting pieces together, or wondering why he'd not noticed. "And before that?"

"Before that I thought he was hot but annoying. No, wait, I *still* think that he's hot and annoying."

And this time it was Nick who laughed, the way I'd meant him to.

"So, you want to sleep with him, but you can't sleep with him 'cause the job thing…awwwkward. And it's not like you've been the poster child for self-control on that front, but I'm guessing this thing also makes you not want to go wandering, no matter how pretty the trail?"

He was damned close to the truth on that. I wasn't sure I could work up enough interest in anyone else to wander, and the one thing I'd always demanded, even when I'd been juggling two or three lovers, was a real, emotional attraction. And honesty. "Hi, you're hot, but I have this weird bond thing with someone else that's always going to come first...." Probably not going to go over well.

"And he, I presume, thinks you're hot, too, cause he's breathing and hetero male, and he practically sizzles when he's yelling at you, which is Venec's way of emotional communication," Nick finished.

"Nicely delineated, Shune. And your conclusions, having evaluated the available evidence?" I kept my tone light, but his words had burned me a little, left me feeling more raw than I was comfortable with. It mattered what he thought; it mattered what he concluded.

It mattered a lot.

There was a silence. It wasn't a comfortable silence, but I didn't find myself twitching, either. To fill the time while I waited, I let myself listen to the hum of electricity within the house, letting it touch me gently, following the traces out along the wires, and deep into the ground. Wild current and man-made... I much preferred the refined, clarified man-made that ran alongside electricity, but knowing that it was there in the raw form, too, was comforting. If we needed it... I really, really hoped that we wouldn't.

When Nick finally did speak, his voice was as serious as I'd ever heard, this man who joked to keep the boogey monsters at bay. "I was worried, at first. We all were. I mean, it took us months to figure out who went where, y'know?"

I remembered. Pack politics had been dicey, during

training, and even after. It wasn't until the organ-leggers job that we really started to feel properly shaken down. And that was when it had really hit me, this Merge thing, and what it was doing to me. I hadn't thought, at the time, what it might also be doing to the rest of the team.

"We all knew you had the hots for him. Teasing you…didn't make dealing with this easier, did it? If we'd known how serious it was. Or that he… Christ, he does feel the same way, doesn't he?"

And in that instant, Nick went from the coolly calculating pup to aggressively protective little brother, ready to beat up on the boy who didn't appreciate his sister.

"What, annoyed, irritated, frustrated, and really pissed off about the entire thing? Yeah, that sums it up pretty well." I let go of the tendrils of current, letting them slip away like sunbeams at dusk, and spread my fingers palm-up on my lap, as though I could still see traces of it against my skin. "He's better at repressing it, though."

I wasn't used to repressing anything. At all. I dealt with it, I explored it, I figured it out, and then I moved on.

"I'm sorry." For mocking you, for not realizing, for what you're going through, for not being helpful, all in those two words. "It's tougher on you than it is on us, isn't it? I mean, you're juggling all this shit, and worrying about how we're going to react to it, and we're only worrying about how it's going to affect us, if Venec's going to start playing favorites, or acting weird, or we're going to walk in on mad monkey-sex in the conference room." He looked really pained at that. "Could you maybe warn us if you're going to do that? A sock on the doorknob or something?"

"I really don't think that's going to be an issue, Nicky. But yeah, I promise." I frowned, distracted. "Did you feel that?"

"Feel what?"

I held up a hand, not to silence him, but to show the current-traces still resting against my skin; to a Talent it looked like 3-D veins, pulsing greenly against my skin.

"I was testing the wild current around here," I said, almost whispering, although there was no need. Probably. "And then I felt it...can you pick it up?"

I felt him slide into fugue-state next to me, and followed. Stalking current was like trying to move through a room thick-hung with wind chimes; if you brushed one too closely, it would set off a musical chain reaction, scaring away whatever was on the other side of the room.

Or, worse thought, *not* scaring it away.

Years ago, I'd gone snorkeling in Hawaii, and swum into the huge school of gorgeously colored fish. The front of my brain had been going all ooh and aah, but at the back of my brain the thought had come: what if something was diving into the school from the other side? What if that something had teeth—and wouldn't mind eating something larger than finger-length fishlings?

That was how I felt right then, even before it grabbed me.

The shark image was all wrong. This was like being nailed by an octopus, an eight-armed thing with tentacles that dug into you and held on like a thousand tiny grappling hooks that stung like antiseptic on an open wound. I could feel Nick's current-signature flowing over me, surging into where the hooks met magic-skin and melting them away as fast as they were placed, but he was barely keeping up.

Hold.

The thought came, cold and dark and deeper than anything human could manage. Nick ignored it, flowing onto the next series of hooks.

Hold it said again, and the hooks started to untangle themselves. I let out a tiny sigh of relief, resisting the urge to rub my physical—and untouched—arms in reaction.

You are the dogs of the Flame?

The what of the who?

An image came, of current strung out long and bright, the orange-red color a dead giveaway, the magical interpretation of Stosser's unmistakable ponytail. My first image of him, dressed all in black, his hair loose, had been of a satanic candle, too.

Oh. "Yes," I told the voice, feeling Nick tense beside me, ready in case that turned out to be a bad answer. "We're pups."

We are to exchange.

The voice opened—a door? A drawer?—and the scene flowed out and into our memories.

An overhead view of a large room, lit by a red glow that didn't seem to come from anywhere in particular. I didn't recognize it, but there was a sense of familiarity, anyway, as though one or more of the figures below knew it well. The mental camera angle swooped in, and the mike went live.

"They are not objects. They are people. You know this, you helped transform them." If you knew Stosser, you could tell that he was wildly curious about how the

Old One had accomplished that, but knew better than to ask. That was a trap alchemists used to fall into regularly, and the truth was that no human could manage it. Not without paying a price our boss was too smart to offer. I hoped.

The human failed his agreement. They are mine.

The voice that had caught me; it was the same entity that was arguing with Stosser. Okay, I'd known that, I guess, but the knowing sent a cold prickle into every inch of my skin.

"You don't want them." Stosser's voice again, an absolute certainty replacing the curiosity.

The doing was mine. The agreement in my holding. The objects were surety against payment. The human failed to pay.

Stosser's comprehension became ours: the voice we were dealing with was tied to the rules of the agreement, just the same as Wells. We weren't dealing with an all-powerful Old One here, not directly. Or it was, but not all of it, an offshoot still tangled with the world, while the rest of it slept? Maybe: it was still old, and powerful, and scary as hell, but not going to rip the city apart if we pissed it off.

Probably.

Stosser shook that off, and went back to his argument, gathering steam as he went. "Your agreement is valid. Yet. The objects are humans. They contain souls. An older law than your agreement says that you may not take a soul without its permission."

There was a silence, as though the other was searching through pages of parchment, looking for the relevant clause.

This is true. But they were pledged as surety. The balance must be maintained.

First rule: there's a price for everything. I could feel the pressure build, and knew what Stosser was going to say, even as I reached—far too late, since this was a memory, not reality—to stop him.

"Then take me, instead. Let them go, the unwilling souls, and take me in their place."

The door closed, the drawer slid shut, and I was back in my own head again, still staring at the veins of current pulsing on my skin. Now, though, I could follow them into the ground, deep into the stone, to where the creature waited. I didn't know what it was, but I could taste Ian Stosser within it, waiting. Contained. I hadn't known anything could contain Ian Stosser.

"He agreed to it," Nick said, following my thoughts, or simply airing his own conclusions along the same path. "He's held by the agreement."

The Flame burns me; restless and…annoying.

I stifled a totally inappropriate grin at the almost aggrieved tone in the creature's voice, and waited. Something had sent the creature here; sounded like we were about to find out what. Hopefully, it involved getting the boss out of hock.

He suggested a new trade, to please us both, and put final paid on the debt. *We are to exchange for the one in your holding, who owed the original payment.*

I got the feeling, suddenly, that the payment had not been in cash, and shuddered.

You will do this.

It wasn't a question. Nick and I exchanged a glance,

and I could see the same question in his expression as was inevitably setting on mine: How the hell were we supposed to manage that?

"Go get him," I said to Nick. "Tell him...we've got the guy who stole his stuff here. He'll either come, or he'll run. If he runs, drag him back. And don't bother being too careful with him, either."

You couldn't send an unwilling being into this sort of agreement, but this guy had made like a pack rat with two human lives, presumably against their will. I was done playing nice-nice with him. The hell with holding the facts up to light: we were the only ones who could fix this, and we had to do it, now. Somehow.

It was only a couple of minutes later that Nick returned, holding Wells firmly by the ear. Literally—he had the guy in a gentle headlock—and magically, as I could sense the loop of current around Wells's neck. Probably not approved methodology, but we'd gone a bit beyond that.

Wells looked around, like expecting to be confronted with something, and visibly relaxed when it was just us on the porch.

"He tried to run?"

"Like a bunny."

I tsked sadly.

"This him?" I asked the voice, still waiting in the rocks deep below us. I needed confirmation before I took the next step.

Yes.

The client didn't flinch; he couldn't hear our visitor. Interesting. I wondered if that was intentional on our visitor's part, or not. Not that it mattered; I'd just have to explain it in small words.

First, though… "Why did you do it?" I wasn't sure it mattered, but I'd always been curious about the why as much as the who and the how. "How could you do that?" When he looked at me blankly, I elaborated. "Your wife, and your son. Yeah, we know. You took away their lives. You turned them into objects, inanimate possessions. Why?"

He stared at me, his eyes going cold, all hints of the genial host fading, and I understood, and felt stupid for not getting it, before. Venec had known; that's why he'd been hired, the first time. Why he was so angry at himself for not following up on them, after. "That's all they ever were to you, anyway, weren't they? Things that made you look better, things you *owned*."

"They belonged with me," he said, and he didn't sound like a power-mad monster; more like a man who'd been told his team sucked; sulky and belligerent. "They belonged here, not out there. I was taking care of them, protecting them."

"Yeah, well, you should have kept paying for their upkeep then," Nick said, before I could even really process what that bastard had just said. "'Cause we bought your marker, and they're ours now."

Wells's eye brightened, and he tried to stand up in Nick's hold. "You have them back? Oh, excellent! You really are as good as your reputation. There might even be a bonus if—"

"Wow." I thought I was going to be sick. "You really don't get it, do you?"

"Oh, he gets it," Nick said, giving him a gentle shake. "He gets it completely. He just doesn't know that we get it, too. They're free, you bastard."

Actually, we didn't know if they were free, yet, or still stuck in their object-form. If the latter, hopefully Stosser would be able to do something about that, once he got free, himself. Which was the point of this little confab.

"You defaulted on your payment," I said, turning to stare into his face, as grim as I could manage, which right now was pretty grim. "And guess who's here to collect?"

"But...you took them back."

"No, we bought them back," I corrected him, Stosser's plan unfolding in my brain, even without Venec's prompting. "And as per our contract with you, any and all expenses incurred in the execution of our job are paid in full by the client." I smiled, not sweetly. "Guess what just came due?"

His eyes flickered back and forth, then tried to roll back in his head, like they were trying to escape. "You can't do this!"

"You signed the agreement," Nick said.

"I don't have them in my possession! You haven't given them back yet!"

Damn. And also, damn. I wasn't a lawyer or a Council scholar, but that sounded like it was enough of a loophole to get him off.

venec?

With the barriers down, he returned my ping almost immediately.

bit busy here Grumbly dog, distracted and worried.

us too. we have a Situation

fourteen

The contact with Bonnie was brief but thorough, summing up her Situation in the time it took her to think it. Ben was almost grateful to the Merge; trying to explain it all via pings would have been tiresome, and distracting at a time he needed to focus here-and-now.

Fortunately, he wasn't working alone. "Hold up a minute," he said to Nifty. The pup's shoulders lowered, but he didn't let go of the hold he had on the two figures, one in each hard hand, and outside the barrier, in the larger, shadowy space of the garage, Sharon and Lou waited, specially modified stun-sticks locked and loaded in case the warding failed.

"Pull yourself together," Venec told The Roblin. "I have a deal for you."

The Roblin stopped struggling, and the two forms slid together, merging back into one, a gnarled, gray-skinned figure, like tree limbs bound over in badly tanned hide. Venec wondered, idly, how many times it could split like that, and if they each caused equal amounts of trouble, or if it diminished geometrically with each split.

He suspected he wouldn't ever get an answer to that.

"Let it go, Lawrence."

"What?" The pup was moderately outraged. "After the crap we went through—"

"Let it go. It's not going anywhere. Not so long as I have its attention—and interest. Right?"

The gnarled, gray-skinned figure folded its thick arms across its chest, and glared at the human. "But only so long as you are of interest," it said, in a voice to match its form, scratchy and bitter.

Venec nodded at Nifty, who reluctantly released his grip on the imp's shoulders, stepping back a half pace; still within reach if the imp tried to do anything.

They could practically see the fatae testing the wardings again, and knew when it determined that they were still holding.

The garage was cold and damp, but this late at night—or early in the morning—the only other people around were the two guys in the cashier's box at ground level, and they weren't going to come out no matter what noises they heard.

The moment Bonnie and Nick had Translocated out—in a moment of intense frustration that he had to send them out, splitting the team at a time when his every instinct was to gather them together, creating a barrier against all possible threats—Venec had known how to trap the imp.

With minimal instructions to the rest of the pack, he had headed out across town, shrugging into his jacket, letting himself think—no, not think but *feel* intensely about Bonnie, and how frustrating she was. His current swarmed around that thought, the Merge building and intensifying his emotion, almost but not quite reaching the point of him losing control, until the cab's meter stopped working with a little whimper of shorted-out protest, and he had to get out a block early, shoving a handful of bills at the driver, and walk the rest of the way to the garage where his bike was stored. The streets were empty, at this hour, and he was painfully aware of the streetlights that died as he passed underneath.

He had also been aware of the prickling, swirling sensation just outside his awareness. The Roblin was being cautious, watching, waiting...but unable to resist.

The moment Nifty had appeared in the garage, bellowing at him for abandoning them, leaving them at the mercy of the Old One while all he could think about was Bonnie, the damn fatae had scampered in like a rat on the scent of an overturned Dumpster, thinking to catch him away from the warded office, ripe for chaos.

Sharon and Lou had been waiting in the shadows to raise a warding around them; they'd all been locked down so hard and tight, there was nothing for the damned imp to get its claws into, even if it had sensed them.

It had been a risk, but it had worked, and in the end that was all that mattered.

Once inside the wardings, with Nifty's bulk and his own current-lock, no matter how the imp had wriggled or threatened, or how many parts it had split itself into—four, and that had been a surprise—the trap had held, and they had the bastard fair and square.

And if there was one thing a mischief imp hated, it was anything fair and square.

"What?" the imp demanded of Venec, still glaring.

Before they got to the deal-making, Venec wanted to get one thing clear, so there would be no room for misunderstandings. "You had your fun, imp. Christ knows, we were probably irresistible to you, from a certain viewpoint. But Bonnie and I are dealing with this now, so the fun's going to end." Venec was sure he saw the corners of the imp's mouth droop a little at that. "We'd therefore appreciate you getting the fuck out of our city." As tempting as it was to ask for more than that, a mischief imp was a mischief imp, and The Roblin couldn't not be true to its nature. Venec would have to be very careful about what he demanded, and what was promised.

"Big city. Lots of people." The Roblin's fingers twitched, like it was counting all the possible toys it could find.

"Lots of people who are used to dealing with shit on a regular basis," Ben replied. "You'd have to ramp it up pretty high, for that, and while I've no doubt that you're more than capable of it—we know you're here. We can very easily spread the word that anything odd or unusual is your doing. Once people know that…it's not as much fun, is it? Not so much fun to fuck with people if they can see your hands pulling the strings."

Whatever The Roblin muttered under its breath, then, Ben was pretty sure it wasn't polite.

"So yeah, big city. Lots of people. But also, us."

The Roblin managed, without moving its body, to look at Nifty behind him, and the other two just beyond the barrier, and then back at Venec.

"Us…and the rest. And every contact we have, every ally we've made, all spreading your name, telling your every secret."

The Roblin's eyes narrowed, their golden fire brightening. "Not believing you."

Venec shrugged, like it didn't matter a damn's worth to him. "Your boredom, then. Stay as long as you want. But you're not leaving this garage."

"What?"

"Did you think we'd come here without a backup plan?" Of course they had; they'd barely had a front plan to begin with, but none of that tainted Venec's smug confidence. "You'll stay here, trapped, only able to reach those who come here…and everyone will know that you are here. They will laugh at you. The Roblin will become a name not of fear and awe, but amusement and scorn."

He was probably laying it on too thick; Ian used to warn him about that.

"But it doesn't have to be that way. In exchange for your agreement, we will release you, allow you to leave the city unharmed and intact. But!—" and he cocked his head slightly, giving back as fierce a glare as anything The Roblin managed "—only if you agree not only to leave town without any parting shots, but not come back for a period of…seventy years." Nearly a human lifetime, but barely an inconvenience to an imp. "Is that agreeable?" Before the imp could reply, Venec held up a finger, and caught The Roblin's gaze with his own.

"If you cross me," he told the imp, "I will come after you. No matter where you go or how long it takes. And I will be in no mood for mischief. And if you behave… there may be something in it for you, too."

The imp scowled, his old-man face looking even more like a dried apple as he did so. "How can we resist an offer like that? And what is this parting gift?"

Venec smiled then, a cold smile that gave Nifty the chills, even though they were on the same side. "The scent of a human in this city, a man proud of his power, who thinks himself above judgment or punishment, and the promise that we will not retaliate, if you go after him."

The Roblin considered, trying to see where the catch might be lurking, and then nodded. "Deal."

"Nifty, apologize to the nice imp for breaking its arm."

"Twice," The Roblin said, its mood souring again.

"Twice breaking its arm. But you only have to apologize once."

While the pup and imp glared at each other—The Roblin had gotten some nasty bites in during their struggle, and showed no signs of apologizing for those—Venec turned away slightly, craving the illusion of privacy even though it was only the five of them in the garage. It cost him a small fortune to rent the entire space for only his bike, but occasionally it came in handy when he needed a place nobody would wander into accidentally. Admittedly, he had never thought to use it for this, but life was a series of learning experiences, and you either learned, and adapted, or you died.

Benjamin Venec had no intention of dying.

bonita He didn't mean to call her that, had meant to use her last name, or even her usual nickname, but it slipped out. He was more tired than he wanted to think about, if his control was that shaky.

okay? Her response was immediate, as though she'd been on hold for however long the deal-making had taken. Maybe she had.

i'm fine. we have a solution for everyone's problems If they could pull this off. He rather thought they could, though. All it would require was some fast talking, and confidence. *open up*

open up Venec demanded, and I did so without hesitation: whatever doubts I might have about Bonnie and Ben didn't exist when Big Dog Venec was talking. That was interesting, and good to know, and something we were going to have to look at, when there was some downtime. But for now I was taking in the details he was firing at me faster than pings could keep up, and grinning probably like a madwoman as the shape of his plan unfolded. Stosser had been right: Benjamin Venec was an evil, twisted man.

The connection closed with a snap—less by intent than, I suspected, because our energy ran out; the Merge might make the connection instinctive and inevitable, but it was also an exhausting use of current. But I had enough.

"Jacob Wells, I have been authorized to offer you a choice. Either you accept the consequences of your ac-tions, and exchange yourself as per the terms of your original agreement... The one that you broke, with full intent, and knowledge of the consequences..."

I paused, letting him take that in, then continued, "...or we will give your psychic scent to a mischief imp with the tenacity of a bulldog and the sense of humor of, well, a mischief imp. It will make you its personal pet project, plucking bits of dignity and power from you at whim, and turning everything you touch into shit, just for its own amusement, for the rest of your natural life."

The client blanched, and even Nick looked a little uneasy. It was a crap choice we were giving the guy: life as an inanimate object, or being the butt of a mischief imp. I figured sweetening the pot to make him jump our way wouldn't hurt.

"If you choose the latter," I said, as though only just thinking of it, "you would remain within the reach of human agencies. Meaning that your misuse of current to imprison innocent lives would come under the purveyance of the Mage Council."

It wouldn't, actually. They'd be pissed, maybe, but he was a Null, and the people imprisoned were Null, and the Council therefore wouldn't give a damn. But Wells had dabbled without doing his homework, and so he didn't know that.

I wish I could say I felt bad about lying to him. I didn't. I felt bad about that, though.

"Decide now," Nick said, resting a not-meant-to-be-comforting hand on his shoulder. "Your choices are waiting."

"If it was me," I said, switching back into the kind-and-thoughtful mode I'd learned at J's knee, "I'd go with inanimate. Much more...restful, that way. And who knows, maybe you'll find something to trade yourself out of there with, after a few decades. God knows, it's got to be better than having the imp after you—and risking the Old One coming after you again, pissed off because you hadn't paid up."

The Old One wouldn't; the terms had been satisfied. Again, Wells didn't know that, and in his own mind, of course someone would be out for every bit he could claim, because that's what he would do.

I wondered, briefly, watching the calculations cross his face, what the payment due had been. Somehow I didn't see the Old One, or whatever was left of it, being interested in coin, gold or otherwise.

The sweat that broke on his skin when I mentioned the unpaid obligation suggested it wasn't something I wanted to know about.

"All right." His voice practically squeaked with frustration and anger. "All right, I agree."

"To…?"

The words needed to be said.

"I accept the terms of your offer," he said, spitting out the traditional wording with little drops of venom.

And like that, he was gone.

And so was the lurking presence in the stone beneath us.

There wasn't a celebratory wrap-up party for this case. Stosser had taken the dagger and the watch, carefully wrapped and protected, off to some bigwig Council magefest, to see if they could find a way to return them to human form. Sharon had, at his request, gone with him; I had a feeling, like it or not, she was going to learn how to deal with the Council. Better her than me; she could tell when they were lying, while I just had to assume they always were. Nifty was off getting some bite marks treated—I didn't ask; he'd had a really bad year, medically speaking—and Lou and Pietr and Nick all seemed to share my slightly depressed, disconcerted mood. Yeah, we'd won, we'd closed the case, but the things we'd had to do…

The world was messy. Sometimes, when you held something up to the light…you had no choice but to clean it up, too, so nobody else stepped in it. That was a good thing, right?

"There was a message for you, by the way," Lou said, pulling a piece of paper off the message tree and waving it at me when I wandered through the break room looking for I-didn't-know-what. "Some woman called, said you were in luck, there was a vacancy. You're supposed to stop by when you can."

"You getting a new place?" Nick raised himself up off the sofa enough to look at me. "Aw, I liked your apartment."

"It was a little too noisy for me," I said, taking the paper from Lou's hand. "We'll see how this place does."

Pietr just smiled up at the ceiling, a kind of sad, nostalgic smile, like he knew he wasn't going to get any more invites to stay over, in the new place. Instinctively, I reached out—and was met by a hard, impenetrable surface. Huh.

"I'll catch you guys tomorrow," I said. "Gotta go see a man about a wall."

I found him exactly where, no magic involved, I'd known he would be: on the stoop of my soon-to-be-old apartment building. He didn't look up when I stopped in front of him, so I sat down beside him, feeling the cool brick soak through my pants and numb my ass.

There were any of a dozen things I could have said, from the funny to the horrifyingly blunt, from the excruciatingly personal to the offhandedly polite. What came out was: "Would you really have given Wells to the imp, if he'd balked?"

"Of course."

"Of course," I echoed.

Of course he would have. Benjamin Venec didn't bluff—or if he did, and you called him on it, he followed through, which was probably the same thing as not bluffing.

If he had any doubts about what we'd done, about where the high ground was, and where the quicksand waited, he didn't show it.

Dealing with Venec on a daily basis was never going to be a cakewalk. It would, in fact, be the antithesis of everything I'd ever looked for in a relationship: awkward, frustrating, complicated, and with the potential for big ugly meltdowns on a regular basis if we didn't watch what we were doing. And I didn't even know where half of his sore spots and hot buttons were. Hell, I probably didn't even know a quarter of them yet, Merge or no Merge.

But the thought of walking away, of cutting him out of my life, of him cutting me out… It left an ache larger than anything I'd ever felt, even worse than when Zaki died, even worse than my first and worst broken heart combined. Like there was a chunk of my soul that had gone walkabout, and left a stone in its place.

"You shut me out. Today, I mean. Walls back up."

"You found me, anyway."

"You weren't exactly trying to hide." I gestured behind me. "I live here, had to come back sooner or later."

He nodded. "Exactly."

Great. Now he was giving me Zen koans to suck on. I opened my mouth to ask him why he was making things so damned difficult, when we'd gotten past that, when he reached out and put his unbandaged arm around my shoulders, pulling me into what might have, to an outsider, looked like a casual, if uncomfortable, embrace.

I didn't resist; his arm was at an awkward angle at my throat, but it felt okay, and I was afraid that if I said or did the wrong thing, he'd pull away again, disappear behind even higher walls.

"You did well this week," he said. "All of you. Two cases at once, both tied up, wrongdoers punished..."

"Wrongs left wronged," I said, finishing the sentence.

"Yeah. Well. That's not our job, is it? We're not here to save the world, not even our corner of it. Just to identify, isolate, and incriminate the bad guys."

He'd managed to put a finger on exactly the sore point. "What we did went beyond that, though. Forcing Wells to make the choice he made...it went way beyond our charter, such as it is. And it...wasn't very moral."

"No. Not particularly. It was coercion, justified only by the fact that that bastard had imprisoned his wife and son for years, and deserved to be punished." Ben exhaled, his scent thicker in my nostrils than a second before, the smell of ash and dark rum and clean male sweat. "We gave him the choice of what that punishment would be."

His arm at my neck felt a little like a choke hold now,

but I couldn't bring myself to wiggle out of it, even a little. There's a physical metaphor for you, huh?

"We're not supposed to be the judge or jury. Just the investigators."

"I know. But..." His arm relaxed a little, sliding down to rest around my shoulders. "Circumstances—and Ian's grandstanding little stunt—put us in a position where we had no choice. Let him carry the guilt for that, okay?"

I considered the suggestion.

I wanted to argue with his argument, find the hole that J would have found, turn it back on him and somehow make it all black-and-white again, good guys and bad guys. I couldn't. J wouldn't approve—he was all about standing on your own feet and owning your own actions, but J...hadn't ever been here. Or if he had, he'd made different decisions.

He was a different person.

I'd taken this job because I needed the money, and as an intellectual challenge, but also as a way to put myself to good use, to do something that I felt strongly about. I still felt that way, still believed in the cause. Maybe even more so, now. The world we're in isn't black-and-white, or if it is, that's only for Council, people who take themselves out of the scrum. Down here, it's always been shades of gray...and I'm living—working—smack in the middle of it. That grayness was bound to rub off onto us, sooner or later.

My turn to exhale, and I put my entire body into it. Next to me, I felt Ben's body shake a little with laughter. All right, maybe it had been a smidge overly dramatic.

"Don't shut me out," I said. I meant to add "we work

well with it—it made this case possible to close," or maybe, "I don't mind feeling you always rubbing along the edge of my awareness...we'll figure it out as we go along," or possibly, "I kind of like knowing that you're there." But I didn't say any of that, because he turned his head and shifted his arm again, and then his lips touched mine, and I inhaled the scent of warm flesh and a faint hint of aftershave, and felt the rasp of a soft tongue and my fingers were tangled in that dark shag of curls, pulling his mouth harder against mine, and anything I was going to say went purely to hell.

And then my fingers unclenched and his arm fell away, and there was space to breathe between us.

The walls were still up. But I could see where the outline of a door was etched; one that swung both ways. I touched my fingers to his mouth, not sure if it was me, or him who was trembling, and smiled, and got up and went up the stairs, leaving him sitting there alone.

Shades of gray. We'd figure this out.

★ ★ ★ ★ ★

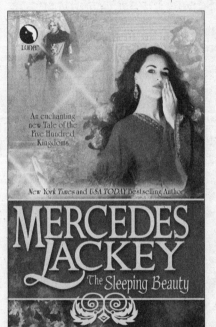